# THE MAN IN THE METH LAB

### A JOE COURT NOVEL

BY
CHRIS CULVER
ST. LOUIS, MO

This is a work of fiction. Names, characters, places, and incidents either are the product of the author's imagination or are used fictitiously. Any resemblance to actual persons, living or dead, events, or locales is entirely coincidental.

Copyright © 2019 by Chris Culver

All rights reserved. No part of this book may be reproduced or used in any manner without written permission of the copyright owner except for the use of quotations in a book review. For more information, address: chris@indiecri me.com

First paperback edition July 2019.

www.indiecrime.com
Facebook.com/ChrisCulverBooks

# Contents

# Chapter 1

Gray storm clouds covered the sky. Goosebumps formed up and down Lorenzo's back and sides as a cold breeze whipped through his thin black jacket. Couples, families, and more than a few individuals trekked along the concrete parking garage's outer walkway to the hospital.

Lorenzo kept his breath even as he walked. Tires chirped and the occasional horn blasted as cars jockeyed for position in the crowded parking structure. Sarah and Blake Nolan—his targets—had just given birth to a little girl in St. Louis's largest Catholic hospital. Sarah was an assistant curator at the St. Louis Art Museum, and Blake was the executive vice president of Nolan Systems, the private security and intelligence firm his father had founded forty years ago. Neither attended church with any regularity, but they gave to Catholic charities.

The moment the couple announced their pregnancy, Lorenzo and his team had started developing files on both individuals. Blake was sleeping with his office assistant, his wife, and a third woman who lived in his neighborhood.

Sarah was faithful to her husband, but she had visited a divorce attorney twice in the past six months.

With their new daughter, Blake might change his ways for a time, but he'd go back to the arms of other women when he grew bored with the monotony of his matrimonial bed. A child would change his life, but it wouldn't change who Blake was—and Blake was a schmuck who didn't deserve his wife or his massive trust fund. Lorenzo would have no problem killing him.

"Morning, Father. How are you?"

The chipper voice broke him from his thoughts. A nurse with brunette hair and oversized but fashionable glasses smiled at him. She was in her early to mid-twenties, and she wore blue scrubs that showcased her pleasantly curvaceous figure. Her ID hung from a lanyard around her neck. Lorenzo had seen her once or twice on his previous visits, but he couldn't remember what floor she worked on.

"I'm good," he said. "How about yourself?"

"I'm going home after a twelve-hour shift," she said, "so I feel great."

Lorenzo nodded and allowed his eyes to travel down her body. He hadn't allowed himself to do that on his previous visits, but he wouldn't be making a return trip after today. In a little over nineteen minutes, it wouldn't matter what the hospital staff thought of him.

"You okay, Father?" she asked, her smile slipping just a little.

"More than all right," he said. "I was just admiring what the Lord hath made. Have a nice day, sweetheart."

The nurse drew in a quick, surprised breath. Lorenzo winked and started walking. Just as he had on his previous visits, he wore a black jacket, black slacks, and a black shirt with a priest's white Roman collar. The outfit had opened the hospital's doors better than any key in existence, but he looked forward to getting rid of it. Even more, he looked forward to getting rid of the bulky bulletproof vest he wore beneath it.

He nodded hello to people as he walked, but no one else tried to talk to him. That gave him a moment to talk to his team. He slipped in an earbud and opened the walkie-talkie app on his phone.

"Overwatch, this is Padre. Confirm that you can hear me."

"Confirm, Padre. Hearing you five-by-five."

Lorenzo had met his radio operator, Deion Shelby, almost ten years ago during Operation Rock Reaper west of Baquba, Iraq. It was a counterinsurgency measure to clear al-Qaeda strongholds north of Baghdad. The fighting had been tough, but Lorenzo's unit had done well.

"Sound off and tell me what you're seeing," he said.

He waited a moment before the first of his team responded.

"Main lobby is clear."

"Skybox has three overnight guests and a lot of traffic. I'm walking the floor."

3

Lorenzo nodded to himself and looked around to make sure no one was watching him. No one was, so he kept his head down and spoke.

"Coffee Shop?" he asked.

"Hey, honey," came Laura Singleton's singsong voice from the coffee shop. "Mike, Doug, and Tom are here with Louise. I can't talk right now."

Reading through the code words, there were three armed police officers and one unarmed hospital security guard within two hundred feet of their planned exit. The security guard wouldn't be a problem, but the police officers posed a serious risk.

"Options?" he asked.

"It'll work out," she said. "I'll give you an update once she has the baby."

Lorenzo had a professional team. If Coffee Shop thought she could handle it, they wouldn't have a problem. He said nothing until he reached the edge of the parking garage. The hospital loomed in front of him.

A covered walkway led to a side entrance and the birthing center. He didn't plan to leave from that door, so he followed a sidewalk to the gargantuan front atrium instead. Sheets of glass stretched several stories overhead, allowing the morning's sunlight to penetrate the building's interior. A line of cars idled at the curb, waiting to pick up discharged patients.

"Bus Driver?" he asked.

"Ready to move," said Cornell North, the man behind the wheel of the ambulance they planned to use as their secondary exfiltration vehicle. Deion—Overwatch—was in the back. Lorenzo had known every one of his team members for over a decade. He had trained for, fought, and survived a war beside them. They were as close as a family, and he trusted them with his life.

"Maintain positions. You know your jobs."

He crossed through the entrance and into the hospital's bustling main atrium. Six people stood in line at the information kiosk near the front door, and another dozen sat on chairs interspersed throughout the space. No one looked dangerous at first glance, but he couldn't evaluate them without slowing. It didn't matter, though. If his team said the atrium was clear, it was clear.

As he walked to the elevators, he found a crowd outside the coffee shop. The shop's doors were closed, and two young people mopped the floor inside. Nobody in sight wore a police officer's uniform. He lowered his chin.

"Coffee Shop, what did you do?"

"Puked on the floor," she said. "They shut down to clean up and sanitize. The police officers moved on. I'm sitting beside the yellow bank of elevators now."

"Outstanding. Thank you. Keep watch."

He took the green elevators to the fifth floor. Once his elevator door opened, he found Josh Knight—Skybox—sitting on an upholstered chair in the lobby and scanning the room while pretending to read on a tablet. His eyes passed over Lorenzo as if he weren't there, but Lorenzo knew his friend had noticed him. He noticed everything.

The Nolans had a large, private room at the end of a winding hallway. A pair of armed security guards stood outside. Coffee Shop and Skybox would neutralize them downstairs. For their sakes, Lorenzo hoped they had kissed and hugged their families before showing up to work that morning. They stepped aside as he walked forward.

"Morning, Father," said the guard on the left.

"Good morning," said Lorenzo. "Is Mrs. Nolan awake?"

"She is. Mr. Nolan came in this morning, too. They're expecting you."

Lorenzo nodded, removed his earbud, and knocked on the door. A woman's voice called out from inside, asking him in.

The morning sunlight from the room's east-facing window gleamed off the polished terrazzo marble floor. Sarah Nolan lay in a hospital bed with a shroud over her chest. She was nursing her newborn. Her husband—Blake Nolan—was on the phone near the room's bathroom, but he hung up upon seeing Lorenzo.

"Father Lorenzo, thank you for coming," said Blake. "I've got the bags packed, and we're just about ready to go."

If the Nolans had gone to church as often as they claimed, they would have had their own parish priest, and they would have recognized that he knew next to nothing about

Catholic theology. The plan would never have worked. Instead, they pretended as if they had known him for years. A little spiritual bravado wasn't a bad thing.

"I'm so glad," said Lorenzo. He looked to the baby and smiled. "How's Scarlett eating today?"

"She's doing well," said Sarah, giving him a relieved smile. "She's my little fighter. The doctors say she'll be okay once she has her surgery."

"I've been praying for all of you," said Lorenzo. He looked to Blake. "While you guys finish up, I'll step out into the hallway. When you're ready, call me back in. I'll take you downstairs to your car."

Sarah nodded, and Blake walked toward him with his hands outstretched. He shook Lorenzo's hand in both of his own.

"Thanks again, Father," he said. "It means a lot that you're here. This has been the hardest week of our lives."

"Faith isn't faith until it's all you're holding on to," he said, squeezing Blake's hand before disengaging from the handshake. He took a step toward the hallway. "I'm glad I could be here for you. Just call me when you need me."

Blake nodded, so Lorenzo left and looked to the security guards.

"I'll be right back."

The guards nodded, and Lorenzo walked back down the hallway toward a family restroom he had passed earlier. Inside, with the door locked, he slipped his earbud back in his ear and spoke into the microphone.

"The Nolans are ready to go. Overwatch, get our bird in the air. Skybox and Lobby, watch for guests. Coffee Shop, check your sight lines and ensure that we are free of a police presence. Bus Driver, get ready to roll."

"We're clear, Padre," said Coffee Shop.

Six months of his life and every penny he owned had gone into this job. He hadn't seen his kids in all that time. He missed them. Compared to his team's sacrifices, though, Lorenzo's loss was minor. Deion Shelby—Overwatch—had missed the birth of his son; Laura Singleton—Coffee Shop—had broken up with her live-in partner; Josh Knight—Skybox—had turned down a lucrative private security contract that could have set him and his family up for years.

Soon, all their struggles would be worth it, though. He drew in a deep breath and closed his eyes. This was it.

"Ladies and gentlemen, as always, it has been a true privilege working with you. Thank you for your trust. Our mission is a go. Repeat, the mission is a go. You know your jobs. Get to it."

In a briefing room, they might have clapped or whooped and hollered. In the field, they confirmed the order and did their jobs. Lorenzo drew in a deep breath to still his nerves and then removed his earbud before using an app to format his phone's internal hard drive. Once the app finished, he threw the phone in the trash and pulled out a hard-shell eyeglasses case from the inside pocket of his jacket. The two syringes inside were intact and ready to go. This would work just fine.

Blake and Sarah Nolan had thought they had a rough week. They had no idea how rough their lives were about to get.

# Chapter 2

Dirt clung to my forehead, my lungs felt tight, and my right knee ached from where I had banged it on the ground, but I felt better than I had in days. Work had been keeping me so busy for the past couple of months that early morning runs through the woods—once a huge part of my daily routine—had become rare events. I had missed the exercise. It felt nice to relax and forget about the rest of the world.

Gray clouds covered the sky from one end of the horizon to the other. Goose bumps formed up and down the exposed skin of my arms as a damp, cool breeze whipped through the trees behind my home. It was mid-September, and yellow, red, and orange leaves dotted the canopy of green over my backyard. It was almost like watching a fire lumber to life. Spring was my favorite season, but fall had a draw all its own, and this one promised to be beautiful.

I inhaled deep lungfuls of the cool, moist air and walked around the side of my old farmhouse, intending to get my spare key so I could get ready for the day. Instead, I stopped in my tracks and groaned as soon as I turned the corner. My mom's SUV was parked in the driveway. I closed my eyes and swore beneath my breath.

"Hey, Joe," she called from the front porch. "Thought you might have spent the night at a friend's house."

"Hey, Mom," I said, jogging toward the porch, where I kept my spare key. "Sorry. I forgot you were coming this morning. I'll get changed. Give me a minute."

Julia Green, my adoptive mother, sat on one of my two rocking chairs. Physically, Mom and I had almost nothing in common. She had a petite, wiry build, high cheekbones, and bright green eyes. At five-seven, I towered over her and had at least thirty pounds on her. Despite that, I knew without a doubt she could kick my ass from one end of the street to the other without breaking a sweat.

"That's okay," she said. "We just got here."

Only when she said *we* did I notice the dog sitting at her feet. He had a sleek brown coat, enormous paws, and a block-shaped head. His yellow eyes had a lively light, and his tongue stuck out of his mouth as he panted. His tail thumped against the ground as I walked toward them.

"Who's this guy?"

"Roy," she said, glancing up at me. "Hold on a minute. I'm texting your dad to let him know I made it."

I stood and plucked a tennis ball from the terra cotta pot beside my front door. Roy fixated on it, as I suspected he would. After checking to make sure there weren't any cars nearby, I threw it as hard as I could to the woods across the street from my house. My old dog used to love retrieving tennis balls from those woods. Roy, however, watched the ball sail away and then seemed to nod before lowering his massive head between his paws and yawning.

"You don't want the ball?" I asked, patting him on the shoulder. He yawned again. I had never seen a dog shrug before, but I could swear that his shoulders heaved for just a second. I furrowed my brow and petted him once more before sitting on the chair beside my mom.

"Roy doesn't exercise," Mom said as she slipped her phone into her purse. "It's one of his little quirks. He'll enjoy living here."

I gave her a bemused smile.

"He's going to live here?"

"Yep," said Mom, nodding. "Roy's a great dog, and he needs a home. You're a great human, and you need a dog. It's perfect."

I kept the bemused smile on my face until I saw she was serious. Then I sighed.

"I thought you came to have breakfast with me."

"I did," she said, nodding. "I figured while I was here, though, I'd drop off Roy."

I tilted my head to the side and reached down to pet the dog. His tail thumped against the deck boards.

"I don't know, Mom. Roy's pretty, but I just lost Roger. I don't know if I'm ready for another dog so soon."

"I know you loved Roger, but you'll never find a better dog than Roy. He's healthy, housebroken, and well-trained. He's also loyal, sweet, and gentle as can be. Kids love him, too."

I shook my head and allowed my voice to grow cold.

"I don't want to talk about kids again."

Mom held up her hands as if she were telling an oncoming freight train to stop. "I'm just saying. If you ever have kids, he'd be okay with them. He's a good dog."

I looked down at him. Roy tilted his head at me curiously before lowering it between his paws again.

"He seems like a good dog. If he's everything you say he is, he'll make a family with kids happy."

Mom shook her head.

"I wish he could, but he's got bite training, so he can't go to a civilian family. Ideally, he'd live with his trainer for the rest of his life, but he and his wife just had twins. They can't care for a new dog and two babies."

I narrowed my eyes.

"What kind of training does he have?"

"He's a cadaver dog," said mom. "Or at least he would have been if he hadn't flunked out of the training program."

I rested my hand on Roy's back. He drew in a deep breath, almost as if he were sighing contentedly. Then he rolled onto his side.

"He likes you," said Mom.

"Why'd they kick him out of the cadaver dog program?" I asked.

"He's lazy," she said. "His trainer took him to three different vets to make sure he's healthy, but every test came back normal. He was too laid back for the program, but he'd be a great friend."

I had wanted a dog again—even a lazy one—and Roy was pretty, but for some reason, I held back.

"He's kind of small," I said.

Mom scoffed. "He's a hundred and ten pounds," she said. "He's huge."

I guess that was big. Before he had died, Roger, my last dog, had weighed about a hundred and forty pounds. He wasn't fat, either. He was just a big, loveable bullmastiff. Roy was big enough that he could use most of Roger's old stuff, so he had that going for him.

"Is he a full chocolate Lab?"

"He's half chocolate Lab, half Chesapeake Bay retriever, and he's got some of the better qualities of both. His chocolate Lab side makes him relaxed and laid back, while the Chesapeake Bay retriever side makes him a little more assertive. He's two and a half, so he's got a long life ahead of him, too. You'll love him."

I blinked a few times and then scratched his neck.

"What do you think, Roy? You want to live here?"

Upon hearing his name, he lifted his head and licked my hand. As silly as it sounded, I missed having a dog lick my hand. More than that, I missed having a reason to come home after work instead of driving to a bar. My old dog had been my best friend. It sounded hokey to admit that, but it was true. Whenever I had a bad day, Roger would sit at my feet and let me know things would get better. He had cared for me unconditionally, and I had loved him. I missed having that in my life. Roy's side rose and fell with his breath as I petted him.

"He can stay for a week," I said. "We'll see how it goes, and then we'll talk about making it permanent."

Mom's shoulders relaxed, and she smiled. "Great. I'll get the paperwork and his food from the car, and then I'll make you some breakfast. You go take a shower. You smell terrible, and you look like shit."

"Thanks, Mom."

She patted my shoulder. "That's what moms are for."

She stood and walked to her car. I straightened and nodded toward the house.

"You want to go inside, Roy?"

He lumbered to his feet and then stretched into a play bow. I thought about throwing him a ball again, but I figured I'd just have to go retrieve it myself. We'd work on that.

I showered while Roy searched my house. After I had dried off and dressed, I found Mom in the kitchen, scrambling eggs. She smiled at me and opened her mouth to say something, but then my cell phone rang. I sighed and walked back to my bedroom to grab it. Hundreds of people knew my cell phone number, but few called me before eight in the morning except in cases of emergency. When I saw the name on the caller ID, I sighed.

*Terepocki, R.*

I answered before it could ring again. Our conversation didn't last long, but by the time Reuben finished speaking, my heart pounded against my breastbone, and every muscle in my body felt tight. I hung up, grabbed my gun and badge from the safe in my closet, and hurried to the kitchen, where my mom was just putting eggs on plates.

"Hey, Mom," I said. "Did I tell you my department hired a new detective a couple of months ago?"

She looked up and nodded. "Yeah. Was that him?"

"Yeah. And he just shot somebody. I've got to go."

# Chapter 3

Lorenzo took the syringes from the case and slipped them into the outer pocket of his jacket before returning to the Nolans' room. Their door was open, and a hospital attendant wearing purple scrubs and holding the handles of a wheelchair stood beside the security team. Lorenzo smiled and held his hands forward for the chair.

"I'll escort Mr. and Mrs. Nolan outside. You can get to your next patient."

The attendant hesitated but then straightened and turned the wheelchair toward Lorenzo. Inside her room, Sarah Nolan was out of the bed and packing a black rolling suitcase while Blake held the baby. He looked as if he'd make a good father. That was almost a pity.

"It looks like you guys are ready to go," he said. Both adults looked at him and smiled.

"What do we do now?" asked Blake.

"You get the bags," said Lorenzo, brandishing the wheelchair. "Your wonderful wife and beautiful daughter get a ride."

By the sour expression on his face, Lorenzo doubted anyone had told Blake to get the bags in his life. It felt satisfying. Blake took his wife's suitcase from the bed and then wheeled it to the security team, both of whom remained outside. The younger of the two guards took the bag without hesitating. It was a stupid move from a security professional. The bag would tie up his hands and prevent him from reaching his firearm in an emergency. He should have known better.

Within moments, Lorenzo pushed Sarah and Scarlett Nolan down the hall while Blake Nolan spoke on his cell phone, scheduling a meeting in his office that afternoon. Blake's company hired a lot of soldiers and former intelligence officers, but he had never served a day in his life. Though Blake was athletic enough to play lacrosse in college, he wasn't a threat.

As they reached the lobby, Lorenzo saw his team's blue and white helicopter landing on the emergency medical helipad not two hundred yards from the hospital's front door. Sarah looked over her shoulder to Lorenzo and then to her husband.

"Looks like somebody's sick," she said. "I hope they're okay."

Blake was still on the phone and hadn't heard, but Lorenzo leaned forward.

"This is a good hospital," he said. "Whoever it is, she'll get excellent care."

She nodded and tightened her grip on her baby. Her husband kept talking. Meanwhile, Nick McCoy—Lorenzo's team member in the lobby—slipped his cell phone into the inside pocket of his sport coat. Though Lorenzo's heart thudded, his breath slowed. A stillness came over him as years of training kicked in. It wouldn't be long now.

He cast his eyes over the room one final time. Two men near the door stood and nodded brief greetings to Blake. Both had thin, angular faces, hard eyes, and skin prematurely wrinkled by excessive sun exposure—probably in the deserts of Iraq or Afghanistan. Each man wore a pair of slacks, a button-down shirt, and a sport coat. Judging by the bulges and folds of fabric, one had a gun beneath his left breast pocket, while the other had a firearm on his right side.

Time seemed to slow. McCoy didn't see them.

*Fuck.*

McCoy reached into his jacket for his firearm. The plan called for Laura Singleton and Josh Knight to take out the Nolans' guards, while McCoy took out Blake Nolan. They would then surround Lorenzo and escort him to the helipad. It'd be over before anyone could even ring the alarm. Once the two men near the door saw McCoy's weapon, though, they'd shoot him in the back, and then they'd shoot Laura and Josh.

Lorenzo couldn't let that happen. He had a Glock 27 on his ankle in case of emergency, but it would take too long to reach it to protect his friend. This was already starting. He couldn't stop it, so he did the next best thing and gave his team a warning.

"Gun!" he shouted. "Two shooters near the door. Everybody down!"

McCoy immediately dropped to a knee, while the two security guards near the door flinched. An older man in a cowboy hat stumbled and fell onto a couch. He'd be fine. Lorenzo couldn't wait for his team to figure things out. He had to get to cover before the shooting started.

"It's okay," said Sarah, her voice tinged with panic. "My father-in-law sent them."

The moment she finished speaking, the first shot rang out. The round slammed into the tempered glass panel beside the front door. Then a second shot rang out. A member of the Nolans' security team dropped, clutching his chest. The shooter was the old man on the couch. He was trying to play hero. They could use that.

Lorenzo leaned over Sarah.

"Keep your head down and cover up your baby. We're getting out of here."

Even as the words left his lips, the Nolans' security team returned fire. Half a dozen rounds or more slammed into the old man, likely killing him. Nick McCoy, Laura Singleton, and Josh Knight saw their chance and fired on the security team. Two members of the Nolans' team went down fast, but that left at least one armed man to contend with. Hopefully they'd take him down soon and get out of there before the hospital's own armed security team arrived. Amateurs with guns had already done enough damage for the day.

Lorenzo sprinted toward the front door. The glass panel slid to the left, and he pushed Sarah and her baby outside. Several people huddled behind cars, unsure what to do. Every part of him wanted to run back into the lobby to protect and exfiltrate his team, but his training told him to complete his mission while he still could. Too much had gone into this.

He ran up the sidewalk alongside the building.

"Where are we going?"

Lorenzo hadn't realized that Blake Nolan had been following him. Lorenzo looked over his shoulder and then slowed.

"Take her and run. Just get away from here," he said, thinking quickly. "I'll stop anybody from coming after you."

Blake nodded and took the wheelchair before running down the path. Lorenzo knelt to take the firearm from his ankle. It was a nice weapon, although it was small for his hand. He pulled back the receiver to chamber a round and then positioned his feet shoulder-width apart. Blake was about thirty feet away. Lorenzo locked his right elbow in a slight bend and lowered his left.

The world disappeared as he zeroed in on his target. It was an easy shot. He blew the air from his lungs and felt his heart slow. As Blake's right foot dropped to the ground, Lorenzo squeezed the trigger twice. The rounds tore through Blake's unprotected back with a pop of blood. He dropped straight down.

Lorenzo sprinted just as Sarah Nolan rose from the seat. Her mouth was wide open, and tears streamed down her face. Her baby cried. Upon reaching her, Lorenzo wrapped his arms tight around her so she couldn't move.

"Hush, hush, hush," he whispered, already reaching into his pocket for the syringe. He popped the protective casing off with his thumb and jabbed it into Sarah's neck. Every muscle in her body went rigid, and she gasped.

"Sorry, dear," he said, depressing the plunger. "This is nothing personal."

Sarah stared at him with surprised, terrified eyes. He dropped the syringe and lowered her to the ground, all the while keeping a hand over her mouth to muffle her screams. Her muscles relaxed, and her eyes turned glassy as sedatives coursed through her system.

He reached for the baby and plucked her from her mother's grip. The baby screamed, so Lorenzo cradled her in his arms and gently shushed her.

"It's okay, sweetheart," he whispered. "I've got you."

Sarah tried to say something, but only a gasp escaped her lips.

"It's okay, Mrs. Nolan," he said. "Your daughter's safe. My people will be in touch."

Even with enough drugs in her system to knock out a horse, she cried. Unlike her husband, she'd live. That was part of the plan. Lorenzo needed her alive to needle her father-in-law into paying the ransom. Scarlett Nolan's grandfather was worth almost four billion dollars. He was also a war criminal who deserved to rot in prison for the rest of his life.

Lorenzo cupped the back of the newborn's head to hold it steady and then sprinted toward the helipad. The gunfire in the lobby had ceased, but he didn't know who had won. He didn't want to leave a member of his team behind, but he had a job to do.

The whine of the helicopter's engine carried on a soft, early morning breeze. As he approached the helipad, the helicopter's rear door popped open. A man about Lorenzo's age stepped out. He had brown hair and a full beard, and he wore a navy blue fight suit with the sleeves rolled up, exposing forearms crisscrossed by tattoos. Lorenzo didn't recognize him. His footsteps slowed.

"Come on, Padre!" he shouted. "We've got to move."

Lorenzo stopped. He had always been uneasy with the helicopter, but it had been an integral part of the plan. The hospital had easy access to the interstate and major roads, which made for a quick exit. Unfortunately, that ease of exit ensured a rapid police response once the shooting started. Already, Lorenzo could hear distant sirens closing in on their position. The helicopter had promised a clean getaway, but only if he could trust its pilot.

"Where's Thomas?" asked Lorenzo.

"No time to explain. Give me the baby and get in."

This wasn't right. Lorenzo shook his head and took a step back, already looking for another option. Even with a shootout in the hospital's main entrance, there were dozens of cars streaming into and out of the campus. He could jack one of them and have the driver take him to the West County Mall. Then he could shoot the driver full of a sedative, steal another car, and find his team. First, though, he needed to get rid of this guy.

"No good," said Lorenzo. "Take off and get out of here. We'll meet at the farm and talk later."

He turned to run. Lorenzo heard the shots a split second before they hit slammed into his back. His breath caught in his throat, and he fell to his knees. Footsteps pounded behind him. The baby cried, so he tried to cradle her and prevent her from becoming injured.

A pair of hands rolled him over. Two unfamiliar men stood over him. Both had brown beards, and both wore the identical flight suits of air ambulance paramedics. One held a gun. Lorenzo tried to breathe, but his lungs wouldn't inflate. The second man, the one without the gun, plucked the little girl from his hands and then ran toward the awaiting helicopter. The gunman squeezed off two shots. Both hit him in the chest. Lorenzo gasped again as pain exploded across his rib cage.

He rolled onto his belly, but his ribs and shoulders hurt so much he couldn't push up. Pebbles and grit bit into his skin as the helicopter's engine whined during liftoff. It disappeared within seconds.

For a few moments, Lorenzo lay on the tarmac, trying to catch his breath. Then, footsteps pounded around him. He tried to roll over and raise his firearm to protect himself, but he could barely move. Then Laura Singleton and Josh Knight grabbed him by the armpits and dragged him across the helipad and grass to an ambulance.

The moment he was inside, Lorenzo's team slammed the rear doors shut, and the heavy ambulance took off. Laura cut his shirt. Then she straightened and sighed.

"We saw what happened," she said. "Doesn't look like anything penetrated your vest. Can you breathe?"

He nodded and tried to sit up, but it hurt so much it made his breath catch in his throat.

"Stay down. You might have broken ribs. We don't want them penetrating your lungs," she said, pressing him down to the ambulance's floor again. Around him, his team gave him wary, confused looks.

"Where's Nick?" he asked, shuddering as pain swept through him.

Laura looked to Josh Knight with a worried expression on her face.

"What happened?" asked Lorenzo.

"He got shot in the neck," said Laura. "We left him there. If we took him, he'd bleed out before we could get him help. If he stayed there, though, the hospital would whisk him right to the ER. They might even think he's a civilian caught in the crossfire."

Lorenzo nodded. He could breathe easier without the vest on, so he took two deep breaths before sitting up. Laura tried to push him down again, but he waved her away.

"I'm fine," he said, blinking. "And good call on Nick. Leaving him gave him the best chance of survival."

"What happened out there?" asked a voice from the front of the ambulance. It was Deion Shelby—Overwatch—and he had a concerned expression on his face.

"The Nolans had a secondary security team in the lobby," said Laura. "A civilian started a gunfight."

"Yeah, but what happened on the helicopter?"

Every eye in the ambulance turned to him.

"Becker screwed us," said Lorenzo. "There were two guys on the helicopter with him. One of them shot me. The other took the girl."

"How do you want to handle this, boss?" asked Josh.

"We find Becker, and we make him hurt," he said. "First, though, drive to the Baptist hospital up the street. We need to ditch this ambulance and get a car. If we're lucky, we've got another minute to get out of here before the police show up."

Cornell North, their driver, hit the switch to turn on the ambulance's lights and siren. It called attention to them, but they were near two of the busiest hospitals in the Midwest.

Ambulances blew through this area dozens of times an hour. As they drove, Lorenzo felt himself calming some.

Laura Singleton slid to the ground to sit beside him.

"It's a big world, Renzo," she said, her voice a whisper so the others couldn't hear them. "You think we can find Becker?"

Lorenzo nodded. "He's got an ex-wife and a boy in some podunk town south of here. Once we get rid of this ambulance, you and I are going redneck hunting in St. Augustine. We'll find Becker and his friends even if it means burning that entire goddamn county down around them."

# Chapter 4

I wolfed down a couple of eggs and grabbed a piece of toast to go and was out the door within five minutes of Reuben's call. I hated to leave Roy so soon after getting him, but he'd be fine in the dog run for the day. It had plenty of room for him to walk around in and a big doghouse in case it rained. He'd be okay.

As a detective with the Sheriff's Department, I covered cases all over St. Augustine County. The address Reuben gave me put him outside Dyer. It had a gas station, a building that once held a drugstore, and the county's only working pay phone. Residents could buy milk and bread at the gas station, but the nearest bank and grocery stores were fifteen miles away in the town of St. Augustine.

After twenty-five minutes in the car, I arrived at the crime scene. The home was tiny and reminded me more of a cabin than anything else. Its cracked stucco exterior, sagging roof, chipped yellow paint, and shuttered windows all spoke of better years. There were already four police cars out front, including Sheriff George Delgado's unmarked SUV.

I parked on the lawn out front beside one of the cruisers and walked toward Officer Katie Martelle, who was standing near the home. At twenty-three, Katie was just five years younger than me, but her complete lack of cynicism made me feel much older. Everybody in the department liked her, and it wasn't hard to see why: She was kind to everyone she came across, even those who didn't deserve it. That made her a special kind of person. Had she been a teacher, every elementary school in the state would have clamored for her services.

"Morning, Katie," I said. "You got the logbook?"

"Yes, ma'am," she said, holding out a clipboard for me to sign. I signed my name and noted the time before handing it back to her. "Detective Terepocki and Sheriff Delgado are behind the building with the body."

I nodded. "Fill me in on what's happened."

She hesitated. "I'm just maintaining the logbook, ma'am."

I smiled but didn't let it reach my eyes. "You're a police officer at a crime scene, Officer Martelle. When'd you arrive, what have you done, and what has everyone else done?"

She fumbled a notepad from her utility belt and then flipped through pages.

"My shift started at seven, and I directed traffic by the high school until I got the call to come out here at 7:34. I got to the scene at 7:56."

I nodded. "Good. Who was here when you arrived?"

"Sergeant Reitz. He told me to set up a perimeter and start a logbook. Sheriff Delgado arrived at five after eight, and he took over."

"Has anyone talked to the neighbors yet?"

She, once more, hesitated and then lowered her chin. "There aren't any neighbors. We're pretty far out in the country."

I looked around. A farmer had planted a field across the street with corn, while woods stretched beside the house in either direction. I nodded.

"Thanks," I said. "Good work. Keep it up. And please don't call me ma'am again. I'm twenty-eight. You can call me Joe like everybody else, or you can call me Detective Court. Either way works for me."

"Okay...Joe," she said. "Thanks."

I nodded to her and walked around the house, where I found my partner and my boss conversing. I nodded to them both and walked over.

"Morning," I said, looking from Reuben to Sheriff Delgado. "Can I talk to you in private, George?"

The sheriff nodded, so the two of us stepped away from Detective Terepocki. A rickety picket fence with flaking white paint partially surrounded the backyard and separated it from the woods behind the home. Tufts of grass pockmarked the hardscrabble landscape. The air held a damp, fetid odor that made me wonder whether a sewer pipe had broken nearby.

Once I was far enough that Reuben wouldn't overhear us, I leaned in toward my boss and lowered my voice.

"What's going on?" I asked. "Reuben called me at home and said he shot somebody."

"He wasn't lying," said Delgado. "Body's in the house. Caucasian male. According to his license, he's forty-six years old, and he lives in St. Augustine. His name is Jay Pischke."

I furrowed my brow. "How does Reuben know Stinky Jay?"

"That's what you're going to figure out. I've placed Detective Terepocki on administrative leave pending a full investigation. I'm heading back to our station, so I'll take his firearm with me and drop it off with Darlene McEvoy. Her team will run ballistics on it. The case is yours. Good luck."

I immediately shook my head. "We should bring in the Highway Patrol. They can investigate. Reuben's my partner."

Delgado narrowed his eyes and crossed his arms.

"You telling me you can't work this case because of a conflict, or that you're not interested in working it because Reuben's your partner?"

"The optics are bad," I said. "I'll work the case, and I'll follow the evidence, but he is my partner. If I find out this was a righteous shooting, the victim's friends and family will say I was biased. If I arrest Reuben for murder, no cop in the state of Missouri will work with me. We need to bring in outside, neutral investigators."

31

Delgado leaned forward slightly and stood on the balls of his feet. He did that sometimes. I figured he meant it to make himself look taller and more intimidating. It didn't work. Delgado could hurt my career, he could give me crappy assignments, or he could chew me out in front of my colleagues, but nothing he did would intimidate me. I wouldn't let him.

"If you're scared of how others will perceive your investigation, maybe you're not ready for this kind of case. You say the word, and I'll take you out of the field. You can get a nice desk set up in the station. I've always appreciated the quality of your paperwork."

I tilted my head to the side. "If you put me behind a desk, who's going to work the speed trap for you?"

"I'll find some knucklehead," he said, smiling. "Contrary to your opinion, you're hardly indispensable, Detective."

I nodded and crossed my arms. "Be that as it may, Sheriff, you've only got two detectives on staff, and one of them shot a guy this morning. I'll work the case, but this is a bad idea."

"Objection noted," said Delgado, his voice flat. "Work the case, Detective. Good luck."

"Okay," I said, forcing myself to smile. "Since you're going back to the station, please take Detective Terepocki with you. I'll get a formal statement from him in the office."

Delgado looked down and then shifted his weight from one foot to the other.

"That's how you want to play this?" he asked, narrowing his eyes at me. "You want me to treat him like a suspect in a murder investigation?"

"I want you to treat him as you would anyone found holding a firearm at the scene of a deadly shooting. If you want this case handled some other way, call in the Highway Patrol."

Delgado considered me before taking a step back.

"You want to dig your own grave, go right ahead," he said. "Don't blame me if you find yourself buried alive, though."

"Thank you for your wise counsel," I said, still smiling. "Now, if you'll excuse me, I've got a case to work."

I turned around before he could respond. Terepocki straightened and nodded hello as I walked toward him.

"Hey, Reuben," I said. "You okay?"

He nodded. "As good as I can be."

"I'm working the case, but Sheriff Delgado's going to take you to our station. I'll talk to you there. I'll do what I can to get this sorted out quickly. Okay?"

He nodded and walked toward Delgado. They left a moment later. Sheriff Delgado and I had never gotten along well, but our relationship had come to a head during a recent investigation into a serial murderer. I disagreed with some of my boss's judgment calls—particularly as they related to the media—and he disagreed with my assessment of his abilities. I also called him a moron to his face. We closed the case, but a lot of people had gotten hurt. That was the past, though. I needed to focus on the present and the future.

In a normal shooting, I'd look at the scene, search for evidence, talk to witnesses, and try to figure out who pulled the trigger and why. In this case, though, I already knew my partner pulled the trigger. The investigation started and ended with Reuben. If his story matched the crime scene, we could close the investigation today. If it didn't, we'd have a problem.

I walked around the home. Time had aged the exposed wood trim to a deep gray, while cracks striated the stucco exterior. Plywood covered many of the windows, and even from outside, I could smell mold and rotted wood. Inside, a frayed brown and orange carpet covered the floor. Little light penetrated the interior, but even in the gloom, I spotted water stains on the walls and ceiling. It was amazing the building hadn't collapsed.

Dr. Trevor Sheridan, the forensic pathologist St. Augustine shared with several surrounding counties, leaned over the body of a middle-aged man in the home's northeast corner. Kevius Reed, a newly hired forensic technician with our crime lab, photographed two cardboard boxes full of beakers and chemicals beside the front door. I nodded to both men.

"Morning, guys," I said. "What have we got?"

"According to his wallet, the victim is Jay Pischke," said Sheridan. "He's been shot four times in the chest within the past hour. I'll tell you more when I get back to my lab."

I nodded and looked to Kevius and the array of bottles and beakers in front of him. "What have you got, Kevius?"

He looked up at me and raised his eyebrow. "Meth lab. I called Ms. McEvoy already. She's on her way."

Ms. McEvoy—Darlene—was our lead forensic scientist. She was a good lab scientist, and I liked working with her for the most part. I had only worked with Kevius once before, but he seemed competent. He had just graduated from college a couple of months ago, so he still had a lot to learn, but he was trying. I appreciated that.

"You walk through the rest of the house yet?"

He nodded. "Yeah. There are boxes in the kitchen, but I wanted to focus on this first."

It was probably the right call, so I nodded.

"Where's the kitchen?"

He pointed to a closed door at the back of the house. I thanked him and started walking. The kitchen was small but surprisingly clean. The yellow linoleum tile curled beneath the cabinet's toe kick, but the cabinets hung onto the walls evenly and without a sag. Three hunting rifles leaned against the wall beside the back door, while stacks of cardboard boxes and plastic milk crates holding gallon-sized jugs of water reached nearly to the ceiling.

I took out my cell phone and snapped pictures. The boxes had no labels, and thick packing tape sealed them shut. I took one off the shortest stack, photographed it, and then put it on the ground, where I used my keys as a knife to break the tape. Inside I found thirty packages of freeze-dried lasagna, macaroni and cheese, and beef stroganoff. I grabbed the next box and found containers of powdered milk.

I took a step back and considered. St. Augustine, like a lot of counties in rural Missouri, had a problem with meth. It was cheap, easy to produce, and extraordinarily addictive. It ruined the lives of a lot of people. We had a lot of meth cookers, but few stocked their kitchen this well.

I walked back into the living room. My position by the kitchen gave me a perspective on the room I didn't have before. A pair of rounds had ripped through the plaster beside the front door and out the stucco on the other side, leaving two holes through which I could see the sky outside. If Reuben had been standing anywhere near that door when the victim fired those shots, he had ample justification to fire back.

Still, that left me with dozens of questions. Why did the victim have months' worth of supplies in his kitchen? Why did Reuben drive to the middle of nowhere to see him at seven in the morning? If he was working a case, why didn't he call me first? What—if anything—was he hiding?

I had more questions than answers, but that was okay. The answers would come in time. I hoped they'd be worth hearing.

# Chapter 5

I spent almost two hours at the house. Besides the boxes of freeze-dried food in the kitchen, I found four boxes of newborn diapers, two boxes of baby wipes, four cases of premixed infant formula, half a dozen clean baby blankets, and an infant's Pack 'n Play in the back bedroom. It was enough stuff to keep an infant happy and healthy for weeks, and yet, I had found no sign of an infant. That worried me.

I left Sergeant Bob Reitz in control of the crime scene and drove to my station in downtown St. Augustine. My department worked out of an old Masonic temple the county had purchased about thirty years ago when the Masons left town. For years, my colleagues and I had heard the County Council promise to fix the building's intermittent heat, drafty windows, and leaky slate roof, but we never believed those cheap bastards would actually pony up the money.

Then, out of the blue, they did. I was glad Sheriff Delgado was only in his fifties. An older man might have had a heart attack.

Already, construction crews had torn that beautiful historic building apart. The plans called for them to gut the building from top to bottom. When the construction crews finished, we'd have a gym, a modern forensics lab, windows that kept out both the rain and wind, and a roof that didn't leak. If I kept my job until then, I'd even have a private office somewhere on the second floor. As much as I loved the building the way it was, I'd love it even more when it no longer rained indoors.

I parked and entered through a side door. The construction crews had already torn apart the first floor and parts of the basement, forcing most of the station's operations to the second floor. I took the stairs up and found Trisha, the day shift's dispatcher, in the second-floor conference room behind a desk. Telephone and computer cables dangled from the ceiling and connected to the phone, computer, and fax machine on the desk in front of her. She smiled at me and put her cup of coffee down.

"Morning, Joe," she said. "I hear you've been busy."

"Yeah," I said. "Did George bring Reuben in yet?"

She hesitated. "Did you really arrest your partner?"

"He's not under arrest, but I did bring him in to get an official statement."

Her shoulders fell, and she breathed out a relieved sigh.

"Good. It's bad business to arrest one of our own."

"Maybe," I said, shrugging. "If that's where the evidence takes me, that's what I'll do, though."

She nodded but said nothing. I left her in the conference room and walked down the hall to the storage closet that had become the office Reuben and I shared. The room was about three hundred square feet and had ample floor space for two desks, four file cabinets, and a stack of chairs in the corner. Three big windows allowed in so much light I could almost wear sunglasses on a bright day. Unfortunately, they also leaked so much we couldn't put furniture or paperwork anywhere near them for fear of a rainy day.

Reuben sat at his desk, typing. I leaned against the doorframe and crossed my arms.

"You want a lawyer?" I asked.

He looked up from his computer and considered me.

"Do I need one?"

I raised my eyebrows and shrugged. "You're entitled to one. I'm not looking to jam you up, though. I've got a team at the house, and the coroner's got the body. You know how these investigations work. I want to find out what happened."

His lips curled into a tight smile. Reuben had brown eyes, light brown skin, and freckles around his nose. His gray hair was cropped close to his scalp. When I first met him, I didn't think much of him. He seemed fine, but I didn't think I needed a partner. Then, we visited the family of a young man who had died in a car accident. The victim had been nineteen, and he had commuted from his parents' house in St. Augustine to St. Louis every morning to attend classes at the University of Missouri-St. Louis.

He died driving home after a night class. It was a Wednesday. The victim drove a fifteen-year-old four-door sedan. The guy who hit him drove a full-sized pickup that weighed over three tons. The truck driver switched lanes and didn't see the kid's car. He clipped the front quarter panel at eighty miles an hour, knocking his car off the road. The victim overcorrected, hit a semitruck, and died.

When we got to that kid's house to tell his parents their son had died, Reuben took over. He was compassionate, patient, and kind. He had been my partner on paper from his first day on the job, but that was the moment he became my partner in reality. I liked him, and I hated what I was about to do.

Reuben turned back to his computer.

"I'm just about done with my statement," he said. "I'll print it out for you and sign it."

"Good," I said, nodding. "How'd you know Stinky Jay?"

He glanced up at me before focusing on his computer again. "I'm a detective. It's my job to know people—especially the troublemakers. How do you know him?"

"I've arrested him for trespassing," I said. "Let's stick to you, though. How'd you meet him?"

Reuben said nothing. Then he pushed back from his desk and sighed as he looked at me.

"Did you know he was a bouncer at Club Serenity?"

Club Serenity was a strip club by the interstate owned by a man named Vic Conroy. Conroy was the closest thing

St. Augustine County had to a real gangster. In addition to the strip club, he owned a massive truck stop and a motel. Young women started by working the truck stop parking lot as prostitutes and then moved on to working the strip club when they turned eighteen. They picked up men at the club and took them to the motel for paid trysts. When they got too old to sell themselves, most moved on, but some became maids or clerks. It was a veritable cozy—and sleazy—triangle.

We had tried to make cases against Conroy in the past, but he had good lawyers, and he took care of the men and women who worked for him. On the rare occasion we found someone willing to speak against him, they disappeared before trial. Conroy might have bought them off, but more than likely, he put a few of them in a grave somewhere.

"If you were trying to use Stinky Jay to get at Vic Conroy, you should have told me," I said, tightening my crossed arms. "That's what partners do."

"Conroy's got his fingers all over this county. Based on the things I've seen since moving here, it would shock me if he didn't have somebody in this department on his payroll."

I blinked and said nothing, hoping I had misheard him. Reuben stared at me with cold, flat eyes.

"So you don't trust me," I said.

"It has nothing to do with trust."

A warm feeling spread from my core to my skin. My jaw clamped tight as I ground my molars against one another. I drew in a long, controlled breath, hoping that would keep my temper from bubbling over.

"You may not have known me well, but you were my partner," I said. "I put my life in your hands. If you didn't feel comfortable telling me about the cases you were working, you should have asked for a reassignment. And if you don't trust anybody in this department, do us all a favor and quit. You don't need to be here."

He grunted but said nothing.

"Call your lawyer," I said, turning to leave. "We'll talk about it when she gets here."

He raised an eyebrow and gave me a bored expression but said nothing. My skin felt hot and muscles all over my body trembled as I walked out of the room. I didn't care whether Reuben liked me, but trust was another matter. If he didn't trust me, I didn't have room in my life for him.

I walked to Trisha's conference room, cursing under my breath the entire time. Reuben and I barely knew each other, but we swore the same oath when we became police officers and put on the same badge every morning. We hadn't run into serious trouble together, but if we had, I would have risked my life for him. I would have fought for him. It pissed me off to know he didn't even respect me enough to talk to me about concerns about me and our department.

"Back so soon?" asked Trisha. Her smile disappeared as I walked toward her. "You look mad. What's wrong?"

"Nothing we can deal with right away," I said, nodding toward one of the spare workstations the department's new IT team had set up. "You mind if I use this?"

"Go right ahead," she said. "Just to warn you, though, it's been loud in here. The phone lines have been busy today."

"Okay by me," I said. She nodded, so I sat down and logged in.

A modern police department had access to a mind-boggling amount of information. Reuben may have put me in a bad mood, but I was a professional with a case to work. I started by looking up Stinky Jay's arrest record. We had picked him up twice for public intoxication, once for possession of marijuana, three times for trespassing, and once for disturbing the peace by creating a noxious odor in a place of worship. I didn't know what to think about the last one, but none of his offenses had involved violence. When he was last arrested, the arresting officer described him as polite and cooperative.

I looked him up on the license bureau's database next. He shared an address with a young woman named Jennifer Corkern. She was twenty-four, and she had blonde hair and blue eyes. She looked pretty even in her license picture. Like Stinky Jay, she had a lengthy arrest record, mostly for prostitution. She had last been arrested at the Wayfair Motel, which meant she was one of Vic Conroy's girls.

I logged out of my computer and walked to Trisha's desk, where I waited for her to finish routing an officer to a fender bender by the interstate. When she finished, she looked at me and gave me a tight smile.

"When Reuben Terepocki's attorney gets here, tell him to call me."

Trisha peeled off a sticky note from a stack beside her monitor and wrote herself a note.

"Will do. You going anywhere in particular?"

"I'm going to visit a pimp. Wish me luck."

# Chapter 6

C lub Serenity occupied a single-story windowless building with an asphalt shingle roof and a parking lot big enough to accommodate semi-trucks. It wasn't even eleven in the morning, but almost a dozen cars had parked around the building. My old cruiser shuddered over a cattle guard as I turned into the lot. Why a strip club that was miles from the nearest cattle ranch had a cattle guard, I didn't know, but I tried not to judge.

I parked beside a maroon minivan with tinted glass and a yellow sign suction-cupped to the rear window warning other drivers that there was a baby on board. Hopefully, the driver had left the kid with a sitter.

I locked my cruiser and walked toward the building. When I was young, my biological mother had danced in a similar club in East St. Louis. She could have made a reasonable living taking her clothes off for money, but Erin didn't have enough sense to take care of herself. For brief periods, we had apartments, but we lived out of her car most of the time. I didn't know when she crossed the line from stripping to prostitution, but she lost herself—and me—after that.

A wooden wedge held the club's frosted glass door open. Music wafted outside. A no-smoking sign adorned the door-frame.

"Once more unto the breach," I said to myself, checking to ensure my badge was visible on my belt.

Inside, the lights were low, the music was loud, and a top-less pregnant woman danced on an elevated stage about thir-ty feet from the entrance. Six men sat on stools and watched while her hips gyrated to the music. A woman about my age in a bikini at least two sizes too small for her ample chest walked toward me and bit her lower lip as she touched my arm.

"You're cute," she said, her eyes flicking down my body. "See anything you like? I won't charge the first time."

I furrowed my brow. "What are you offering?"

She stepped close enough that she could have kissed me had she wanted.

"You can have whatever you want," she said, her voice low and sultry. That didn't narrow her offer down very much, but I shook my head, anyway.

"I appreciate the offer, but is Jennifer Corkern around?"

The dancer straightened, and the flirtatious smile left her lips as she stepped back.

"You'll have to talk to Vic about her."

I looked toward the stage and the pregnant woman and the men who were clearly enjoying themselves.

"I see," I said, pulling back my jacket to show her my badge. "Where is he?"

She crossed her arms and gave me an annoyed expression before looking toward the back of the club.

"Third door back."

I thanked her and walked toward a small hallway at the rear of the club. Two of the men near the stage stopped ogling the dancer and stared at me as I passed, but most of them couldn't take their eyes off the pregnant woman.

The back hallway led to a pair of restrooms, a dressing room for the club's dancers, and an office with its door open. A middle-aged man sat behind a gargantuan desk in the center of the room. I knocked on the doorframe and waited for him to look up.

"Hey, sweetheart," he said. "Come on in."

Conroy was in his late forties to early fifties. Not a single hair graced his head, causing the room's overhead light to bounce off his polished scalp as he moved.

"I'm Detective Joe Court with the Sheriff's Department," I said. "A girl out front sent me back."

He studied me for a moment. It didn't feel sexual, but it made me feel exposed.

"You're attractive enough that you don't need the cop schtick. Take your top off and let me see you move."

I reached for my badge. "My clothes are staying on."

He leaned back and crossed his arms. The office was small but clean. His desk had little clutter.

"Okay," he said, nodding. "This isn't an audition. If you're a real cop, why are you here?"

"I'm looking for Jennifer Corkern. She's one of your dancers."

"*Was* one of my dancers," he said. "She flaked out on a lot of shifts, and when she showed up, she was coked out of her gourd as often as not. I can't make a schedule if I don't know who will show up, and I can't put a girl on the floor if she's so high she's liable to fall off the stage."

I nodded. "You still turn her out at your motel?"

He didn't even blink before responding.

"This is a busy club, and I don't turn out anybody. What the girls do when they're off the clock is their business."

It was a smooth, practiced answer from a man accustomed to talking to the police. Conroy ran the biggest illegal enterprise in the region, and he did it in the open. Everybody knew where he made his money, but we couldn't prove anything. He knew how little leverage I had. I wouldn't rattle him with questions. I was lucky he hadn't kicked me out already.

"How about Jay Pischke?" I asked. "People like him?"

Conroy blinked a few times and tightened his arms across his chest.

"Stink's one of my bouncers. Yeah, people like him."

"How about customers who touched your girls? Did they like him?"

Conroy shrugged. "We make sure everybody walks away happy. Sometimes that's hard."

"Did anyone take particular exception to Jay's actions at the club?"

Conroy paused and then shook his head. "Even if somebody did, I won't talk about it. People come to this club expecting discretion from its manager. They'll have it even if I have to kick them out."

I nodded. "You know Reuben Terepocki?"

For an instant, he drew in a breath, and a glimmer of recognition flashed over his eyes. Then, he shrugged once more.

"I don't know everybody who comes to the club, Detective."

I crossed my arms. "Reuben is six-one, and he's got light brown skin, freckles, and gray and black hair. He was a vice detective in Kansas City, so he's familiar with your line of work. Sheriff Delgado hired him two months ago."

"I might have met him, but I don't remember him. You got a card?"

I reached into the inside pocket of my jacket for a business card. Conroy looked at it and then nodded.

"If I think of anything, I'll call you, Detective," he said. I nodded and turned to leave when he called out again. "It's lunch time. Special today is a wagyu beef hamburger with gorgonzola cheese, caramelized onions in a balsamic vinegar reduction, and a bed of arugula on a rye bun. It's the best burger in town, and we serve it with the best fries in town. My chef went to culinary school."

My stomach grumbled, but I ignored it.

"I try to avoid eating at strip clubs."

"This is a gentlemen's club, but your loss," said Conroy, tilting his head to the side and shrugging. "If you change your mind, we do a great Sunday brunch, too. It's free with the purchase of five or more lap dances."

"Those lap dances come with a happy ending?"

Conroy grinned and leaned back. "Everybody walks away happy in my club. I guarantee it."

"I don't doubt that," I said, turning to go once more. This time, I didn't stop before reaching my car. The trip was a waste of time, but that was common in my job. I only needed one lead. If I had to turn over ten rocks to find it, so be it.

I left and drove to a fast-food place for a hamburger that wasn't as good as the one Conroy described. Then I drove to the bungalow Stinky Jay and Jennifer Corkern shared.

No one answered when I knocked on the door, so I took out my notebook and jotted down my name, phone number, and a quick note requesting that Jennifer call me back. Then I slipped it into the mailbox by her door and looked through the front window. The home's interior looked neat and clean. The living room had two couches and a television above the fireplace. I couldn't see toys, baby swings, changing mats, or anything else baby related.

Since I was there, I walked around the house in case someone was in the backyard and hadn't heard me. The home had two bedrooms but no nursery as best I could tell. Jay and Jennifer might have lived together, but they didn't seem to have a baby, and they didn't keep drug paraphernalia out in the open.

Why, then, did the meth lab have cases of diapers, wipes, and formula? Why did it have a crib? And why did Reuben drive there before work without telling any of his colleagues? I couldn't answer any of those questions yet. Death investigations were almost always frustrating in the beginning, but this one pissed me off. Reuben had been my partner. I deserved better than the runaround.

As I walked back to my car, I called Trisha.

"Hey, it's Joe," I said. "Has Reuben Terepocki's attorney arrived yet?"

"Not yet, but I hear he's on his way," she said. "He's driving down from St. Louis."

"Good. I'm on my way in, and I want answers."

# Chapter 7

When I got to my station, Reuben and his lawyer—a man named Paul Bellamy—were sitting in the office Reuben and I shared. Detective Terepocki sat behind his desk, while his attorney sat to his right. I sat behind my desk and used an app on my cell phone to record our conversation.

"Okay. For the record, I'm Detective Joe Court, and I'm interviewing Detective Reuben Terepocki about the shooting death of Jay Pischke. Sitting in on this interview is Detective Terepocki's attorney, Paul Bellamy. Do you agree to talk on the record, Detective?"

Reuben leaned forward to rest his elbows on his desk. "Yeah."

"Good," I said, nodding and taking a pen from my desk so I could take notes. "What happened this morning?"

Reuben looked to his attorney before raising an eyebrow. "How long have you been a detective, Joe?"

I allowed my lips to form a thin line. "Long enough to know the investigating officer asks the questions during an interview."

He straightened and crossed his arms.

"I shot Jay Pischke in self-defense."

"Good. Did you go to the meth lab specifically to meet Mr. Pischke?"

He nodded. "I needed to talk to him."

I nodded again and jotted down a few notes before looking up and holding his gaze.

"What did you need to talk to him about?"

Before Reuben could answer, his attorney cleared his throat and leaned forward.

"That's irrelevant to your investigation, Detective Court."

I darted my eyes toward him.

"I don't know what's relevant yet," I said. "You two can stonewall me if you want, but it'll be harder to clear Detective Terepocki if he doesn't talk. What do you want to do?"

Reuben spoke before his lawyer could respond.

"An informant told me I should talk to him. I had never met him, but I tried going by the home he and his girlfriend shared. I left him multiple messages, none of which he returned. When a second informant told me he believed Mr. Pischke was staying in the house in Dyer, I drove out to see him early in the morning, believing he would still be there. There was nothing improper about it."

It sounded like a prepared statement. I wrote it down and then narrowed my eyebrows before looking at him again.

"What did you hope to get out of your meeting with Mr. Pischke?"

"He worked for Vic Conroy, so I had hoped to turn him into an asset."

"You thought he would flip on Conroy?" I asked.

"Maybe," said Reuben. "I planned to groom him for a while first."

Harry Grainger, the former sheriff, had tried the same tactic for years, but he failed every time.

"What happened when you got there?"

"I knocked on the door. Mr. Pischke opened, saw my badge, and pulled a pistol from his waistband. I removed my weapon from its holster. He backed up and opened fire. I then shot him in the chest four times."

I nodded. "How many times did he shoot at you?"

"I don't know. It happened fast. I fired four times. I hit him every time."

"Did you identify yourself?"

Reuben leaned forward. "He saw my badge, Detective."

"But did you verbally identify yourself?"

He let out an exasperated sigh and covered his face with his hand. "Yeah. Before firing, I said I was a police officer. I then asked him to drop his weapon. Instead, he shot at me."

I wrote that down. "And you had never seen him before, and he had never seen you?"

The lawyer spoke before his client could say anything.

"Based on the facts at hand, that's irrelevant."

Unfortunately, Mr. Bellamy was right. Under Missouri's law, a police officer could use deadly force if he believed someone threatened him or someone else with serious bodily injury. Events that happened two or three days earlier mattered little. Based on what I had found at the crime scene—the gun in Jay's hand and the gunshot residue on his clothes and body—Reuben had ample justification for firing.

Reuben and I kept talking for another half hour, but I didn't learn anything new. I thanked him for coming in and then stood to leave. Reuben's story didn't have many details, but it didn't seem obviously false. I'd investigate and ensure the scene matched what he told me, but, so far, this looked as if it were a righteous shooting. Still, the case nagged at me. I stopped in the doorway before leaving the room.

"Why did he have diapers?" I asked.

Reuben and his attorney had huddled behind his desk. They stopped talking.

"Excuse me?" asked the attorney.

"Diapers," I said. "When I searched the meth lab, I found freeze-dried food, jugs of water, medicine, sleeping bags, guns, and almost a dozen boxes of ammunition. I also found diapers, baby wipes, a Pack 'n Play, and infant formula. Why did Stinky Jay have the baby stuff? He doesn't have a kid."

"I can't help you, Joe," said Reuben. "There was no baby there when I arrived."

And that was a problem. I had a homicide to work, but already my mind had drifted to other matters. If Stinky Jay and Jennifer Corkern had an infant together, and if Jennifer did as many drugs as her former boss implied, that baby could be in danger with Jay dead. I needed to find them both before somebody got hurt.

I walked to the parking lot, where I found Old Brown, the decrepit cruiser Sheriff Delgado had ordered the department to keep on reserve for me. Old Brown had four hundred thousand miles on its odometer and a suspension that made it feel as if I were floating down the road. Rust had eaten through the floorboards in the back so thoroughly that the department's mechanic had bolted old license plates to the frame so prisoners wouldn't fall through, and the air conditioner spewed exhaust in the driver's face when turned on. Still, it ran, and it had a working laptop and an internet connection.

I sat in the front seat and called up Jennifer Corkern's arrest record. No one had arrested her in the past year, but uniformed patrol officers had questioned her outside the homes of suspected drug dealers on multiple occasions. Since few drug addicts strayed far from their favorite dealers, it was a good lead.

As I turned on my cruiser, the fan belt squealed, drawing pitying glances from two construction workers outside on a smoke break. I ignored them and backed out of my spot. Though I hadn't seen him in years, I knew Jennifer's dealer and had questioned him a couple of times for various drug offenses. Where some dealers got into the business to make money, this guy got into it because he loved the product. It made him easy to manipulate.

I drove to his address and found a single-story cottage with white clapboard siding and a porch swing. I parked out front and stepped across the crumbling walkway to the porch. Someone had turned the television up so I could hear it through the front door. He was watching a game show.

I pounded on the door.

"Sheriff's Department."

Something thumped to the ground inside, but nobody answered my knock. I pounded again.

"Sheriff's Department. I'm just here to talk. You run, this is going to suck for you."

The volume on the TV lowered.

"What do you want to talk about?"

The voice belonged to Tony Bosa, my target.

"You know Jay Pischke or Jennifer Corkern?"

The voice hesitated. "Everybody knows Stink and Jenn."

"Jay's dead. Open the door. I want to talk."

The deadbolt retracted with a thud, and the door squealed open a moment later. Tony had a thin face and trimmed black goatee. Red striations streaked the whites of his eyes as if he were high, but I couldn't smell dope.

"What happened to Jay?" he asked, blinking.

I ignored him and looked over his shoulder into the room. The overhead light fixture only had one working bulb, and it cast a dim light over the interior. Nicotine had stained the walls a dull yellow, and foot traffic had worn the carpet down so I could see the matting beneath. An upholstered couch sat across from an enormous television. A young woman wearing nothing but pink panties and a white tank top sat and watched us. She had a forty-ounce bottle of malt liquor in her hand, but she dropped that once she saw me watching her.

I looked to the man.

"Nice to see you again, Tony."

His eyes opened wide. "How do you know my name?"

"I'm a police officer," I said. "I know everything."

"Really?" he asked, furrowing his brow.

I considered him, wondering how much he had smoked, and then shook my head.

"No, I'm not omniscient," I said. "I'm going to look around and make sure everything's okay."

He shook his head. "You can't do that. I've got rights."

"That's true. You have rights," I said, nodding and then tilting my head to look around him. The girl in the couch had stood to get dressed. "How old is the pretty girl with the pink underwear?"

He smirked. "She's legal."

"Maybe, but I'd bet my last nickel she's not twenty-one. Step outside, Mr. Bosa. I'm placing you under arrest for supplying alcohol to a minor," I said. I looked over his shoulder again. "And miss, once you get your pants on, I need you to step outside, too. If you run, you won't like what happens."

She nodded and pulled on her jeans. I led Bosa outside toward my cruiser and secured his hands behind his back with zip ties. Bosa had broken the law when he gave his date booze, but it was a class-B misdemeanor. If I took him in, it'd take me half an hour to process him and another half hour to fill out the paperwork. I didn't plan to waste that much time. This was about leverage.

Once I had his hands secured, I sat him down on the backseat of my car.

"So you know Jennifer Corkern. Have you seen her in the past couple of days?"

Bosa refused to look up. "I have nothing to say."

I nodded. "All right. You sit tight for a few minutes. I'll talk to your girlfriend."

He grunted and drew his legs inside the car so I could shut the door. Since my car lacked rear door handles, and since it had a welded cage that separated the front seats and backseats, he'd be safe there for a little while. I walked back to the house and found Bosa's date in the front room, sitting on the couch. She could have passed for seventeen, but not twenty-one.

I leaned against the doorframe and crossed my arms. She looked at me but said nothing.

"What's your name and how old are you?" I asked.

"I don't have to tell you shit."

I nodded and reached for my cell phone.

"If that's how you want to play this, that's how we'll play this."

I snapped her picture. She gave me a dirty look but said nothing. After a recent tragedy, I had made it a point to get to know the administrators at the local school district. That would come in handy. I texted the girl's photo to the guidance counselor at St. Augustine High School and asked whether he knew her. Within three minutes, my phone rang.

"Detective Court," came a cheery voice from my phone. "This is Rajendra Gavani at the high school. It's good to hear from you."

I had only met Mr. Gavani—the high school's new guidance counselor—once, but he had seemed like a nice guy. He was about thirty, and the county had hired him from a school district in south St. Louis County. He had tried to flirt with me at our first meeting, but he was aware enough to realize I wasn't interested and stopped. It was refreshing to see.

"You, too, Mr. Gavani," I said. "I've just found this young lady in a house in St. Augustine. You recognize her?"

"Her name is Ava Lockheart. She's sixteen, and she's a sophomore. According to the nurse's office, her mom called her in sick this morning."

Gavani gave me her parents' names and phone numbers, so I thanked him and hung up. Then I called Trisha and asked her to send me some additional officers.

Ava's shoulders rose and fell as she breathed. Tears came to her eyes.

"Are you going to arrest me?"

"No," I said, shaking my head. "I'll turn you over to your parents."

She looked up at me. "What about Tony?"

"You're sixteen. Tony's a twenty-nine-year-old drug dealer who supplied you with alcohol before having sex with you. What do you think should happen to him?"

She said nothing. Then she looked down.

"He said he loves me."

"If he loved you, he'd tell you to stay in school, and he'd wait until you were older to have a relationship."

By the look she gave me, I didn't know whether she was about to burst into tears or hit me. She blinked and then crossed her arms.

"You don't know what you're talking about. You don't even know him."

"Miss, I put men like him in prison for a living. I know him better than you think."

She blinked. Then the tears started falling.

"You're a bitch."

"People have called me worse," I said, holding out a hand. "Now come on. I've got backup on the way. Once they get here, I'll take you home."

# Chapter 8

Ava lived in a middle-class brick ranch home with a basketball hoop in the driveway. Her mom met us at the door. Mr. Gavani at the school had already called the house, but he left the details for me to explain. I told Mrs. Lockheart where I had found her daughter and what she had been wearing and drinking. A lot of parents—dads especially—would have been mad, but Ava's mom drew her into a hug and told her everything would be okay. Then she thanked me for bringing her baby home. I told her I was just doing my job.

I hated that Bosa had put Ava in that situation. She should have been able to date whoever she wanted. She should have been able to make her own mistakes and to learn and grow from them. Tony Bosa wasn't some boy in her geometry class, though. He was a predator who gave alcohol to a young woman half his age so he could take advantage of her. I'd enjoy sending him to prison. That I could possibly pry some information from him about Jay Pischke and Jennifer Corkern made it even better.

I stayed with Ava and her mom for about fifteen minutes before heading back to my station. Officer Marcus Washington had driven Bosa from his house, and both men were waiting for me in our makeshift second-floor lobby. I thanked Marcus and then walked Bosa to a windowless storage room we used as an interrogation booth. The air conditioner hissed, and construction workers hammered something downstairs as Bosa and I sat on opposite sides of a card table.

I forced a smile to my face and put my phone between us on the table to record our conversation.

"First, are you comfortable, Mr. Bosa? If you're thirsty or hungry, I can bring you something."

"I'm fine," he said.

I didn't care about his comfort level, but at this point in an investigation, I'd give him whatever he wanted so he couldn't later tell his lawyer I had starved him or threatened to withhold water. It made it more likely that my interrogation would stand up in court.

"At the moment, you're under arrest for providing alcoholic beverages to a minor," I said. "You have the right to remain silent, but if you talk, I can use whatever you tell me against you in court. If you'd like, you can have an attorney. If you can't afford one, the court will provide you a public defender free of charge. Do you understand those rights?"

"Yeah. Sure."

"Good," I said, nodding. "Would you like to talk to me?"

He shrugged and slouched. "I don't know what we've got to talk about."

I forced my shoulders to relax.

"How about we start with Ava, then. What's up with her?"

He cocked his head to the side and furrowed his brow.

"I rolled up to your house and found her drinking a forty-ounce bottle of Olde English malt liquor on your couch," I said. "Did she bring the drink, or did you give it to her?"

He said nothing, so I leaned forward and lowered my head.

"This is your turn to tell me what happened in your own words. If you don't talk, a judge will find you guilty of giving her booze and send you to jail for six months. Your choice. If you didn't do anything wrong, though, talk to me."

He narrowed his eyes at me, thinking. In the end, my question didn't matter. Whether he had given Ava the bottle or had merely allowed her to drink it in his house, he had still violated the same statute. Finally, he nodded.

"She brought it. Said she got it from some guy at Waterford College. You ask me, you should arrest him."

"You got a name?" I asked, reaching into my jacket for a pen and notepad. He hesitated and then shook his head.

"Nah. You want, I'll ask her. She'll tell me."

"I believe she would," I said, nodding and flipping through my notepad to a blank page. "She's a pretty girl."

He crossed his arms but said nothing, so I shrugged and let my head hang low again.

"There's nothing wrong with saying a girl's pretty," I said. "And Ava is certainly pretty."

He furrowed his brow. "You into girls?"

I shrugged, getting into the role. "Nothing wrong with it if I were."

"Nah, nothing wrong with that," he said. His eyes traveled down my face and to my chest before he nodded. "Yeah, she's hot."

"How old is she?" I asked. "She looks like she's about twenty."

He shrugged. "Eighteen, nineteen, something like that."

"Nothing wrong with hooking up with a nineteen-year-old in the middle of the day. We've all been there," I said. He didn't hesitate before nodding his agreement, so I pushed forward. "Did she go to your house so you two could fool around?"

He looked away and said nothing. Now that I had given him the rope, I needed to push him off the platform so he could hang himself. I held my breath for a moment to slow my heart.

"Look, man, I got to be honest with you," I said, leaning back and matching his posture. "Either she came to your house to have sex with you, or she came to your house to drink and maybe pop some pills. If she came to hook up, that's one thing. If she came for drugs or booze, that's a problem. So what was it? She come for sex or dope? I know she didn't come for the atmosphere. Your house was a shit-hole."

He ran a hand through his hair before sighing and looking down at the table.

"She came because she wanted to fool around," he said.

"And did you have sex with her?"

He narrowed his eyes. "What kind of question is that?"

"Did you have sexual intercourse with her?" I asked, allowing a measure of ice into my voice. "I found her in your living room in her underwear. Did you have sex with her?"

"Yeah," he said. "What's it matter? Like you said, there's nothing wrong with hooking up with a girl in the middle of the day—especially when she looks like she's twenty years old."

She looked like she should have been playing youth soccer, but I kept my mouth shut.

"That's all I wanted to hear," I said. "The truth. Ava showed up at your house with a forty-ounce bottle of malt liquor. You two had sex, she drank some malt liquor, and you watched a game show. That right?"

He nodded.

"Great," I said, balling my hands into fists beneath the table so he wouldn't see how revolting I found him. The conversation left a bitter taste in my mouth, but I forced myself to smile anyway as I reached for my phone. "See how easy that was? It took twenty minutes to drag that out of you.

If you had been honest earlier, you could have been out of here by now. Unless you like it here. Do you like it here?"

"Shit no," he said, a smile forming on his lips. "I've got a job. I've got stuff to do."

"I hear you," I said. "Before you go, though, I need your help. The law says you committed a misdemeanor by letting Ava drink in your house."

"That isn't right," he said. "I told her she shouldn't have been drinking. She's underage."

"I'm not here to jam you up," I said. "You help me out, I can forget that I found her with booze. I need to know about Jennifer Corkern. Does she have a baby?"

"Jenn?" he asked, screwing up his face. "Nah. She doesn't have any babies. Stink didn't want them."

I nodded.

"Did Jay have a baby with someone else?"

He shook his head. "Nah. Jay loved Jenn too much to get with anybody else."

"You know where she is?"

He shook his head again. "She used to come by some, but I haven't seen her for a couple of weeks. You should check out her club. I bet Vic Conroy knows where she is. He knows everything in this town."

That might have been true, but his answers would come with a cost I couldn't afford. Still, I nodded.

"I'll go by the club and ask," I said. "When did you last see Jay?"

He thought for a moment. "'Bout two nights ago. Saw him at Tommy B's. Boy was slinging cash around like it was nobody's business."

Tommy B's was a dive bar downtown. The booze was cheap, the main room smelled like body odor and bleach, and the crowd got rowdy late at night. We made a lot of arrests there.

"He go to bars and sling around cash a lot?"

"Nah," he said, shaking his head. "Stink makes good money at the club, but he must have had ten grand."

That was more money than a bouncer made in three months, making me wonder where he got it. Not only that, it was a lot of money to carry around. You couldn't put that in your wallet and go on with your day. If he carried that around to the bar, he likely carried it around elsewhere, too, and yet we hadn't found it on his body. I made a note reminding me to ask Reuben about it.

I nodded once more and glanced at him.

"Thanks for your help."

He raised his eyebrows. "So, can I go?"

"No," I said. "You're under arrest for statutory rape in the second degree. Ava is sixteen. The age of consent in Missouri is seventeen. For future reference, if your date shows up to your door with a backpack and a story about sneaking out of class, do us all a favor and keep it in your pants."

He called me a bitch, but I ignored him and left the room. Marcus Washington stood outside. I hadn't known he was listening, but he held out his hand toward me to shake.

"That was impressive work in there, Joe," he said, covering my hand with his own massive one. "As a dad of two little girls, I could watch you send shitheads to prison all day."

"You're too kind, but thank you," I said, smiling. "Do you mind taking him down to booking? I'm still working a homicide. He just showed up in the middle."

Marcus nodded. "I'm on it, boss."

I thanked him and then checked my phone to make sure it had recorded everything. It had, so I emailed the audio file to myself so I could include it with my report. The arrest had given me an hour or two of paperwork, but I'd do it gladly to get a predator off the street. If I could just figure out where Jennifer Corkern was, it might turn into a nice day.

Somehow, I didn't get my hopes up.

# Chapter 9

W hile Marcus led Tony Bosa to booking, I walked to my office, where I spent the next hour and a half typing up my handwritten notes and filling out the paperwork that would send Tony Bosa to prison for statutory rape.

A judge could sentence him to seven years behind bars, but he'd probably plead to a lesser felony to avoid a trial. Either way, we'd get him off the streets for a while, and he'd have to register as a sex offender for the rest of his life. He deserved far worse.

After filling out the paperwork, I took out my phone to call Sheriff Delgado with an update, but I couldn't even dial before somebody knocked on my door. I glanced up and found Trisha with a sheepish smile on her face. I asked what she needed, but then I noticed Vic Conroy standing behind her. I put my phone down and crossed my arms.

"Mr. Conroy," I said, leaning back. "What can I do for you?"

"I've been thinking about our meeting this morning," he said. "There are some things I'd like to add to our conversation."

"Do you know where Jennifer Corkern is?" I asked.

"No, but I know a few things that could put your partner's shooting of my employee into context."

I narrowed my eyes. "When I talked to you this morning, you said you didn't know Reuben."

"I said I didn't remember him," said Conroy, gesturing toward a chair in front of my desk. "I offered you a chair in my office."

I considered him for a moment. My instincts told me to throw him out, but my training and experience told me to hear what he had to say. Almost assuredly he'd lie to me, but the best lies all contained an undercurrent of truth.

"Have a seat, Mr. Conroy," I said, glancing at him and then to Trisha. "Thanks, Trisha. I've got it from here."

"If you need anything, Sergeant Reitz and I are down the hall. Bob's finishing up paperwork."

I nodded and gave Vic a fake smile.

"My dispatcher thinks you might try something," I said. "You're not stupid enough to attack a police officer in her station, are you?"

"No, ma'am," he said, matching my smile and sitting. "Scout's honor."

I looked to Trisha and softened my voice. "We'll be okay."

She hesitated and left. I put an elbow on my desk and rested my chin on my palm.

"What do you want, Mr. Conroy?"

"Let me start by apologizing for our brusque meeting this morning," he said, reaching into his jacket. I lowered my hand and opened the center drawer of my desk, where I kept my firearm when I was in the office. He pulled out a pair of tickets and slid them across the desk toward me. "Those are good for two free lunch specials next time you're in the club. Our burgers are the best in town. We get our beef fresh from a local farm. It's never frozen. Once you get my meat in your mouth, your life will never be the same."

I thought about responding with a double entendre of my own involving a meat grinder, but I had spent most of the day on my feet, and my eyelids felt heavy. I flicked the coupons back across my desk with a fingertip.

"Fuck off, Mr. Conroy."

He laughed and smiled the first genuine smile I had seen from him as he put the coupons back in his jacket.

"You don't suffer fools lightly, do you, Detective?" he asked. "I'll add that to your profile."

"I don't have a problem with fools, but you're not a fool," I said. "What do you want?"

He crossed his legs.

"First things first, I feel like we got off on the wrong foot when I asked you to take your clothes off in my office. I apologize."

I shrugged. "No problem. You're not the first person to ask me to take my top off."

He grinned. "I am sure of that. That's why I'm here. I'd like you to give a thought to working for me."

"So we're back to you asking me to take my top off."

"No," he said, shaking his head. "I'm asking whether you'd like to work security at my club. Jay did a great job at making the girls feel safe, but with his death, I've got an opening. I think you'd fit in well. It'd only be two or three nights a week, so you could even keep your job here. Plenty of police officers work off-duty security jobs. Why should they get all the money?"

"I don't need the money, but thank you."

"Pay is considerable—thousand bucks a week," he said. "It's not enough to make you rich, but it could make you comfortable when added to a detective's salary."

I leaned closer to him and raised my eyebrows.

"You and I both know a part-time bouncer's salary isn't anywhere near a thousand bucks a week," I said. "Watch what you say next, Mr. Conroy, because you're close to offering a bribe to a police officer."

He smiled. "You could just say no. You don't have to threaten me."

I nodded, my lips straight. "In that case, no thank you. If that's all you've got, I'll call an officer to see you out."

He crossed his arms and appraised me as he leaned back. "How well do you know Mr. Terepocki?"

I folded my hands together on my desk and sighed.

"I'm not here to shoot the shit with you. What have you got?"

"Reuben Terepocki is an enforcer for Pete Marino with the Kansas City mob."

I snorted and pointed toward the door. "Get out of here."

"I'm not kidding, Detective," he said, his voice flat. "KC mob isn't what it used to be, but they've still got legs throughout the state. You know my business. I own a gentlemen's club. My competitors aren't always upstanding members of the local chamber of commerce. Sometimes it helps to know people, and I know your partner. He's not who you think he is."

Conroy stared right into my eyes. I shook my head.

"I don't believe that."

He ran a hand across his mouth and chin before leaning forward.

"The world doesn't care what you believe, honey," he said. "Facts are facts. Since you're the skeptical type, though, ask yourself something: How much do you get paid?"

I raised my eyebrows. "That's none of your business."

"Is it more or less than a hundred and twenty grand a year?"

I shook my head and crossed my arms. "I'm not answering that."

"Your partner turned down a job paying a hundred and twenty grand a year to come here," said Conroy. "He's a public employee, so you can look him up. The *Kansas City Star* has a database online."

It was probably twice what Reuben earned here. I blinked a few times, processing that.

"Okay," I said, my voice a little softer. "What's your point?"

Conroy laced his fingers together and leaned forward. "Your partner is healthy, intelligent, and productive. He closes cases. He's a good detective. Why would a detective making a hundred and twenty grand a year quit his job in a major, cosmopolitan city to come here and work for half his salary in St. Augustine?"

It was a good question, but I shook my head anyway.

"It's none of my business."

"Maybe you should make it your business," said Conroy. "He's your partner. Two kinds of people end up in St. Augustine: those hiding from their past, and those who have nowhere else to go. I know your story, so I know what you were hiding from. Why is Reuben here?"

I closed my eyes and shook my head again. "I won't dignify that with a response."

Conroy nodded and reached into his jacket again. This time, he pulled out a cell phone. I leaned back and waited. He flicked his finger across the screen and paused for a moment before turning the phone to me.

Conroy had spooled up a video. By the angle, it came from a surveillance camera suspended near his club's front entrance. When he hit the play button, I felt like the entire world shifted. My throat tightened, my stomach dropped into my feet, and my heart nearly stopped.

On the video, Reuben Terepocki walked through Club Serenity's front door and punched Stinky Jay Pischke in the face. Then he kicked him on the ground. Three people rushed over to break up the fight after that, including Vic Conroy. Then Conroy and Reuben disappeared off camera.

"Shit," I said, closing my eyes and leaning back. Reuben had lied. I had asked him to his face whether he knew Stinky Jay, and he looked right in my eyes and said no. I swore under my breath.

"Did your partner not tell you he and Jay got into a fight last week?"

I put my hands behind my head and tilted my neck so that I was staring at the ceiling, mostly because I didn't want to see the smug look on Conroy's face.

"What were they fighting about?"

"Jay's a loyal employee who's been with me for a long time. Your partner was trying to shake me down. He wanted two grand a week on behalf of his friends in Kansas City. If I didn't pay up, they'd torch my club. Jay was trying to protect me. I can take care of myself, but it was a touching gesture. I never thought Reuben would come after him afterwards."

If I believed Reuben was some kind of mob enforcer, it would make sense, but it would take an awful lot to convince me of that. I said nothing as I ordered my thoughts.

"Here's another possibility," I said. "Reuben was a vice detective in Kansas City. You're a pimp. More than that, Reuben's good with women, especially young women. He's like a dad. My guess is that he's been talking to some of your girls, maybe the ones who work your truck stop. You're afraid Reuben will build a case against you, so you came here to muddy the waters as much as you could. You're doing everything you can to tarnish a good detective's reputation before he destroys everything you've spent your life building."

Conroy frowned and considered before shrugging.

"Maybe you're right," he said, lumbering to his feet. "But maybe you're not. Talk to your partner. See what he has to say. I'm sure you'll do the right thing."

"Don't worry," I said, standing. "I will."

I walked him out of the building and then returned to my office, where I called Reuben's cell phone. He answered after three rings. His voice was slurred.

"This is inappropriate, Joe. If you need to talk, call my lawyer."

"If I did, would you amend your statement?"

He paused and then sighed. "What do you want?"

"You ever been to Club Serenity?"

"No," he said. I clenched my jaw and said nothing, hoping he'd correct the lie. He didn't.

"And you had never met Jay Pischke before today?"

This time he paused.

"If you want to continue this conversation, call my lawyer."

He hung up before I could respond. I swore under my breath and tossed my phone onto the desk before pacing the room. I refused to believe Reuben was a criminal without more evidence, but this wasn't right. As a former vice detective, he should have had a special interest in Vic Conroy. He should have been looking into his prostitution ring. That was his job and his area of expertise. He had every reason to know Club Serenity's bouncer, dancers, and owner. He had no reason to lie, and yet he did.

I plopped down in my chair and swore.

"What the hell are you hiding?"

# Chapter 10

The car was silent save Laura Singleton's soft snoring. Lorenzo had met Laura over a decade ago at the Baghdad Country Club. It was the only bar in the Green Zone, a heavily fortified area in the Karkh district of central Baghdad. The Country Club occupied a cinder-block building within a cluster of villas that Saddam Hussein's buddies had once lived in. When you wandered in, you dropped your guns off in a vault and left the outside world behind.

The bar had run out of things a lot—supply lines were hard to keep up in a war zone—but it had a bartender named Heidi who poured generous shots and was easy to look at. When he visited the first time and ordered a Manhattan, he had almost forgotten that he was sitting at a white plastic table in a gravel courtyard and listening to eighties music pumped through tiny speakers attached to an iPod. For a few hours, that bar had let him leave the war.

The Country Club didn't survive long, but Lorenzo had appreciated having it around. When he met Laura the first time, she had been an MP assigned to work with the Green Zone police. General Order 1 forbade US soldiers from drinking while serving in Iraq or Afghanistan, but people did anyway, and MPs like Laura dutifully arrested them.

When she walked into the bar, Lorenzo saw a beautiful woman wearing a tight black tank top, jeans, and hair pulled behind her head in a utilitarian tail. She hadn't worn make-up, but she hadn't needed it. The sun had tanned her skin to a golden brown and bleached her hair to a honey-colored blonde. She had smelled like vanilla. After smelling only the sweaty grunts in his fire team for weeks, she was a welcome distraction.

"Sir, put down your drink. I'm taking you home."

She had a Midwestern American accent—she was from Minnesota, as he would later learn—so he assumed she was a junior staffer at the embassy. Her tight top showed off her lean, athletic body, and her jeans did little to hide her long legs.

"How about you let me buy you a drink first?" he had asked. "If we're going home together, I'd like to know a little about you."

"Call me Laura," she said. "Now come on. We need to go, sir."

He downed the rest of his bourbon in a gulp and left a twenty on the bar. Instead of leading him to the embassy compound, Laura led him to a dusty green MP's Jeep. He spent the night in the brig, but she stayed and talked to him until dawn. It was one of his favorite memories. He and Laura spent time together after that, but they couldn't have a real relationship because of their differences in rank. He liked her, though, and she liked him.

As he looked at her now and watched her chest rise and fall with her breath, he wondered whether this would be their time. He was almost forty, and she was thirty-three. They had their entire lives ahead of them. Maybe this time it would work out.

He rubbed his hands together. It was four in the afternoon. Xavier Becker, Thomas Becker's son, had come home from school half an hour earlier. His mother, stepfather, and baby brother were still out. Thomas Becker was smart enough to know he'd have to disappear after betraying his former partners, but before he did, he'd see his son. It's what every good father would have done, and Thomas was a good father. Lorenzo just needed patience.

Laura stirred and then blinked her green eyes as the sun's rays landed on her face. She straightened and then adjusted the visor before looking at him and smiling.

"How long was I out?"

"Little over an hour," he said. "You needed the sleep."

She nodded and then yawned. "Is the kid here?"

He nodded. "Yeah. No sign of Thomas, though."

"He'll show," she said. "He loves Xavier."

They drifted into a comfortable silence for a few minutes. Then Laura cleared her throat.

"What happens after this job?" she asked.

Lorenzo glanced at her and then back to the road. They had parked about half a block from the home Tara Madison shared with her husband, Wesley, her son Xavier, and their infant son, Joshua. Fifteen years ago, Lorenzo had been an usher at Thomas and Tara's wedding. The marriage didn't last, but it had produced a good kid in Xavier.

"I was thinking about spending time with a friend of mine. She just got out of a relationship with some moron who didn't appreciate her."

"Anybody I know?" she asked, reaching behind her to pull her hair back.

"I'd say you know her pretty well," he said, glancing at her. "I've been waiting ten years to ask her out. It's time."

Laura nodded, her face serious.

"Before you hook up with her, want to fool around with me? I hear it's been a while for you. You might be rusty. Wouldn't want to jump into anything with rusty equipment."

"You'd be willing to do that for me?" he asked. She nodded.

"Anything for a friend," she said.

He smiled at her. She winked.

"I've missed you," he said.

"I've missed you, too," she said, nodding toward the road. "We'll talk about us later. Now, I think our friend just showed."

He followed her gaze to the left. A thin man just a shade under six feet tall walked down the road. His blue sweater and jeans hugged a frame corded with ropy muscles. Thomas had boxed in the Army. He didn't have the speed or strength to go pro, but he could best Lorenzo in a hand-to-hand fight. Until this morning, Lorenzo would have done anything for him. They had been family. Now they weren't.

Lorenzo chambered a round in his pistol and opened his car door just as Thomas passed the shadowy alcove in the woods in which he and Laura had parked. Bottles and cans that had once held cheap beer littered the ground around their car. He even saw a few condom wrappers. Evidently, this was a popular parking spot.

"Hey," said Lorenzo. Thomas whirled around and reached for his waist. Laura shot him in the chest with a Taser. He gasped as the barbs struck him and caught on his skin. As he reached for the wires to pull them out, Laura squeezed the Taser's trigger. Fifty thousand volts coursed through the tiny wires, and Thomas fell to the ground, trembling as every muscle in his body contracted as hard as it could at once. He would have screamed if he had the ability.

Laura held the trigger for a good fifteen seconds before letting off. It gave Lorenzo time to walk toward his former friend and inject him with a measure of suxamethonium chloride—a very fast-acting muscle relaxant—in the thigh.

Thomas looked at Lorenzo with black, hate-filled eyes.

"You mother—"

Lorenzo balled his hand into a fist and punched him in the face, likely breaking his nose. Thomas's head snapped back, and blood trickled down to his chin. Laura squeezed the handle of her Taser again. Once more, Thomas convulsed in pain.

"Something you were saying?" asked Lorenzo.

Laura held on for about thirty seconds, long enough for the drugs to kick in and paralyze him. After that, it wasn't hard to roll him over and secure his hands and legs with zip ties. They put duct tape over his mouth before dropping him in the trunk of their car.

"Nick McCoy was shot. He's probably dead," said Laura. Thomas narrowed his eyes, but the drugs didn't let him react otherwise. She ran a fingernail across his cheek. "It's not your fault, but you'll pay for it anyway. Nick was like a brother. If I had my way, I'd cut off your fingers one by one with garden shears and force you to eat them. Then I'd burn you alive. Renzo's nicer than me. He'll make it quick if you answer his questions. Otherwise he leaves, and I start chopping. Think about that on the drive."

She slammed the trunk lid shut and looked at her partner.

"You ready?" she asked.

"If I had known that's why you wanted the garden shears, I would have suggested bolt cutters."

She tilted her head to the side. "Bolt cutters would be too easy. The handles give you leverage. Garden shears will take more time. It'll hurt more."

"I didn't know you were so scary."

"You never gave me a reason to show you," she said. "Let's get going. The drugs will only be effective for fifteen to twenty minutes."

"Yes, ma'am," said Lorenzo, already walking toward the front seat. They got in and drove, settling in for what promised to be a long, dark night.

# Chapter 11

Until Vic Conroy walked into my office, I had thought I'd finish up my paperwork, go home, have three or four drinks, and take a long bath before bed. It would have been a nice night. Now, though, my mind wouldn't stop working. Reuben was a good cop. If he wanted to investigate Vic Conroy, he would have done it right. He would have filled out reports and applied for search warrants. Somebody should have known something.

I grabbed my phone and called Sheriff Delgado. As his extension rang, I paced by my desk.

"Sheriff, this is Joe Court. I wanted to ask you something about Reuben Terepocki. You got a minute?"

"Maybe one or two," he said. "I've got a budget meeting with the County Council at Café St. Clair."

Café St. Clair had opened about two months earlier on the first floor of a Victorian mansion down by the river. I hadn't been in yet, but it had drawn rave reviews from just about everybody I knew who had eaten there. The owners would make a fortune during Spring Fair week, but for now, they contented themselves by serving very expensive, rich French food to the locals and those men and women from St. Louis willing to drive an hour for dinner.

"I'm working Reuben's shooting and making good progress. I've got a question, though. Was he working any long-term cases with you?"

Delgado paused and drew in a breath. "He's your partner. You should know his caseload."

"Is he investigating Vic Conroy for anything?"

Delgado paused again. This time, I counted to five before he spoke.

"Conroy's a big fish. Has he come up in your investigation?"

I considered and then tilted my head to the side. "Jay Pischke, the guy Reuben shot, was a bouncer at Club Serenity."

"That your only connection to Conroy?"

Now it was my turn to pause and think. If I told the boss the truth, he'd tell me to write an official report detailing Conroy's visit and accusation. Even if Reuben was clean, people down the line would read that report and question his integrity. It would plant a seed of doubt in their minds. It'd hurt his career and reputation. If I wrote him up, I wanted to be right.

"That's it for now," I said. "I'm just doing my due diligence."

"Good," said Delgado, breathing a little easier. "He's not working on anything with me. You keep working the case. I'll read your reports later."

I thanked him for his time and then wished him good luck at his dinner meeting. After that, I sat down and laced my fingers together. If Reuben was working a case against Conroy as he claimed, he was doing it off the books. Not only was that dangerous, it was pointless. Without proper documentation and without the proper warrants, nothing he found would be admissible in court. It was stupid, and Reuben Terepocki wasn't stupid.

I didn't know what was going on yet, but I spent the next half hour writing a report that detailed Conroy's visit and my thoughts on the case so far. Instead of saving it to the department's cloud server and making it part of the official record, though, I emailed it to myself. If I had to file it later, I could. For now, I needed information.

Since I didn't know anybody who worked in Kansas City's police department, I called their switchboard. The operator connected me to their liaison officer. I had to twist a few arms and fax a letter on my department's letterhead, but they agreed to send me a digital copy of Reuben's personnel file—including any citizen complaints made against him in the past twenty years.

After that, I stretched my arms above my head, yawned, and turned out the lights on my way out the door. Before going home, I drove by the grocery store to pick up a bag of dog food for Roy. He was just a dog, but I looked forward to seeing him all the same.

I parked in my driveway and walked to the backyard. Roy was in the dog run, but when he saw me, his tail wagged, and he stretched. As I opened the gate, he licked my hand. As much as I flattered myself to think he cared about me that much, more than likely he was excited because he smelled the dog food I had bought.

I put the food away inside the house while he went to the bathroom in the yard. Then we went for a walk. I watched the sun set, while he stopped and smelled things. Whenever I got too far ahead, he'd trot to catch up. Then he'd lick my hand, and I'd walk again. It was a welcome break from my day, and I hoped it would become routine.

About a quarter of a mile from my house, my steps slowed. Then they stopped when I saw Susanne Pennington's mailbox. Roy nuzzled my hand before trotting off into some nearby woods to smell something.

Until a couple of months ago, Susanne had been my friend, one of the few I had. Unfortunately, she killed herself. I drove her to the hospital, but the doctors couldn't save her. It had been a hard day.

Though I didn't know it until shortly before her death, Susanne had been wealthy. Most of everything she owned went to food banks and shelters for women around the Midwest, but she left her house and a hundred acres to me. A cleaning service came by once a week to dust and flush the toilets to make sure they still worked, and I checked the mail two or three times a week. I had a key to the front door, but I couldn't make myself go inside.

Darren Rogers, a local county councilor, had already made me an offer to take the property off my hands. He acted as if he were doing me a favor, but he and I both knew his offer was less than a quarter of what the property was worth. He assumed he could take me for a ride because I was distraught at my friend's death. I told him that if he contacted me again, I'd consider it harassment.

As I stared and looked at the home of a person I had loved and lost, though, I wondered whether, maybe, I should have accepted. I could have sold Susanne's house and my own and left St. Augustine County. My mom had been a well-respected captain in the St. Louis County Police Department before she retired, and her name still carried a lot of weight in law enforcement in St. Louis. The county or city police departments would have offered me a job if I applied. I would have had a new start.

But then, I'd always know what I left behind.

I had lived in St. Augustine County long enough to make it my home. Its rolling hills, jagged limestone cliffs, deep woods, and open fields were beautiful, but that beauty hid a rot at this county's core. St. Augustine was built on blood money. When I tried to expose that, a friend died.

I became a cop to help people, but if I abandoned St. Augustine, I'd be no better than the people who had corrupted it. This county was my home, and I didn't plan to give up on it.

I patted Roy's shoulder. He looked up at me with his tongue hanging out. I couldn't help but smile in response.

"Hey, buddy," I said. "Let's stretch our legs tonight and see what there is to see at your new home."

# Chapter 12

After walking Roy, I made dinner—pasta with spinach, bacon, and parmesan cheese—and then poured myself a stiff drink. The dog and I sat together on my couch and listened to a John Coltrane album as I thought through my day. I didn't know what to believe about Reuben. He had lied to me over and over, but that didn't mean he was a murderer.

I went to bed at a little before ten, but I tossed and turned for at least an hour before falling asleep. And then when I fell asleep, Roy woke me up by licking my face and whining. I pushed him away and forced my eyes open. My heart thumped against my chest, and my T-shirt felt damp with sweat. I must have been having a nightmare. My nightmares weren't always bad, but I had them three or four nights a week. Roger had gotten so used to them he didn't even wake up when I tossed and turned. They were still new to Roy, though.

I pet the dog and coaxed him back onto the foot of the bed. It took another hour to fall asleep again. Unfortunately, I didn't get to sleep long because my alarm rang at a little after six. I groaned and covered my face with a pillow, but that didn't drown out the sound. Roy hopped off the bed, wagged his tail, and stared at me with a big grin on his face as if he were telling me it was time to play.

I rolled over and slapped the alarm clock to turn it off. Then I lifted my head and looked at the dog. He nuzzled my hand, so I stroked his cheek. He practically purred.

"So you're a morning person," I said, blinking and nodding.

He stretched into a play bow, so I swung my legs off the bed and led him to the kitchen, where I made a pot of coffee while he ate his breakfast. After he ate, he pawed at the back door, so I let him outside. He bounded off to the woods behind my house, while I sipped my coffee and checked my cell. Nobody had contacted me in the night. As one of only two detectives in the county, I didn't get too many mornings without at least one call. It was nice.

While Roy sniffed around the yard, I showered, dressed, and got ready for the day. Normally, I tried to sleep in until at least seven, but I had an appointment in Kirkwood—an upper-middle-class suburb west of St. Louis—that morning. At a quarter to seven, I put Roy in the dog run, filled his water bowl, and scratched his cheek before leaving.

The drive was easy even in early morning traffic, but the closer I drew to the city, the tighter the knot in my stomach became. I was meeting my biological brother and Detective Mathias Blatch for breakfast to go over an old police file. I didn't want to do it, but Ian had begged. He seemed like a good kid, but I worried he'd get less out of this than he wanted and learn more about our biological mother than he cared to know.

Until three months ago when Ian showed up on my porch, I had thought I was an only child. As a detective, I made it into the news cycle more often than I'd want, so crazy people sometimes contacted me wanting crazy things. Ian wasn't crazy, though. I found that out when I ran a background check on him. He did well in school, although his teachers knew he was brighter than he let on. He didn't play sports, but he had a lot of friends—including a girlfriend a year ahead of him in school. I talked to his teachers and the principal at his school, and I followed him on Instagram. I even called his local police department to see whether they had a file on him. They didn't.

Ian was exactly the person he said he was: a healthy, well-adjusted fifteen-year-old kid who lived with his adoptive parents in St. Charles, Missouri. After high school, he'd go to college, major in computer science, and make more money in a year than I'd make in a lifetime as a detective. Despite everything I knew about him, I didn't understand why he contacted me or what he wanted from me. That unnerved me.

I pulled into the parking lot of an upscale diner three blocks from Kirkwood's historic center. As soon as I opened my door, the bells of the old Lutheran church and school to the south rang, calling kids into class. Cars streamed into and out of the parking lot of the middle school down the road. The air held a hint of ozone. My brother and Detective Blatch sat outside the restaurant on a wooden bench.

"Sorry I'm late, guys," I said, crossing the parking lot toward them. "I got a later start than I expected. Has anyone put our name in for a table yet?"

Ian nodded but stayed seated. Mathias stood and flashed me a tight smile. When I first saw Mathias's shaggy black hair and thin, angular face, I thought he was just another cop working a case. I hadn't noticed his kind eyes, easy smile, or infectious laugh. No one in the world would call him handsome, but I enjoyed looking at him now. He was a good man. It had taken me time to see that, but now I couldn't help but notice it.

"Hey, Joe," he said. "How's life in St. Augustine? You shot the sheriff yet?"

"Yeah, but not the deputy."

Mathias smiled, while Ian narrowed his gaze.

"You shot your boss?" he asked.

I smiled at my brother and shook my head. "It's an old song by Bob Marley. I used to listen to him when I was in high school. I thought it made me cool."

Ian grunted and looked down at his phone. Mathis shook his head and drew in a breath.

"Kids these days, huh?" he asked. "They don't appreciate the classics."

I smiled and nodded. Ian continued texting somebody, so Mathias and I talked for a few minutes while the restaurant got our table together. After about ten minutes, the coaster-sized pager the host had given Mathias buzzed and flashed red. A hostess led us to a wooden booth near the kitchen in the back corner of the restaurant. Most people would have hated the table, but it was perfect for our purposes.

We ordered breakfast and then asked the waitress for privacy. With every table in the building full, she seemed more than willing to avoid us for a while. Once she left, Mathias put a thick manila file folder on the table.

"This is it," he said. "Everything we've got on the murder of Erin Court. I've warned you before, and I'll warn you again: These are copies of official documents. I've taken out the autopsy pictures, but I've included the medical examiner's written report. It might be hard to read."

Ian drew in a deep breath and looked to me.

"Mathias has briefed me on the case, but I've never looked at the file," I said. "I've worked a lot of homicides, though. The reports and notes stick with you. They might give you nightmares. You don't have to look."

He considered and then looked away.

"I need to do this," he said.

"Okay," said Mathias, opening the first page to the summary report. "The victim was Erin Elizabeth Court. She was born March 23, 1968. Died July 4, 2007. Patrol officers found her body in an abandoned lot on East Delaware Street in Dutchtown. The initial call came from a real estate agent with a listing half a block away. It was a Wednesday. The call came in at 7:30 in the morning. The first officers arrived at the scene fifteen minutes later. They confirmed that the victim was dead."

"The victim was my mom," said Ian.

"You remember anything about that day?" I asked, leaning forward. He blinked and then shrugged.

"Not much," he said. "Mrs. Martelle—she was our neighbor—was watching me. When the detective told me Mom had died, Mrs. Martelle gave me a hug so tight I couldn't breathe. Everything after that was a blur."

"The lead detective on the case was a woman named Mary Petrosini," said Blatch. "She still works in the city. She's a good cop, and she busted her ass on this case. The medical examiner's office conducted an autopsy. Erin's cause of death was catastrophic injury to the heart, lungs, liver, and larger blood vessels due to multiple gunshot wounds to the chest."

Ian balled his hands on the table and sat straight but said nothing. I held up a hand so Mathias would stop.

"Ian," I said. "You have nothing to prove. We can stop right now."

His lips moved, but no sound came out. Mathias and I said nothing. Ian closed his eyes and breathed in.

"Did she suffer?"

Mathias shook his head.

"The ME's notes say her death would have been almost instantaneous."

He nodded. It seemed as if he had needed to hear that.

"Why would someone do that?"

Blatch looked at me before drawing in a slow breath and looking to his folder again.

"That's a tough one to answer," he said. "When Detective Petrosini picked up the case, she interviewed your mom's neighbors and a few of her friends. As best we could tell, your mom had no enemies, and she didn't owe anybody money. The two of you lived a quiet, happy life together. Everybody said she was a good mom."

My jaw clenched tight. Erin wasn't a bad person, but she was a terrible mother. When I lived with her, we had lived in her car and begged for food from restaurants at closing time. The little money she earned by selling herself, she blew on drugs. I was an afterthought at best.

"If she was such a good person, why would someone kill her?" asked Ian.

"Detective Petrosini had several theories," said Blatch. "Are you sure you want to hear them?"

Ian nodded. "Yeah."

Blatch blinked and pulled the file toward him so he could flip through the pages.

"The medical examiner's autopsy found indications of a long history of intravenous drug use," he said, glancing at me before looking down again. "We also have strong reason to believe she was a prostitute. It's possible she was killed during a drug deal that had gone wrong. Detective Petrosini also considered that she might have been killed by a client."

"My mom wasn't a hooker, and she didn't do drugs," said Ian, his voice loud enough it stopped conversation at the table next to ours. They looked at us but returned to their breakfast before I could say anything to them. I softened my voice and leaned forward.

"Mathias is right, Ian," I said. "Erin had problems with drugs her entire life. It's why she lost custody of me."

He considered me and shook his head. "Maybe she had problems when you were young, but she was a good mom."

"That's what her neighbors and friends said, too," said Mathias, stepping in. "Can you tell me about your trust fund?"

Ian closed his eyes and held up a hand.

"Mom left me and Joe her estate. There's nothing illegal about that."

"She left us a very large estate," I said. "Erin never worked a day in her life, and she left me almost a quarter of a million dollars when she died. I don't even know how much it's worth now. She left you an apartment building worth at least a million bucks. Where'd she get that much money?"

Ian used his thumbs to spin his glass of orange juice.

"You didn't even know her. When was the last time you even saw her?"

I answered without hesitation. "January 2nd, 2005. Erin overdosed on heroin at a New Year's party and was taken to the hospital. My social worker thought I'd want to see her. When the doctors left, she asked me to go to her dealer and buy her a hit. When I refused, she slapped me and told me to get out."

He looked at the table. "I was alive then. I don't believe you. She took good care of me."

"Fourteen years ago, you were a baby. You were probably with Lacey Rayner. She covered up a lot of Erin's messes."

As Ian exhaled, his nostrils flared, and he gripped his glass hard enough that his fingers trembled.

"You don't know what you're talking about."

"Let's take a step back, guys," said Mathias. "Erin was a complicated person. You guys knew different sides of her, and you have very different lives now. You both have nice adoptive families. That's more than many people have."

I gave Mathias a weak smile and nodded.

"Mathias is right. You've got good parents. Focus on them," I said. "You've got great memories of Erin, and that's wonderful, but if you dig into her past, you won't like what you find."

Ian rolled his eyes and swung his legs out from beneath the table.

"Can I go now?"

"Of course," I said. "Do you want a ride?"

"I'll get an Uber," he said, grabbing the file before either of us could stop him. I stood to get it back, but Mathias shook his head. Our waitress took that as her opportunity to drop off breakfast for three. At least we wouldn't go hungry. For a few minutes, I ate my omelet and Mathias ate his pancakes in silence. Then he put down his fork and leaned forward.

"You were a little hard on him," he said.

I nodded and felt my throat tighten. "I'll text him later and apologize."

Mathias looked down. "I looked him up. He's a good kid."

"He had a shitty mom, though."

Mathias tilted his head to the side. "He doesn't see it like that."

I looked toward the windows at the front of the restaurant. Ian sat on the bench out front, waiting for his ride.

"While he was living with Miss Sunshine-and-Roses in Shangri-La, I was living with a foster father who drugged me, raped me, and threatened to kill me. Erin didn't even try to contact me after the police arrested him. I needed her, and she refused to show up. Instead, Julia Green took me home. She and Doug made me part of their family. They stood up for me when I couldn't stand on my own.

"Erin isn't worth Ian's time. If he doesn't learn that from me, he'll learn it on his own, and it'll hurt."

Mathias nodded and poured syrup over his pancakes. I started eating my omelet again. When I looked up, I found him watching me.

"He deserves to know what happened to his mom," he said.

Before I could respond, my phone buzzed. I pulled it from my purse and found a text message from Trisha, telling me the fire department had just found a body inside a house. I needed to get back to St. Augustine ASAP. I texted her back to let her know I was on my way. Then I took thirty dollars from my wallet.

"Thank you for coming this morning," I said. "It means a lot that you're here."

He leaned back and gave me a wistful smile. "Sounds like you plan to leave me to eat breakfast alone."

"Yeah, sorry," I said. "There's a body on the ground back home. I'll make it up to you, though. We'll get lunch when I'm in town next. My treat."

He tilted his head to the side. "Understand that I don't come cheap at lunch. It'll involve soup *and* salad—not just one or the other. The restaurant might even have table-cloths."

I smiled. "Tablecloths sound good. I've got to go, though. I'll talk to you later."

Mathias smiled. "Good luck, Detective."

"Thanks," I said. I hurried out of there and jogged to my car. Normally, I ate lunch alone. It gave me time to pause and reflect on my morning. I enjoyed being alone, but I didn't mind the idea of Detective Blatch interrupting my solitary existence for a time. Everybody—even me—needed friends.

When I reached my car, I called Trisha.

"Hey," I said. "Tell me about this body."

# Chapter 13

T risha directed me to an address in a housing development called Rolling Hills Place west of the town of St. Augustine. Six years ago, when I first became a police officer, the site was a soybean field owned by an old St. Augustine family. A developer bought it about five years ago and put in grass. It had taken a while to get the permits—and bribe the right county councilors—but now it was a thriving upper-middle-class neighborhood.

I turned off a small county road onto newly laid blacktop. Each home sat on four or five acres of rolling land. By now, the developer had sold or built upon most of the lots, but the enormous yards and lack of mature landscaping made the development feel incomplete, like it would become a neighborhood full of children and families one day, but it wasn't there yet.

I followed the blacktop to a single-story brick home that jutted from the empty landscape. It had a three-car garage out front and big picture windows overlooking the expansive front lawn. A metal for-sale sign waved in the morning breeze on the front lawn. Chances were it wouldn't sell soon with the front windows cracked and black soot staining the brickwork. The roof was intact, but I could smell burnt insulation even from inside my car. The charred remains of a pickup truck were in the driveway.

By the time I arrived, the firetrucks had left, but the fire marshal's red SUV, three police cruisers, our forensics van, and a van from the coroner's office remained. I parked out front and grabbed a fresh notepad from the pack I kept in a box on my backseat. Then I jotted a few notes about the conditions at the home upon my arrival, the time of day, and the address. My notes wouldn't make it to court, but they could be helpful later.

Then I got out of the car and snapped pictures with my cell phone. Two or three minutes after I arrived, Sheriff Delgado and Fire Marshal Paul Cluney stepped out of the house. Cluney was fifty or fifty-five. His bald scalp reflected the morning sun like a mirror as he walked and talked with the sheriff. They turned as I walked toward them.

"Morning, Detective," said Cluney. "The sheriff was just telling me you've got a new partner."

"I do," I said, nodding. "Unfortunately, he's a little busy this morning. You're stuck with me. I hear we've got a body inside."

Cluney turned to Sheriff Delgado.

"Yep. We believe it's a man, but the body was burned beyond recognition," said the sheriff. "This guy's killer is a cold son of a bitch. He cut off every finger on the victim's left hand with garden trimmers and left them in a pile beside the corpse."

I opened my eyes wide and whistled.

"That's a bad way to go," I said, looking toward the coroner's van. "Are his genitals intact?"

Neither Cluney nor Delgado said anything, but they gave me weird looks.

"It points to a particular pathology," I said, lowering my chin. "A killer who cuts off his victim's fingers before murdering him might be after information, but a killer who cuts off a man's fingers and penis is trying to humiliate him and take away his manhood. If his genitals are intact, we should look for a business partner. If our killer cut off his twig and berries, we should look for a jilted lover."

Both men shifted on their feet. Delgado cleared his throat and looked down.

"Take that one up with Dr. Sheridan," he said.

I nodded. "Why do you think the killer used garden shears?"

"My guys found them beside the body," said Cluney. "They tried not to touch anything, but it was a fire, and we had to move fast. Somebody might have kicked them. I'll give you a written report in a day or two, but it looks like the body was the point of ignition. Your killer likely sprayed him with an accelerant and lit him on fire. I don't know whether he was alive or dead when that happened."

"I assume Dr. Sheridan has the body and fingers," I said, looking to Delgado. The sheriff nodded. "What about the truck in the driveway?"

"Similar to the house," said Cluney. "The arsonist doused the interior with an accelerant and ignited it. Cab didn't have any bodies. Your forensics lab will have to confirm the accelerant, but it looks like common gasoline."

I drew in a deep breath, preparing myself for the investigation ahead of me.

"I'll walk through the house and see what I can see. Has anyone talked to the neighbors?"

"Dave Skelton and Bob Reitz have," said Delgado. "Unfortunately, there weren't many people around last night. The house behind us is for sale and empty like this one. The family across the street saw a sedan drive by but didn't pay much attention. Husband said it came at ten. Wife said it was more like midnight. The family to the west heard noises, but they chalked it up to the wind. The family to the east has infant twins. They were so tired Bob said they almost fell asleep during the interview. They didn't see a thing."

"When did you guys get here?"

"First responders arrived at 1:51 A.M.," said Cluney, nodding. "A man near the highway called in an explosion at 1:35 A.M. He thought his neighbors were blowing off fireworks, but I think it was the truck's gas tank. Once it warmed up enough, the vapor exploded."

I jotted down the time.

"And just to confirm, we haven't ID'd the body yet?" I asked, looking to Delgado.

"Nope," he said. "Body was too far gone to recognize. His clothes were incinerated, and we didn't find a wallet anywhere. The pickup was burned, and the plates were removed."

"Anything else I should know?" I asked. Cluney shook his head, but Delgado looked to the fire marshal.

"Can you give me a minute with my officer?"

Cluney nodded and then wished me luck before heading toward his SUV. Delgado waited until the fire marshal was out of earshot before crossing his arms.

"Where are we on Terepocki?"

I grimaced. "Reuben's case is more complicated than we thought. Before I can move on, I'll need reports from the coroner and the crime lab. I'm also expecting his personnel file from his time in Kansas City. Once I have those, I'll compare the physical evidence to Reuben's recollection of the shooting and go from there."

Delgado tilted his head back and blinked.

"Why do you need his personnel file?"

I blinked and considered before answering. "When you were in the hiring process, did you have any suspicions about his background?"

Delgado cocked his head to the side.

"How could a shooting in St. Augustine have anything to do with anything Detective Terepocki did in Kansas City?"

"I've got a witness who says Reuben has tried to shake down at least one business owner in town. If he's dirty here, he was probably dirty in Kansas City, too. I'm looking for corroboration."

"So you're fishing," he said.

"I'm working a case you put me on, and I'm following the evidence. If that's a problem, we can call the Highway Patrol for help right now. Meanwhile, you'd free me up to work this case. How's that sound to you? It sounds great to me. I'd just as soon wash my hands of Reuben Terepocki entirely."

Delgado held my gaze for a few seconds, but then he looked away and took a slow step back. Then he brought a hand to his brow.

"What have you found so far?"

"Reuben lied about knowing the victim, for a start," I said. "He said the two had never met, but I've seen video that shows them getting into a fistfight. Beyond that, I'm still working."

Delgado swore and then cleared his throat.

"Document everything you find. I don't want to arrest a detective and have it blow up in my face."

"I'll do my job."

He nodded and walked toward the fire marshal's SUV. Delgado hadn't even been sheriff for a year, but he looked as if he had already aged a decade. Everything in St. Augustine County had a price tag, and our politicians were among the most venal I had ever heard of. Before becoming sheriff,

Delgado had been a decent detective. He would have done well for himself in St. Louis or Kansas City. He could have worked in a detective bureau until he was sixty and then retired a hero. People would have looked up to him.

The sheriff's office here, though, wasn't a law enforcement gig at all; it was an exercise in survival. For now, the County Council was giving him what he wanted: a bigger budget, a renovated station, more patrol cars, and more officers. But the moment he stopped doing their bidding, they'd bring out the knives.

That was how this place worked. You either cooperated with the powers that be, or they'd flay you alive. When he got the job, George may not have realized that, but he did now. He was the County Council's pet, and, one day, they'd put him down like they had done to every sheriff before him. It was only a matter of time.

I walked through the house, but the coroner had already removed the body, and Darlene McEvoy and her team had dusted the doorknobs for prints and vacuumed the carpets for fibers. Since the homeowner had already removed the furniture, there was nothing left.

In the front room, flames had charred the window seat, cracked the front window, and burned the wooden miniblinds and carpet. Fortunately, the fire hadn't lasted long enough to spread beyond the one spot in the living room. Blood spattered the carpet, but it hadn't formed a pool. If the killer had stabbed or shot the victim here before setting him on fire, there'd be a bigger spot.

I left the house. Sheriff Delgado and the support staff had left, but two police cruisers remained outside. Officer Emily Hayes walked toward me and smiled.

"Morning, Joe," she said. "I've got the logbook. I didn't see you go in."

I nodded and looked around.

"Dr. Sheridan and Darlene left, I see."

"Yeah, but Dr. Sheridan asked me to tell you to call him," she said. "He had something to tell you about Jay Pischke."

I made a mental note to call him when I could.

"You see anything I should be aware of?"

"Nope," she said, shaking her head. "It's been quiet. Bob Reitz is talking to the woman who lives next door. She just came home."

If she just came home, she hadn't seen a thing. I nodded anyway.

"I'm done with the house for now. When you get a chance, seal the front and back doors. I'll check out the truck."

She nodded and went to her cruiser. The truck was trashed. I couldn't tell where the fire started, but it had consumed everything but the vehicle's metal body and frame. The engine block still radiated heat. I walked to my car and grabbed a pair of nitrile gloves and a flashlight from my evidence collection kit. Then I got to work.

As Delgado had said, the license plate was gone, taking with it the easiest way to identify the vehicle's owner. I had other options, though. Heat had shattered the front window and rendered the vehicle identification number on the lower right portion of the glass unreadable. Our lab might have been able to lift it, but I had something else to check first.

I opened the driver side door and ran my gloved hand across the frame before feeling a slight bump. The truck's manufacturer had installed a metal plate with the VIN etched onto it on the doorframe. The flames had blackened that plate, but I could deal with that.

I grabbed a pencil from my evidence kit and then held a piece of paper to the plate to make a rubbing. Within moments, I had the seventeen-character VIN etched onto the paper as if I had written it. I shut the door and looked up to see Emily Hayes signing the front door's seal.

"Hey, Emily?" I shouted. She turned and looked at me. "You mind if I use your cruiser's laptop?"

"Go ahead," she said.

I jogged to her cruiser and sat in the front passenger seat. Her cruiser's internet connection was a little slower than what we had in the office, but it was more than adequate to search the license bureau's database. My pickup belonged to a forty-two-year-old man named Thomas Becker, and he lived in Rogers, Arkansas. I doubted that the murderer had torched his own car, which meant I likely had my murder victim's name.

I stepped out of the cruiser and pulled out my phone. Dr. Sheridan answered quickly.

"Hey, doc," I said. "This is Detective Joe Court. I've got a probable name for the murder victim you picked up a few minutes ago. Thomas Becker."

"Morning, Detective," he said. "Give me a moment. I'm in the car."

I waited for thirty or forty seconds and listened to him drive.

"Thomas Becker," he said. "I'll see whether I can confirm that for you."

"Thanks," I said. "I appreciate it. If you need anything, let me know. I'll see whether I can track down this guy's next of kin."

"Before you do that, we need to talk about Jay Pischke. Darlene McEvoy and I have found evidence we need to discuss."

I straightened but looked to the ground.

"What'd you find?"

"The kind of stuff I'd prefer to speak about in person," he said. "This can't wait."

"That sounds ominous," I said.

"It isn't good," he said. "I'm still in St. Augustine. Meet me at the abandoned house where we found his body. I'll walk you through our findings."

I nodded to myself. "Okay. I'm on my way."

He thanked me and then hung up. Emily smiled as she walked toward me.

"You find what you needed, Detective?"

I nodded. "That and more. I'll see you later. I've got to go meet the coroner."

# Chapter 14

When I arrived at the meth lab, I found a white Mercedes out front. Dr. Sheridan leaned against his car with his cell phone held to his ear. He waved as I parked but stayed on the phone for another minute. When he hung up, he smiled.

"Sorry about that," he said, slipping his phone into the inside pocket of his jacket. "My assistant and I were just working out our schedule today."

"That's okay," I said, nodding toward the house. "You said you had things to show me?"

"I do," he said, walking toward the building. "Darlene McEvoy and I have been in contact since yesterday. She and I agree on our findings."

I followed him to the front door. The seal was still intact. He nodded toward it.

"If you'll do the honors," he said. I glanced at him, wondering just what he could have to show me, before reaching into my pocket for my keys. I used the sharpest one to cut the foil and tape seal. The interior looked as it had on my last visit. I glanced at the doctor.

"We're here," I said. "Your show now."

He nodded and wrung his hands together in front of him.

"Before I say what I'm about to say, please know that Ms. McEvoy and I have given this a lot of thought and discussion. We're following the evidence and interpreting it given the totality of our experiences and findings."

"You're a good coroner, and I know your findings will be justified," I said. "Tell me what you've found."

"Jay Pischke died from injuries caused by gunshot wounds to his torso."

I nodded and crossed my arms. "That's not in dispute."

"I'm leaning toward calling it murder instead of justified homicide."

I straightened and drew in a breath. "You've got my attention. What have you got?"

"Well, first, consider the body. When I arrived at the crime scene, I found Mr. Pischke in a prone position with his arms ninety degrees to his body. I found a Hi-Point C9 pistol four inches from his right hand. Field tests found gunshot residue on both Mr. Pischke's right and left hands. If you'd like pictures, my assistant can send them to you."

"I'll take your word for it," I said. "Go on."

"Upon rolling Mr. Pischke over for transport, I found four perforating gunshot wounds to his torso and chest."

I nodded. "That's consistent with Detective Terepocki's account of the shooting."

116

Dr. Sheridan looked down and paused. "How tall is Detective Terepocki?"

I considered and then shrugged. "He's not a basketball player, but he's not tiny, either. Six-one, maybe a little more."

"Three of the rounds penetrated the victim's thoracic cavity and ricocheted against the rib cage before exiting the soft tissue of the abdomen or lower back. One round went cleanly through, allowing us to track its trajectory through the body. It entered the body at a twelve-degree downward angle."

By his tone, Dr. Sheridan believed that was important, but I didn't know what he was getting at. I told him so, and Dr. Sheridan nodded.

"Detective Terepocki said he shot your victim from the doorframe, right?" asked the doctor. I nodded, so the doctor positioned me near the door. Then he walked to the part of the room where we'd found Stinky Jay's body. "If Detective Terepocki shot Mr. Pischke from the doorframe, I would expect a downward or upward angle of two to three degrees if both men were standing this far apart. A twelve-degree downward angle, though, shows the victim was on his knees when Detective Terepocki shot him."

I blinked and then drew a slow breath.

"Is it possible Mr. Pischke was standing for the first shots and then fell to his knees?"

The doctor nodded. "It's possible, but all four entry wounds are oblong. I couldn't testify to this in court, but my experience tells me all four shots came when the victim was on his knees."

I said nothing as that sunk in. Then I swallowed hard and nodded.

"Anything else?"

"A few things," said Sheridan. "I X-rayed Mr. Pischke's body. He had two cracked ribs, both of which displayed remodeling. If I had to guess, he sustained the injury a week prior to the shooting. That's unrelated to the shooting, but I noted it in my report."

I nodded. "Mr. Pischke was a bouncer at Club Serenity. He and a patron got into a fight about a week ago."

"That's one mystery solved at least," said the doctor. "Darlene and I found several other oddities. I found a pistol near Mr. Pischke's right hand, leading me to believe he held it in his right hand before dying. Mr. Pischke, though, had a callus on his left middle finger where a pencil would have rested. He had no such callus on his right hand, which leads me to believe he wrote with the left hand. In addition, Darlene McEvoy photographed two coffee mugs in the kitchen with their handles oriented to the left. Right-handed individuals wouldn't hold a mug in their left hand like that."

I nodded. "Even if he's left-handed, he might still shoot with a right-handed grip."

"That's possible," said Sheridan, "and I'd expect a defense attorney to make that same argument. It's another oddity, though."

"It is," I admitted. "Anything else?"

He nodded toward the wall beside me. "As I understand it, Mr. Pischke fired at Detective Terepocki. Do we know who fired first?"

I glanced behind me at the bullet holes.

"According to Detective Terepocki's statement, Pischke."

Sheridan licked his lips, blinked, and then sighed.

"We've got a problem, then. This is Ms. McEvoy's area, so if you want details, you'll have to talk to her. The rounds fired by Mr. Pischke's firearm penetrated the drywall to the left of the doorframe. They then passed through the insulation and perforated the clapboard siding outside. We checked the trajectory of those rounds. This time, the angle is sharply upward. He wasn't on his feet."

At once, I felt a weight hammer into me. I closed my eyes, unsure whether I should be angry or sad. Dr. Sheridan cleared his throat.

"I'm comfortable writing a report that leaves Mr. Pischke's manner of death uncertain, but there are details about this case that don't add up. Despite my investigation and consultation with Ms. McEvoy, I'm left with significant questions—none of which have easy answers."

I nodded but said nothing as I tried to process what he told me. After a minute, I forced myself to nod.

"Thank you for bringing all this to my attention. This is an open investigation. I'll work until I come to a satisfactory resolution."

Sheridan blinked a few times and then crossed his arms.

"I came to you as a courtesy and because I trust you," he said. "Scandals disappear in your department. I won't let this one go."

I softened my expression.

"And I'm glad for that. If I were in your place, I wouldn't let it go, either," I said. "We have to be careful here. Reuben has given his life to law enforcement. If he murdered Jay Pischke, I'll send him to prison, but I won't ruin a man's reputation because there are details of a crime scene I can't explain. If we go public with this before we can prove our case, everybody loses—Reuben most of all. I won't let that happen."

Sheridan took a step back and nodded.

"What do you want to do then?"

"I'll keep working the case. I won't let anyone bury this. I promise."

Sheridan crossed his arms.

"I hope you're not just saying that."

"I'm not," I said. "I've got to get back to work, but I'll keep you informed of my findings."

Sheridan nodded, but he didn't seem convinced. I left anyway. The conversation left me feeling a little annoyed, but the coroner had good reason not to trust people from my department. When I reached my car, I sat in the front seat and called Reuben Terepocki's attorney to request an interview. He said he'd talk to his client and return my call when he could.

After the call, I allowed myself to sink into my front seat. I had only worked with Reuben for a short time, but I had liked him. We had arrested dozens of people and even sent a few to prison for lengthy stays. Now I wondered whether we had done the right thing. Did he cheat on those cases? Did he lie or hide evidence? For all I knew, we could have sent innocent people to prison.

I felt sick. As much as I wanted to keep this quiet, I needed to tell Delgado the whole truth. His phone rang twice before he picked up.

"Hey," I said. "It's Joe Court. I've got an update about the Reuben Terepocki investigation, and you won't like it."

"Tell me what you've got."

I led him through Dr. Sheridan's findings and then my own investigation so far, including the video Conroy had shown me. When I finished, Delgado went silent. Then he swore under his breath.

"You did good keeping this quiet. We don't need the media involved."

"What do you want to do?" I asked.

"Keep working your case. Follow up on Pischke and find out why Reuben beat him up. Also see whether you can get that video from Vic Conroy. And next time you talk to Reuben and his lawyer, I want to be in the room. I want to see how he reacts when he's caught in a lie. If we're lucky, we'll find an explanation for everything."

I waited a moment, but he didn't continue.

"And if we're unlucky?"

"It'll get ugly around here," he said.

That seemed like a fair statement. Delgado had nothing else to say, so he wished me luck before hanging up. I tossed my phone to the seat beside me, leaned my head back, and sighed. With what we had so far, Delgado could fire Reuben and survive an appeal to our union, but that didn't mean Reuben had murdered anyone. After twenty years in law enforcement, he deserved the benefit of my doubt, but that was wearing thin.

I searched through the evidence collection kit on my backseat for a new seal for the meth lab's door, already dreading what I had to do next. Even with these new findings in the Jay Pischke shooting, I had Thomas Becker to deal with. That meant I had a next-of-kin notification ahead of me. The dead were the easy part of my job. The living made things complicated.

# Chapter 15

Forest Park was an enormous public park on the western edge of St. Louis. Though it couldn't compete with Central Park in New York or the English Garden in Munich, it was a wonderful park with some of St. Louis's best amenities, including its art museum, history museum, and zoo. Now, it was a meeting place.

Josh Knight drove the van, while the rest of Lorenzo's team crowded in the back. This was a meet-and-greet, so they wouldn't face opposition. Still, backup didn't hurt—especially when confronting the CEO of Nolan Systems. Deion Shelby turned around from the front passenger seat as Josh turned from Skinker Boulevard and onto Lagoon Drive. This part of the park held a public golf course. Though it had an easy exit, it was too open for their needs.

"Everybody, check your radios," said Deion.

Lorenzo slipped the earbud into his ear and tapped the microphone. The rest of his team looked at him, so he was evidently broadcasting.

"Will the radios work in the woods?" he asked.

Deion nodded. "At the distances we'll be at, we shouldn't have a problem."

Lorenzo nodded. A few minutes after turning the van into the park, Josh pulled to the side of the road near the head of a walking trail. He'd stay in the car, but the rest of the team would take positions on the trail and surrounding woods. They had planned this meeting for months, so everyone knew where to stand, where to aim their firearms, and how to escape if things went wrong. If Gerald Nolan made a single wrong move, he'd never see Lorenzo's team again.

He'd also never draw another breath.

Lorenzo pulled the minivan's sliding door open and stepped onto the grass beside the road. A squirrel scurried from the nearby woods and across the street toward a pond. A pleasant breeze blew. It was sweater weather. Had it been a Saturday, kids and families would have covered every inch of grass. Today, few people walked the paths.

One by one, his team stepped out of the van and walked toward their positions. Laura came last. She squeezed his hand.

"Stay safe," she said. "And be smart. Do the right thing here."

He gave her a curious smile and nodded.

"I will. Don't worry."

She nodded and hurried down the trail. She'd jog about half a mile before turning into the woods to hide behind a big silver maple tree about a hundred yards off the trail.

Lorenzo gave his team five minutes to get into place before walking.

Since he didn't have Scarlett—or even know if she were alive—Lorenzo would have to bluff his way through the meeting. That was easier said than done. Gerald Nolan ran one of the largest private intelligence companies in the world, a lofty perch he arrived at only after running covert operations with the CIA for over twenty years. The rewards were worth the risk. If Lorenzo's bluff succeeded, he and his team would become rich beyond their wildest dreams. If it failed, the Nolan family would bury Gerald beside his deceased son. Either way, Lorenzo and his team would walk away just fine. Their preparations had ensured that.

He followed the trail into the woods. Even at this time of year, the forest canopy still snuffed out the sun's rays, leaving the forest interior dark and almost gloomy. The thick shade would have been a welcome respite on hot summer days, but in the fall, it turned a cool but comfortable day into one that was cold and damp. The air held the fetid odor of thick, wet mud.

Lorenzo walked for almost seven minutes before reaching a small stone bridge. A shallow, dry ravine ran beneath it, while a tall, well-built man with chiseled cheekbones sat on the bridge's rail as if it were a bench. Gerald Nolan wore a sky-blue Oxford shirt, navy slacks, and polished black shoes. He could have stepped out of a Brooks Brothers catalog. His company had conducted dozens if not hundreds of hostage negotiations, so he understood the informal protocol demanded by meetings such as this one. Nolan was unarmed, but he was dangerous all the same.

"Mr. Nolan," said Lorenzo. "Stay seated."

"I will," said Nolan, his cold, gray eyes drilling into Lorenzo. "Before we begin, we should dispense with the unpleasantries. I'm unarmed, but I assume you're not. My son is dead, my daughter-in-law is distraught, and I've had to deliver next-of-kin notifications to the families of three members of my personal security team. Your man, Nick McCoy, is alive and recovering under guard in St. Louis. I propose a trade.

"In return for my granddaughter, I will arrange for your colleague's safe removal from police protection. You can transfer him to a facility of your choice, where he can recover. In addition, I will give you forty-eight hours to leave the country and disappear. Take whatever resources you have and begin a new life. I won't come after you. You have my word."

Lorenzo drew in a breath. The offer changed nothing. Everybody was already in too deep.

"This isn't a negotiation, Mr. Nolan," he said. "Nick knew the risks. I'm sorry for what happened, but we'll take care of his family. They'll take care of him. Even if you could get him out of the hospital, Nick's not in play."

Nolan considered him and then tilted his head to the side.

"Are you sure that's a decision you can make on your own?" he asked. "You've got a team to consider. How do you think they'll react to your unilateral decision to leave one of their own behind?"

"I'm not leaving him behind," said Lorenzo. "I'm continuing the mission, and if you value your granddaughter's safety, you'll stop talking right now. My team and I have Scarlett. At the moment, she's safe in a crib with one of my team members. She receives two to three ounces of Enfamil Premium newborn formula every two to three hours. We hold and comfort her when she cries, and we swaddle her in thick blankets when she sleeps. We treat her as if she were one of our own."

Nolan blinked but said nothing.

"We'll never hurt your granddaughter," said Lorenzo, continuing. "You needn't worry about that. If you refuse to deal with us, she'll grow up safe and sound somewhere in eastern Europe or Israel. You'll never see her again, but she'll know all about you and your family. She'll know you abandoned her. Is that what you'd like?"

Nolan, again, blinked but said nothing.

"We want twenty million dollars cash," said Lorenzo. "In exchange, you will have your granddaughter back. Once you have her, you will never hear from us again. We understand that your company has considerable capabilities, but so does my team. You'd regret coming after us."

Nolan crossed his arms and then looked down.

"You murdered my son and abducted my granddaughter for twenty million dollars."

Lorenzo crossed his arms. "If we could have pulled off the job without killing Blake, we would have. You're a soldier, Mr. Nolan. So are we. Your son was in the way. It wasn't personal."

Nolan nodded but kept his eyes downcast.

"I was a soldier once," he said, his voice low. "Now I'm a father and a grandfather. You're a father yourself, Mr. Molena."

Lorenzo drew in a sharp breath but tried not to let his surprise—or fear—show.

"We're not here to talk about me," he said. "We're here to talk about Scarlett, your granddaughter. You've heard what we want. You have two days to get the money together. We'll be in touch."

Lorenzo turned to leave.

"If you take another step, you'll watch me bury your ex-wife and sons in Phoenix, your sister and mother in Seattle, and your cousin and his family in Portland. I will wipe your entire family from existence. Then, when I'm done with your loved ones, I'll flay you alive and dump your body in a game preserve in Tanzania. The spotted hyenas will devour you whole, bones and all, so that there's nothing left and no one to mourn your death. You will disappear."

Lorenzo swallowed hard but didn't move.

"If you make a move toward any of them, you'll never see your granddaughter again."

"You don't have my granddaughter," said Nolan. "Mr. Becker contacted me yesterday. He asked for considerably less money as well."

Lorenzo turned and considered the older man. He had spent his last dollar for this mission, but money didn't matter if he was dead. As long as he was alive, he could recover. He lowered his chin to speak into the microphone at his throat.

"Abort mission," he said. "Cornell, take the shot. Josh, fire up the car. We're getting out of here."

Lorenzo kept his eyes on Nolan, expecting him to pitch forward at any moment with a hole in his back. Nothing happened, though. He lowered his chin once more.

"Repeat, abort mission. Cornell, take the shot."

Again, nothing happened. Lorenzo swallowed hard.

"Cornell, can you hear me?"

"He can hear you fine," said Nolan, standing. As the older man reached into his pocket, Lorenzo reached behind him for a firearm. Before he could clear his holster, a suppressed firearm barked behind him. A round hit a tree about a foot to Lorenzo's right, sending bark flying. Lorenzo released his grip on his firearm and raised his hands.

"What'd you do to my team?"

Nolan pulled his phone from his pocket. "I made them a better offer than you did."

Lorenzo spoke into his microphone.

"Laura, you there?"

His heart pounded so hard he could feel the blood coursing through his system. He counted to three before Laura spoke. Her voice sounded forced and rough.

"It's over, Renzo," she said. "Nick survived. Nolan offered you a trade. One of ours for one of his. You turned him down."

Lorenzo's hands trembled, so he put them in his pockets. A bead of sweat formed on his brow as he studied the woods around him. Every muscle in his body felt twitchy. He had an exit strategy, but it depended on his team. Without them, he was dead.

"We don't know whether he's telling the truth," he said. "You saw Nick go down. You thought he was dead."

"If there's even a chance he's alive," said Laura, "we have to take it."

A dull pit grew in Lorenzo's gut.

"Nolan's lying to us. We're a team."

"We stopped being a team the moment you turned your back on Nick," said Laura. "If they had shot me instead of him, what would you have done? Would you have abandoned me? Would you have gotten me the best lawyer money could buy, or would you have done your fucking job and been a leader?"

Lorenzo cleared his throat and then licked his lips.

"Come on, honey," he said. "If you're in position, you need to take the shot."

"Don't call me honey again," said Laura.

Lorenzo swore under his breath. If he ran to the east, he'd find Laura and maybe Cornell. If he ran to the west, he'd find Deion. All of them had firearms.

"Cornell, if you're in position, take the shot," he said, his voice hard. "We'll figure this out later."

He held his breath and prayed someone would fire a shot. No one did. Then Cornell spoke.

"What do you want me to do, Laura?"

"Hold fast," said Laura. "If Renzo moves, put two into his head."

Laura emerged from the woods about two hundred yards to the east and walked toward him. She pulled a pistol from a holster on her leg.

"Don't do this," said Lorenzo. "Nolan's lying to you."

Laura raised the weapon.

"Renzo's secure. Return to the secondary location," she said over the radio. "I'll join you shortly."

Lorenzo thought about turning and running, but he didn't think she'd shoot him. She had to listen to reason. As the rest of the team confirmed her orders, she removed her earbud and lowered the microphone but kept the pistol pointed at his chest.

"Don't do this, Laura," he said. "I made a judgment call about Nick. You disagree, but that doesn't mean I'm wrong. Nolan set us up."

"Mr. Nolan contacted Khalid, my former fiancé, this morning. Khalid contacted me on Mr. Nolan's behalf," she said. "He didn't set *us* up. He set *you* up. I thought if I gave you the chance, you'd do the right thing and come clean. You put money before the team, though. We'll find Mr. Nolan's granddaughter. That's the cost of forgiveness. I had hoped you'd join us, but I can't trust you. I'm sorry, sweetheart, but it's over."

Lorenzo didn't know whether he should beg or run, but Laura made the decision for him. She squeezed the trigger. Lorenzo heard the shot and felt the round hit his chest. He had been shot twice before, and it had hurt both times. This time he felt cold.

His knees gave out, and he fell to the trail. The mulch beneath him felt soft.

"I'm sorry," he whispered.

Laura appeared before him and put a hand on his cheek. She cried, but she didn't help him.

"I'm sorry," he whispered again. She put a finger to his lips.

"Me, too, honey," she said.

Lorenzo should have traded for Nick. He should have run with Laura when he had the chance. Now it was too late. Even as he died, though, something nagged at him.

His team killed Blake Nolan. Gerald Nolan wouldn't hire the people who murdered his son to find his granddaughter.

Lorenzo tried to warn her, but the words wouldn't come out. Laura held him and cried. Then, her eyes darted up, and she lifted a hand. Several shots rang out in rapid succession. Laura's head snapped back, and she fell as a fine mist of blood erupted from her forehead. Around him, Lorenzo knew a similar fate had befallen the rest of his team. That was why Nolan had brought them together.

In all his life, Lorenzo had never wished ill on a child, but he hoped Gerald Nolan never found his granddaughter. She'd be better off being raised by strangers than by a monster.

# Chapter 16

With two murders to investigate, I had to budget my time well. Until Reuben Terepocki and his attorney agreed to come in for questioning in Jay Pischke's murder, I needed to focus on Thomas Becker—my burned victim. According to his driver's license, he lived in Rogers, Arkansas, near the Missouri border. Assuming he didn't run into too much traffic on the drive, Mr. Becker died five and a half hours from home. He might have pissed people off in Arkansas, but they wouldn't drive him all the way to St. Augustine to kill him. We were looking for a local.

I drove to my station. With the construction ongoing, my colleagues had desks throughout the building. The office I shared with Reuben felt isolated and empty. It was quiet. In our old bullpen, someone had always been talking on the phone, typing, or joking near the coffeemaker. I never thought I'd miss that noise, but I did. Since I lived alone, most of my life was silent. I hadn't realized how lonely complete silence felt until I lost the little contrast my office provided. That was my problem, though. My victim deserved my attention.

I looked Becker up to see whether he had a criminal record. He had speeding tickets in Arkansas and Missouri but no felony arrests. By all appearances, he was a solid citizen. That changed things. He probably wasn't killed during a drug deal gone wrong or to send a message to a rival gang. He was tortured because he pissed somebody off. My investigation needed to start at home.

Next, I called the police department in Bentonville, Arkansas, and let them know I had a victim from their part of the world. The sergeant I spoke to promised to send officers out to Becker's house to make sure no one had broken in. He also said he'd ask around the station about Becker and see what he could find. I appreciated the effort. After fifteen minutes on the phone, I thanked him for his time and hung up.

Next, I checked Becker out on social media. Based on the number of posts he made on Facebook, I wondered how he had time to do anything else. He had almost two thousand friends and kept his privacy settings loose. On his last birthday, over three hundred people wished him well. I didn't even know three hundred people, let alone three hundred people who liked me enough to wish me a happy birthday.

After looking through several hundred posts, several things became clear. Thomas Becker supported the military and military causes. He was also a helicopter enthusiast. About a dozen of his friends called him Chief, which made me wonder whether he had been a crew chief on a helicopter, or whether he had been a chief warrant officer in the Army.

Besides the military angle, he seemed to have a core group of fifteen or twenty people who commented on his posts and on whose posts he commented. I wrote their names down.

More important than his friends, though, was his son, who played basketball at St. Augustine's middle school. According to his Facebook posts, Becker made it to almost every game, which made me wonder whether he had a place in town.

None of Mr. Becker's posts on Facebook mentioned an ex-wife or significant other, but Becker's son had to have a mom somewhere in town if the kid lived here. I called the middle school's front office and spoke to the assistant principal. She had three kids named Becker in the school, but only one played basketball: Xavier. He lived with his mom, Tara Madison; her husband, Wesley Madison; and his baby brother, Joshua.

After hanging up with the school, I ran quick background checks on both Tara and her husband, but neither had ever been arrested for anything but minor traffic offenses, and neither had any outstanding warrants. Like Mr. Becker, they looked as if they were solid citizens. I hoped at least one of them would be home in the middle of the day. I grabbed my keys and purse and headed out.

The Madison family lived in a single-story brick home on a nice piece of property outside the western edge of the town of St. Augustine. The landscape rolled to a creek at the base of the house, and soybeans swayed with the breeze in fields surrounding the home. A small dog barked from the front room. Before I could open my door, a woman appeared in the doorway behind a glass storm door. She was in her late thirties or early forties, and she had blonde hair pulled back from her face. Navy hospital scrubs covered her torso and legs. When she saw me looking at her, she pressed her lips into a thin line and crossed her arms.

As I walked toward her, she opened her door.

"Can I help you, Officer?"

I said nothing until I reached the porch. Then, I reached to my belt for my badge.

"Afternoon, ma'am," I said. "I'm Detective Joe Court. Just to confirm, are you Tara Madison?"

She blinked and leaned against the doorframe before crossing her arms.

"Yes."

"Do you know Thomas Becker?"

She nodded.

"He's my ex-husband."

Even though she and Thomas had divorced, there would still be feelings—good and bad—between them. They had a child together. This would be hard. I allowed the stillness of our placid surroundings to enter my voice even as my stomach tightened into a knot.

"Is there somewhere we can talk?" I asked.

"We can talk here," she said, fluttering her eyelids. "Is Thomas okay?"

I shook my head.

"No," I said, my voice low. "I'm sorry to inform you we found him this morning in a home in St. Augustine County. He's dead."

Her nostrils flared as she breathed in, and she clenched her jaw. I hadn't expected an angry response, so I didn't yet know what to think of it. She looked down and blinked.

"Someone from the hospital would call if he had a heart attack. You're a police officer, though. How'd he die?"

"It's a murder," I said. "I'm working the case now. Did Mr. Becker have any siblings or parents I should call?"

She considered. Then her expression softened some.

"I'll call his mom," she said. "She and I always got along well. She should hear about this from family."

I nodded. "I appreciate that. Can you think of anyone who would want to harm your ex-husband?"

"Thomas lived in Arkansas. He didn't come to St. Augustine often, so I wouldn't know."

I took out a notepad from my pocket and started scribbling notes, but not because I thought they would help me any. I wanted to give her time to think about her answer and why she had just lied.

"Did Mr. Becker get along with Xavier?"

She licked her lips. "When they saw each other, they got along okay."

"And how often was that?"

A baby cried somewhere in the house.

"Christmas and his birthday. They didn't see each other often," she said. "This isn't a great time."

"I understand," I said, nodding and reaching into my purse. I took a business card from my wallet and held it toward her. "When you and your husband have time, I'd very much like to continue this conversation. I can talk to you here or wherever you feel comfortable."

She took the card and blinked a few times.

"Thank you for coming by, Detective," she said. "If we need to talk again, I'll give you my attorney's number."

I straightened and forced a smile to my face.

"Okay. Thanks."

She shut the door. I stayed still to think. Every other word out of her mouth had been a lie. Thomas lived in Arkansas, but he came to their son's basketball games. She would have seen him, and even if she hadn't, Xavier would have talked about seeing his father. Tara Madison may not have been my murderer, but she was hiding something. I needed to find out what.

# Chapter 17

Tara watched as the detective climbed into her old brown cruiser and drove away. Her arms and legs felt heavy, her chest felt cold, and her throat felt tight. She drew in a slow breath and blinked as her eyes grew moist. Thomas was dead. She had expected that, but to hear the words come out of the detective's mouth had still shaken her. She closed the front door and brought a hand to her brow. The baby continued to cry.

"God damn it," she said, closing her eyes as a tear rolled down her cheek. "God fucking damn it."

She leaned against the wall and allowed gravity to pull her down to a seated position. Her chin trembled despite her attempts to stop it. She had stopped loving Thomas a long time ago, but he was still the father of one of her children. He was a good dad, too. This would break Xavier's heart.

She closed her eyes and leaned her head back again.

"God damn it," she said once more. As she sat with her head against the wall, the hardwood floor creaked and groaned as heavy footsteps plodded down the hall.

"Are you going to get Scarlett, Tara?"

She clenched her jaw and inhaled a slow breath through her nose.

"Fuck you, Shane. And fuck your stupid brother, too. And fuck that goddamn baby while you're at it."

Shane paused. "What'd the cop want?"

She opened her eyes and looked up. A tear slipped down her cheek. Shane Weaver was thirty-nine years old and had a full head of brown hair and a matching beard. Acne scars pockmarked his cheeks, while heavy, thick calluses covered the palms of his hateful, stupid hands. He and his brother were her ex-husband's best friends. They were morons, but she had cared for them when she was young. Now, she needed them out of her life.

"Why did you come here?" she asked.

"What kind of question is that?" he asked, crossing his arms. His biceps strained his plaid flannel shirt.

"I hate you," she said. "I hate everything about you."

"Your boy loves me, though," he said, smiling. "I can't be that bad, can I?"

She looked down at the hardwood. "He won't love you when he finds out you got his father killed."

Shane said nothing for a moment. Then he dropped his arms to the side.

"Thomas is dead?"

"Yeah," she said. "Your best friend's dead. Someone murdered him yesterday. I bet you know why."

Shane hesitated and then squatted beside her.

141

"I'm sorry," he said, his voice low.

"My son's father is dead. I don't give a shit about your feelings right now."

Neither said anything for a moment. The baby's cries became almost hysterical. It made Tara ache, but she didn't move. Shane cleared his throat.

"I don't know the first thing about babies, Tara," he said. "What do I do?"

She sighed and stood and walked to the nursery, glad she had worn the thick nursing pads that morning.

"She's hungry."

The nursery had light blue walls, navy blue carpet, white trim, and new white furniture. Tara crossed the room to the bassinet and took the tiny infant into her arms. Shane and Andy didn't tell her where they had gotten her, but she was only three or four days old. The little girl had a full head of black hair and bright blue eyes. She was tiny, even for a newborn. She should have been in the hospital.

"Hey, sweetheart," she whispered in a singsong voice. The little girl didn't stop crying, but she settled some as Tara patted her back. "Do we have an empty tummy?"

Tara looked to Shane, who stood in the doorway.

"Go to the kitchen and put a bottle of premixed infant formula in the bottle warmer. Set it for two minutes."

He hesitated and then mocked holding a child up to his chest.

"Can't you, uh, you know..."

"Breastfeed her?" she asked.

"Yeah. You're breastfeeding the other one, aren't you?"

"I breastfeed my son, and he's not here," she said. "I'm a hostage, not a nursemaid. Warm up the fucking bottle."

The little girl's cries became frantic, and she rubbed her face against Tara's chest. Tara rubbed her back and raised her eyes at Shane. He threw up his hands and left the room. Tara bounced around the room to calm the baby before settling into the rocking chair in the corner. Wesley had restored that chair before Joshua was born. It had been his grandmother's, and it was beautiful. She wondered what he'd think when he came home and found her ex-husband's two best friends and a strange newborn in the house.

Shane returned a few minutes later with a tiny bottle. Tara rubbed it against the baby's cheek until she rooted. Then she sucked.

"Andy and I will go," he said. "You've just got to tell me what to do with the baby, and we'll take care of her."

She narrowed her gaze at him and shook her head.

"No," she said. "I let you two idiots take her, she'll end up dead like Thomas."

He nodded and shifted his weight to lean against the nursery's doorframe.

"I've been thinking about that," he said. "What if he's not dead? That cop might just be trying to rattle us."

She didn't bother looking up. Instead she smiled at the little girl.

"That's so stupid, I'm not even going to comment," she said, in the singsong voice she reserved for young children. "Thomas is dead, and it's your fault."

He crossed his arms. "Yeah, well, we didn't mean for this to happen."

She looked up and then grabbed a burp cloth from the nearby changing station.

"Where are Scarlett's parents?"

"You don't need to know to take care of her," said Shane. "But if you take care of her, we'll take care of you. Don't you worry about that. You'll get paid for this."

She threw the cloth over her shoulder and patted the little girl's back.

"I don't want money," she said, dropping the singsong voice. "What have you done?"

He said nothing. Tara patted and rubbed Scarlett's back in an upward motion until she burped. Then Tara pulled her from her shoulder in time to see her eyes shutting as she fell asleep. She'd give her a minute, but then she'd change her diaper and wrap her up with a blanket.

Tara glanced up. "Where are this girl's parents, and how did you get her? Talk or learn how to care for a sick newborn overnight."

He straightened, and the expression left his face.

"You think she's sick?"

"She's not well," said Tara. "She's trembling, she feels warm, and her breath is shallow—even for a child her age. She's stressed, but it might be something else."

"You're a nurse," he said. "She'll be okay. Right?"

"Take her to a hospital and let a doctor examine her. That's the only way you'll know," said Tara. She softened her voice and tried a different tactic. "Where are her parents? Just give her back. Let them take care of her. She's not your responsibility."

"Her parents are dead," said Shane. "At least her daddy is. Her mom is...I don't know. Maybe she's alive, maybe she's not."

Tara carried Scarlett to her son's changing station and changed her diaper. During the process, the little girl woke and kicked but then fell asleep again as soon as the blanket was on her. She wasn't lethargic, but she rarely woke up and didn't eat well. Tara had a bad feeling about this. She looked at Shane.

"Tell me how you got her."

Shane didn't give many details, but as soon as he mentioned a helicopter, a hospital in St. Louis, and a plot to make a lot of money, she knew what had happened. The story about the raid on the hospital in St. Louis had been all over the news, but she'd never imagined her ex-husband—helicopter pilot or not—had been involved. It was a nightmare.

She carried the baby back to the bassinet and swaddled her in a blanket. Then she and Shane stepped into the hall.

"What the hell were you three thinking? People died in that hospital. You know that?"

He nodded. "Thomas thought he needed the money."

She balled her hands into fists.

"Why did he need money?"

"It's for Xavier," said Shane. "The X-Man. You're going to take him to Virginia. Thomas would never see his son again."

Tara took a step back.

"How did Thomas know about Virginia?"

"Xavier told him," said Shane. "It's true then, huh? You and that dickless wonder you married would leave with your new family and start a life somewhere else, somewhere Thomas couldn't go."

"It wasn't like that," she said, hating that she sounded so defensive. "There's nothing in St. Augustine for Xavier. We've been talking about moving. All right? Most of Wesley's family lives on the East Coast. The schools are better, our jobs would be better, and our house would be nicer. We'd have a better life there."

"Except that you'd be taking a boy from his daddy," said Shane, crossing his arms. "You take a man's child, he'll do a lot of things to get him back."

It was true. She looked at Scarlett. No matter what happened, Tara had to keep her safe. She couldn't let an infant get hurt if she could help it.

"I know who this baby is. She's been on the news."

Shane shrugged. "So?"

She closed her eyes and counted to ten in her head before speaking.

"Her grandfather is Gerald Nolan. Do you have any idea who that is?"

He blinked but said nothing.

"He owns a private security and intelligence firm," said Tara, speaking slowly. "He could send a literal army after you. What the hell were you thinking? You'd murder his son, ransom his granddaughter back to him, and then ride off into the sunset?"

"We didn't kill the man's son," said Shane, puffing out his chest. "That was on Lorenzo Molena's crew. We just took the kid from them."

"Oh," said Tara, nodding, her eyes wide. "That makes it all better."

"You always thought you were smarter than us," said Shane.

"You didn't even have a plan, Shane," she said. "You idiots just showed up at my house with a baby and asked for help."

"Now that wasn't our fault," said Shane, holding up a finger. "We didn't want to come here. We had a whole house set up with food and water and stuff for the baby. Then Stinky Jay got shot and ruined everything."

Tara held up a hand to shut him up.

"I don't want to know about your stupid plan, and I don't want to know who Stinky Jay is," she said. "We need to figure out how to get this baby back to her family."

"Andy's working on that," said Shane. "We needed a place to lie low for two or three hours. Okay? Me and Andy will sort this out. We'll take the baby, and you won't even see us again."

"No," she said. "Because you showed up here, I'm now part of the conspiracy. That St. Augustine detective knows something's up. I'm not going to prison because you two came to my house, and I'm not going to let this little girl die in your care."

Shane considered her and blinked. "What do you propose doing, then?"

"That baby's grandfather is a dangerous man. He will come after you in force," she said. Shane nodded and then shrugged.

"I'm a dangerous man."

"Yeah. So was Thomas, and he's dead," she said. "We'll go to your cabin for a few days. Wesley can take care of Xavier and Joshua. I'll take care of Scarlett. Once we're safe, we can make long-term plans."

Shane thought before nodding.

"That's not a bad idea," he said, nodding. "You're not saying that just to get me off your back, though, are you?"

She smiled. "If I wanted you off my back, I would have told that cop the truth."

"Good," he said. "Thomas is dead—and I'm sorry about that—but me and Andy are lookin' to make a score. You get in our way, I'll put you down. I don't want to do it, but I will. This job's too important."

Tara balled her hands into fists and felt waves of nausea and heat pass through her. Her legs felt weak. She had grown up around the Weaver boys. They came from bad stock and brought ruin wherever they went. It was part of why her first marriage imploded.

"Like it or not, we're in this together," she said, her heart thudding against her chest. "You don't make threats against your business partner, especially when she's the only person keeping the baby you hope to ransom alive. Now shut up and help me pack a bag. We need diapers, wipes, and all the formula in the house. Wesley can buy more."

Shane nodded. "Where's the bag?"

"I'll get it," she said. "You wait here."

She walked away, but when she turned into the garage where she and her husband stored their luggage, tears came to her cheeks, and her stomach roiled. She held her breath so she wouldn't vomit. Her stomach stopped cramping, and the cool air chilled her face and hot skin. She brought a hand to her face and stayed still for at least a few minutes.

"What the hell am I doing?" she asked.

She didn't have an answer. She only knew she had to keep Scarlett—and her husband and family—alive. As she walked toward the wire shelving unit at the back of the garage, Shane called out from the house.

"What's taking you so damn long?"

She closed her eyes, drew in a breath, and put on a strong, confident persona she hoped would keep her alive even as every muscle in her body trembled.

"I'm getting it, Shane. Cool your jets."

She pushed aside a box full of tennis rackets and balls to expose an old, leather duffel bag. Wesley, her husband, was an EMT. He carried a pistol on a holster on his ankle on every shift. It violated just about every rule on the books, but he wasn't the only paramedic to carry a weapon. She hated having a gun in the house, but Wesley ran into a lot of crazy people at work. He had to protect himself. Now, for the first time, she wished they had bought two firearms instead of one.

As she reached for the bag, she whispered.

"How the hell am I going to get out of this?"

# Chapter 18

I was about halfway back to my station when Darlene McEvoy with our crime lab called. She didn't call often, but when she did, it was important. I pulled into the parking lot of a nearby strip mall and answered.

"Darlene," I said. "It's Joe Court. What can I do for you?"

"Hey," she said, her voice soft. "Are you somewhere we can talk for a moment?"

"I'm in my car, but sure," I said. "What's on your mind?"

"Reuben Terepocki," she said. "I know you like to play things close to the chest, but I don't trust him."

She wasn't the only person with that assessment, so I nodded even though I was alone.

"I'm still working the case, but I've already talked to Dr. Sheridan about the evidence you two found. As soon as his lawyer returns my call, I'll talk to Reuben and see what he has to say about everything. I'm hoping this will blow over, but it's not looking good for him. Your findings were pretty damning."

"I know," she said, drawing in a deep breath. "I've worked in this department almost twenty years. We've had officers

151

steal from the evidence vault, and we had a detective who took bribes to let a weed dealer know when we were making sweeps, but we've never had a cop murder somebody. That'll hurt this town."

"We'll do what we can," I said. "The situation sucks, but we're professionals. I don't know what'll happen with Reuben, but we'll follow the evidence. That's all we can do."

"You're right," she said. "I hate this. Until this case, I liked him. He seemed like a good cop, and he was great with kids at crime scenes. He was like Mr. Rogers with a badge." She paused. "I'm glad you're working this case. We need someone like you."

My stomach twisted just a little, and I went quiet.

"What do you mean by someone like me?"

"You do what's right even though it hurts," she said. She paused. "I used to think you didn't care about anybody, that you wanted to move up in the department and then move on when a better job came your way. After the Apostate case, though, you could have gone to St. Louis or Chicago or even Washington. You didn't leave, though. You stayed here. I misjudged you."

I softened my voice.

"This is home," I said.

"I'm glad," she said. "Just do your best with Reuben. My lab will support you no matter what happens."

"Thank you," I said. She wished me luck and hung up a moment later. My car was still on and I had somewhere to go, but I didn't put it into drive.

My boss was the biggest jerk I knew. The moment I gave him the slightest pretext, he'd fire me without hesitation. He didn't even bother giving me performance reviews anymore. He just sent me a note that said my work was satisfactory. My colleagues were better, but they only saw me as a detective. I ordered them around at crime scenes and thanked them when they did something well. It had been a while since someone thought of me as an actual human being with real feelings. I had missed it.

Before I could put my car back in gear, my phone rang once more. This time, the caller was Mathias Blatch. My stomach fluttered as I answered.

"Mathias, hey," I said. "Didn't expect to hear from you today. Everything okay?"

"I'm just fantastic," he said in a voice that told me he was anything but fantastic. "How are you?"

"Fine," I said. "What's going on?"

"I'm in the North Patrol Division's headquarters in St. Louis. I need you to get up here. An undercover detective picked up Ian in a crack house. He told the watch commander that he was one of my confidential informants, so she called me. I know he's your brother, but I'm ready to kick his ass up and down the parking lot."

I closed my eyes and squeezed my phone tight.

"Hold off on kicking his ass," I said. "I'm on my way."

He told me to drive safely. After hanging up with him, I called Trisha, my dispatcher, to let her know what was going on. Then I squeezed my steering wheel tight, swore under my breath, and drove north to the city. The North Patrol Division's building was a squat concrete and brick structure with few windows. The US and Missouri state flags hung outside. It looked like the kind of secure facility an occupying force would erect in the middle of a hostile land.

I parked in the lot out front and walked inside. Mathias waited for me in the cramped front lobby, his face red and angry. When he saw me, his expression softened. I smiled despite the situation.

"Hey," I said. "Thank you for calling me."

"They let me put him in an interrogation room," he said. "He's not happy."

I nodded and signed in at the front desk. Then Mathias and I walked to a small, windowless room with a heavy steel table bolted to the floor. Thin, rough carpet covered the walls and ceiling to muffle sound and allow for better recording. Someone had put three folding chairs around the table. Ian sat on one with his head down as if he were asleep. When Mathias and I walked in, he looked up.

"Hey," he said, standing. "Are we ready to go now?"

"Nope," I said, pulling a chair from the table. "Have a seat."

Ian looked to Mathias.

"What is this?" he asked.

"This is an interview," I said. "We're trying to figure out what you were doing at that house so we can charge you with an appropriate crime."

"I wasn't doing anything," he said, crossing his arms and turning his gaze on me.

"I asked you to sit down," I said, allowing a measure of ice into my voice. "Now sit or I'll put you in restraints."

He looked at me and then the chair and sat.

"Better?" he asked.

"Yep," I said. I looked at Mathias. "I assume you searched him when he came in."

"Yeah, and I want my stuff back," said Ian.

"Shut up," I said. I looked to Mathias. "He have anything on him that concerns you?"

Mathias shook his head. "Just a cell phone, his wallet, and keys. He told the officer who picked him up that he took the bus from the Galleria Mall."

I nodded and looked to my brother.

"I'm glad to hear you're getting good use out of St. Louis's public transportation system," I said. "Now what the hell were you doing?"

He looked away and said nothing.

"You said an undercover officer found him," I said, looking at Mathias. He nodded.

"Yeah. He's a gang intelligence officer. He said some of his boys saw Ian walking around and decided to hit a lick and make some money."

I crossed my arms and looked to my brother.

"Do you know what that means, Ian?" I asked.

He shrugged and looked at me. "I can take care of myself."

"Out in the suburbs, maybe," I said. "Out here, no. This is gang territory. Do you understand that? They were going to rob you. If you were lucky, they'd just beat you up and take your shoes. If you were unlucky, they'd drive you around town and make you hit every ATM they found until your account ran out of money. What do you think they'd do when they finished that?"

He rolled his eyes. "Drive me home?"

"They would have shot you in the head and left your corpse in a vacant lot," said Mathias. "I've worked ten cases like that in the past year alone."

My brother rolled his eyes again and shook his head but wouldn't look at either of us.

"Fine. I get it," he said, finally. "You've scared me straight. I won't go back."

"No, you don't get it," said Mathias, standing up. "But you know what? That's not my problem. A detective almost had to break cover to save you. He won't do that again. Next time, you get what's coming to you."

"Okay," said Ian, shrugging. Mathias's face turned red, and he drew in a slow breath before looking at me.

"Can you take him home? If I drive him, I might throw him off a bridge."

"I'll get him," I said, putting a hand on the detective's forearm. He was more muscular than I anticipated. "Give me a few minutes. I want to talk to him. Then I'll drive him home."

"Are you going to tell my parents what happened?" he asked.

"Does it matter?" asked Mathias. Ian shrugged.

"Not really," he said, trying to act cool and unconcerned. I saw through it, though. He shifted on his seat and brought his hands closer to his chest.

"I've met your parents," I said. "They care about you. I'll tell them everything Mathias and I have just told you. They'll deal with you."

He cast his eyes toward the table. I looked at Mathias.

"Can I have the room?"

"Sure," he said. "I'll be outside if you need me."

I smiled at him and watched him leave. Then I pulled a chair around the table so I could sit beside my brother.

"What were you doing at a crack house, Ian?" I asked. "The truth. You're not an idiot. What did you want that was so valuable you'd risk getting shot?"

He looked to the table and shook his head. "You wouldn't understand."

"Try me," I said.

He looked at a spot behind me.

"I wanted to talk to someone who knew Mom before she died. I got three names from that file Detective Blatch gave me. Two of them were dead, but the third lady was still alive. I talked to her sister, and she said Christina hung out at the house where the detective found me. That's it. I wanted to find out what happened to my mom."

I softened my voice. "If that undercover detective didn't call the police, you might have died. Do you understand that?"

He said nothing.

"You got lucky, Ian. If you keep looking for Erin, you may not get lucky again. Multiple detectives have worked that case and couldn't break it. If you keep pushing, you'll get hurt. Erin isn't worth it."

He balled his hands into fists. When he looked at me again, red tinged his eyes.

"Are you done?"

I nodded. "Yeah. Come on. I'll drive you home."

"I'd rather take the bus," he said, standing.

"Too bad," I said. "You're a minor, and you're in my custody. If you don't cooperate, I'll tase you and have uniformed officers throw you in the back of my cruiser."

"You're a bitch. I wish I never found you."

"You're not my favorite brother at the moment, either," I said, putting a hand on his elbow. "Come on. My car's out front."

He grumbled but said nothing. Mathias was outside, waiting for us. He smiled at me but showed Ian a much more neutral expression.

"You get things worked out?" he asked.

"Yeah. I'm driving him home," I said. I hesitated and then lowered my voice so Ian wouldn't hear. "I owe you lunch."

His smile spread. "Yes, you do. I'll call."

I thanked him again before leading Ian outside. Once we reached my car, he looked at me over the roof.

"Your boyfriend's ugly," he said.

"So are you. Now get in the car and shut up. Save your voice. You've got a lot to tell your parents."

# Chapter 19

Ian and his family lived in St. Charles, a midsize town on the Missouri River about half an hour west of St. Louis. His directions led me to an American foursquare with yellow clapboard siding and a covered porch that wound from the front of the house to the side.

"Nice house, but the grass could use a trim," I said. "You should get on that."

"Whatever," said Ian, opening his door. As he got out of my cruiser, the home's front door opened, and Mrs. Miriam Staley, his mom, stepped onto the porch. Wavy white hair framed her oval-shaped face. She smiled as she saw us, but then that smile slipped as I walked toward her.

"Detective," she said, nodding. Ian walked past her to go inside, but she grabbed his shoulder before he could. "Honey, you didn't tell me your sister was coming over. Why aren't you in school?"

He looked down at his feet.

"I got in trouble."

Mrs. Staley straightened.

"Is everything okay, Detective?"

"Please call me Joe," I said, nodding toward a set of padded chairs on the porch. "And we should talk."

I stayed at the house for half an hour. Ian did most of the talking, but I answered questions where I could. By the time we finished speaking, Mrs. Staley had grounded her son for a week and confiscated his cell phone and iPad for the next three days. His school would probably suspend him for skipping class, too.

Ian had done something stupid, but he hadn't gotten himself hurt, and he hadn't hurt anyone else. I warned him that if he showed up in that same neighborhood—or one just as bad—we'd come down on him harder and let him spend the night in jail for trespassing. That wiped the hopeful smile clear off his face.

After the conversation, he went inside to call his girlfriend, and Mrs. Staley walked me to my cruiser.

"Thank you for bringing him home, Joe," she said. "When his father and I adopted him, we didn't think we'd ever have kids. We were already in our fifties. He's a handful."

I tilted my head to the side and smiled. "He's a good kid, and you've done a good job with him. He's a teenager, though. Judgment isn't their strong suit."

She raised her eyebrows and nodded as a tight smile crept to her lips.

"Should I worry about him?" she asked. "I'm asking you as a police officer."

I considered what to tell her before nodding.

"Yeah, but for good reasons," I said. "He's not on drugs, he stays out of trouble, and he's smart. He can do anything he wants with his life. If he keeps chasing Erin Court, though, she'll take him places he has no business going. I don't want to see him hurt, especially over someone like her."

She blinked. "Aside from being his biological mother, who was Erin Court?"

"A drug-addicted prostitute who never cared about anyone half as much as she cared about herself."

She nodded, her eyes distant.

"Thank you for your honesty," she said. I smiled at her and started toward my cruiser but stopped when she called out. "My husband and I would like to have you over for dinner soon. You're our son's sister. I guess that makes us all family."

I hesitated before responding. Ian and I shared Erin Court's DNA, but we weren't really siblings. My real brother and sister—Dylan and Audrey—were both younger than me, so I had seen them grow up. I braided Audrey's hair before school, and I cheered Dylan on at his soccer games. They came to my high school graduation and cheered louder than anyone else in the football stadium when the superintendent handed me my diploma. That was what it meant to have a sibling. Nothing could replicate that.

Besides, Ian didn't need me. The Staleys were great parents. Ian went to bed every night knowing his mom and dad loved him and would do anything for him. He'd never have to beg for food, he'd never worry about losing his house, and he'd always have a home to return to. That meant a lot in this world. If Ian had needed a big sister, I would have jumped into his life with a smile on my face, but he already had everything he could possibly want. I looked down at the ground so I wouldn't have to look her in the eye.

"Thank you, but I don't know if that's such a good idea," I said. "Ian's life is complicated enough. I'd just add to that."

"Oh," said Mrs. Staley, straightening. "I see."

"If he still wants to know more about Erin," I said, quickly, "I can answer questions, but he won't like what I have to say."

She paused.

"No, I don't think that'd be appropriate," she said, shaking her head. "I understand that you and my son are siblings, but, like you said, his life is complicated enough. I'll talk to him about Erin. If you need to get in touch with him again for any reason, call me. I'll talk to him on your behalf. I'll thank you in advance for your discretion, Detective."

A heavy pit grew in my stomach, but I ignored it.

"That sounds good," I said. I turned toward my cruiser but only went a few steps before turning around. "Good luck, Mrs. Staley. You've got a good boy."

"I know."

I nodded and felt the pit in my stomach grow. Then I turned and walked back to my cruiser. For the entire drive home, my limbs grew heavier with each mile, and the pit in my stomach grew into an empty chasm. I had done the right thing. If I was in Ian's life, I'd just screw things up. As long as I stayed away, he'd graduate from high school at the top of his class and go to Caltech or MIT or Carnegie Mellon, and he'd write a program or create some new computer that would change the world. He had that ability. If I tried to stay in his life, though, I'd become an anchor. He needed to free himself from his past, not weigh himself down with more of it.

When I reached the outskirts of St. Augustine, I called my station to make sure nothing bad had happened while I was in St. Louis. Someone had reported a stolen vehicle—a relative rarity in our part of the world—but Sergeant Reitz was taking care of that. I was free to punch out for the day, so I dropped off my cruiser, picked up my Volvo, and drove home.

Roy greeted me as soon as I came home. I knelt in front of him.

"You're easy to be with," I said, scratching his cheek. He leaned into my hand. "I wish everybody was like you."

He stretched into a play bow, so I let him into the yard. He sniffed at the grass before peeing on a tree. Then he climbed back onto the porch and sat down in the late afternoon shade. I didn't know if I believed in reincarnation, but if I came back to life after I died, I hoped I'd come back as a dog. Roy seemed to know how to live.

I left him outside and went to my room, where I changed into a pair of black leggings and a loose-fitting T-shirt. Roy stayed with me while I stretched and then even followed me into the woods for about a hundred yards. He trotted back home after that, but that was okay. It was nice to see him move a little.

I ran until the sun went down, but I ended up right back where I started. That felt like a metaphor for my life.

At a little after seven, I warmed up a chicken and rice bowl from my freezer, poured myself a beer, and sat down in the living room to watch TV. I didn't do that often, so I didn't have favorite shows. Instead, I flipped through the channels, found nothing interesting, and then turned on Netflix. I hadn't opened Netflix in quite a while, but somebody had. My recently watched video list now included *Angels of Sex*, *Ten Rules for Sleeping Around*, and *Below Her Mouth*. It looked like porn with a very thin plotline.

I groaned, picked up my cell phone, and sent Dylan, my adoptive brother, a text message.

*Dude, have you been using my Netflix account to watch soft-core porn?*

I tossed the remains of my rice bowl in the trash as I waited for Dylan to respond.

*Nope. I'm still on Mom and Dad's account.*

I flipped through movies and TV shows until I found a superhero TV show I had started and liked. Then I typed Dylan a message.

*Sure you didn't watch Angels of Sex on my account?*

This time, Dylan's response was quicker.

*I don't need Netflix to see boobs.*

I almost asked him who watched it, but then it hit me: Dylan wasn't my only brother anymore. Ian needed to find another way to watch dirty movies. I changed my password, let the dog inside, finished my beer, and then went to the kitchen for a rocks glass and a bottle of vodka.

Only time would tell whether I'd regret driving away from Ian's house, but for now, I didn't want to feel anything. I poured myself an inch of vodka and drank it down in a gulp. The liquid slid down my throat like velvet. I poured myself another and walked back to the living room to watch a show.

About half an hour later, my phone buzzed. My head felt light, but my body felt good. I was tipsy, but not yet drunk. I looked at the text message on my phone.

*What's your new Netflix password?*

It was Ian. I stared at the message for a moment, considering how to respond. Then I shook my head and held the phone's power button until it turned off. In a year or two, he wouldn't even remember my name. This was for the best. His mom and I agreed. He didn't need me in his life.

I swallowed the last of my vodka and pretended it didn't taste bitter.

# Chapter 20

The next morning when Roy woke me up, my head pounded, and my mouth felt as if I had stuffed it full of cotton balls. The sunlight streamed through my beige Roman shades as if they were tissue paper, sending streaks of orange and yellow light across my hardwood floor. The dog hopped off the bed and then play bowed beside it.

"Hey, dude," I whispered as I stretched my arms above my head. "Give me a minute."

Roy tilted his head to the side and raised his eyebrows as if he were confused. I reached out and patted his cheek. He leaned against my hand then licked my wrist, which made me smile. He was a good dog. If he'd have me, I'd give him a home. As I swung my legs off the bed, my cell phone rang. It was twenty to eight. I should have gotten up at least half an hour earlier so I could have breakfast and make it to work on time, but I'd manage.

I rolled over, grabbed my phone, and groaned when I saw the name on the caller ID.

"Hey, boss," I said, closing my eyes as I answered. "I'm walking out the door now. What do you need?"

"Glad to hear you're on the way," said Sheriff Delgado. "Because Reuben and his lawyer are, too. They want to meet and sort this whole thing out."

I closed my eyes and swore under my breath.

"All right," I said, a moment later. "I'll be there with my case notes."

"See you soon."

The sheriff hung up, and I stood. Roy jumped up as if he wanted to play.

"Sorry, dude," I said. "I've got to go."

I hurried into the kitchen and gave him a cup of food in his bowl. While he ate, I threw on clean clothes, brushed my teeth and put my hair into a loose bun. Within ten minutes of Delgado's call, Roy was in the enclosed dog run behind my house, and I was in my Volvo, driving to the station. I reached the parking lot at five after eight and jogged to my office, where I picked up a few reports before heading to Delgado's second-floor office.

The sheriff had the largest office in the building, but that didn't make it very nice. It had a giant picture window overlooking part of downtown St. Augustine and enough space to hold the sheriff's desk, two separate seating areas, and a small conference table. Unfortunately, his windows—like many in the building—leaked when it rained, water marks stained the walls, and the air held a perpetual whiff of mildew. One day, it'd be a nice office, but it wasn't there yet.

Delgado, Terepocki, and Terepocki's lawyer—Paul Bellamy—sat around the conference table. All three men had coffee cups. Nobody spoke or drank. I put my papers down and pulled out the chair beside the sheriff.

"Morning, gentlemen," I said. "I'm glad to see that everybody's here. Are we waiting for anyone else, or am I the last to arrive?"

"You're it," said Reuben. "You look tired, Joe."

I gave him a curt smile. "I'm working two major cases at the moment, so I'm stretched thin."

"Your workload would be lighter if you had cleared me yesterday."

I kept the smile on my face. "I'm working on that. We've got a lot to talk about, so I'll start."

I opened my files and walked them through my investigation into Jay Pischke's death. Neither Reuben nor his attorney said anything when I finished, so I leaned forward.

"Here's where we stand," I said. "You've lied from the start about this case. I'd like the truth. What's going on?"

Reuben opened his mouth to say something, but his lawyer put a hand on his shoulder first.

"Detective Terepocki has no comment," he said. "I do, though. First, if you arrest him, I'll have him out by this afternoon. My client did nothing wrong. He is a licensed, sworn police officer in the state of Missouri, and he visited Mr. Pischke in good faith in pursuance of his duties. Upon reaching the home, my client announced himself as a police officer. Mr. Pischke pulled out a firearm and shot at my client. My client defended himself.

"According to the law, those are the germane facts. My client believed his life was in danger and reacted. This is a witch hunt. We plan to hold everyone here accountable for their actions."

I had figured Reuben and his attorney would make that argument, so I had a response ready. Before I could say anything about the forensics of the scene, though, Sheriff Delgado leaned forward.

"Why'd you lie about knowing Vic Conroy, Detective?"

Reuben didn't even bother trying to respond. His lawyer was doing the talking for him.

"My client maintains that he's told nothing but the truth as far as he can recollect this entire investigation. Only one person has claimed my client has ever met Mr. Conroy."

Delgado looked to me. I raised my eyebrows.

"Are you calling me a liar, Counselor?"

The lawyer looked at me. "I'm saying that only one person has claimed that my client has met Mr. Conroy. Perhaps you were mistaken."

I looked to Reuben. "It's on video, jackass. You walked into a strip club, beat up the bouncer, and then had a private meeting with Vic Conroy in his office. Insinuating that I'm a liar isn't helping your case."

"If there's video, we'd like to see it," said the attorney.

"We'll send it to you as part of the discovery package after we charge your client with murder," I said. "Fair enough?"

The lawyer considered me for a moment before nodding.

"Suppose there is a video," he said. "Perhaps my client's recollections were incorrect. My client is an adult. There's nothing wrong with patronizing a legal gentlemen's club."

I looked to Reuben. "You go to a lot of strip clubs, Reuben?"

"Please direct your questions to me, Detective," said the attorney. "As to your question, my client's leisure activities aren't germane to the issues at hand."

I shrugged. "Maybe they are, maybe they're not. You must go to a shit ton of strip clubs if you can't remember going to one and getting into a fight with the bouncer, though. That would seem like a memorable night."

"I can smell the liquor in your sweat, Joe," said Reuben. "I'm guessing any night you're sober is memorable."

I straightened. Delgado held up a hand.

"Personal attacks are uncalled for, Detective," he said. He looked to me. "And let's wrap up that line of questioning. Mr. Terepocki and his attorney have said all they plan to say about it."

I nodded and looked at my notes.

"Let's talk about the shooting, then. How was Mr. Pischke positioned when you shot him?"

"My client has already answered that question many times," said the attorney. "We won't answer it again."

"Then maybe answer this: was he on his knees?"

The attorney looked at Reuben with his brow furrowed. Then he looked at me.

"Whether Mr. Pischke was on his knees is irrelevant," he said. "What's relevant is whether my client believed that his life was in danger. To reiterate: Mr. Pischke fired upon my client, who was pursuing his duties as a police officer. Knowing that his life was in danger, my client returned fire and killed Mr. Pischke. That's it. End of story."

"That is one story," I said. "Here's another. Detective Terepocki got into a fight with Mr. Pischke. The club's employees broke up the fight, but it left Mr. Pischke with bruised ribs. Mr. Pischke, fearing for his life, went into hiding. He purchased camping supplies, firearms, and jugs full of water.

"Detective Terepocki used his considerable police resources to track Mr. Pischke down. He then went to the home in which Mr. Pischke was hiding. He forced him to his knees in the living room, took several steps back, and then executed him. Once Mr. Pischke was dead, Detective Terepocki pressed a firearm into Mr. Pischke's hand and squeezed the trigger to make it seem as if he were a danger.

"This was not an accident, and this was not a police officer doing his job. Mr. Pischke died because a police officer abused his position and resources to commit a premeditated murder."

The room went silent. Then the lawyer leaned forward and raised his eyebrows.

"There's a lot of conjecture and circumstance in that story," he said. "If that's what you want to roll with, though, I think we'll be just fine."

I looked at Reuben. "Your lawyer's right. I can't prove my theory yet, but it accounts for the forensics at the crime scene. It explains why you lied, why you went to the house to find Mr. Pischke, and why Mr. Pischke had those supplies at his meth lab. Your story is bullshit. A jury will see it for what it is from a mile away.

"Not only that, I've still got time to find evidence that proves my theory. I've not found anything that supports your recollection of events. Tell me the truth, or I'll send you to prison until you die of old age."

The lawyer stood first, but Reuben followed.

"Thank you for the meeting," said the attorney. "If we feel the need to file an amended witness statement, we will. Good day, Detective."

They started toward the door, but I called out before they could reach it.

"Reuben, you ever meet Pete Marino in Kansas City?"

He and his lawyer turned.

"Who's Pete Marino?" asked the attorney.

"Mob boss in Kansas City," I said, looking from the lawyer to Reuben. "Did you ever meet him?"

"You have me on video getting into a fight with him?"

CHRIS CULVER

"If I did, I wouldn't be asking," I said. "Do you know him?"

"No," said Reuben. He crossed his arms. "Why?"

"I've got a witness who says you used to work for him when you were a detective in Kansas City."

"If your witness represents the quality of your investigative work, I'm not concerned with this inquiry. Good luck, Detective. I won't be answering any more questions."

He and his lawyer walked out. Delgado crossed the office and shut the door. Then he sighed and plopped onto the chair behind his desk. I stayed at the conference table.

"That went well," he said.

"It could have been worse," I said. "He could have refused to come."

He nodded but didn't look at me. "The lawyer's right. Your investigation has turned up a lot of circumstantial evidence, but little he can't explain away at trial. Can you shore it up?"

"I think so," I said. "According to a dealer I picked up, Pischke had a lot of cash when he died. I haven't found that money yet. I also haven't found out why he had it. I'm also looking for Jennifer Corkern, the victim's live-in girlfriend. She might tell us about any beef Jay had with Reuben."

Delgado considered and then blew out a slow breath before nodding.

"Sounds like you're on this. Do what you can to find the victim's girlfriend. I'll talk to the prosecutor and see what he advises. You need to keep the momentum going on Thomas Becker, too. If you need help, I'll ask Bob Reitz to act as your second. He's not a detective, but he's a good cop, and he's smart."

It was more than I had expected, so I nodded.

"Thank you," I said. "I don't know if I need anybody just yet, but if I do, I'll call you."

Delgado grunted and wished me luck before dismissing me. I walked to the hall and rolled my head in a circle to loosen the muscles of my neck. I usually got charged up after going after a suspect hard in an interrogation room, but this conversation had left me feeling drained.

It wasn't even nine in the morning, and I wanted a shot. Instead, I got a cup of coffee in the break room. It was hot, black, and terrible—the same as my mood. I couldn't sit around all day wallowing, though. I had too much shit to do.

# Chapter 21

I choked down about half a cup of coffee before signing out Old Brown, my marked police cruiser. My investigation into Jay Pischke's death was on hold until we found Jennifer Corkern, but my Thomas Becker investigation was in full swing. When I got into the cruiser, I found a full tank of gas and a canister of air freshener on the front seat. Somebody must have taken it out on patrol last night.

I adjusted the seat so I could reach the steering wheel and drove to the home of Tara Madison, Becker's ex-wife. Little had changed from my previous visit except that a pickup truck had parked in front of the garage. I parked behind the truck and walked to the front door. A balding but fit man in his early forties or late thirties opened the door. He held an infant to his chest.

"Can I help you?" he asked.

"I'm Detective Joe Court with the Sheriff's Department," I said. "Are you Wesley Madison?"

He nodded and furrowed his brow. "Yeah. What's wrong?"

"Everybody's fine. I'm here because I'm working a homicide. How well did you know Thomas Becker?"

He straightened. "I've met him. He's my wife's ex-husband. Did Thomas kill someone?"

I blinked but tried to keep my surprise under wraps. Tara, evidently, hadn't told her husband about Thomas's death.

"Mr. Becker is deceased," I said. "Someone murdered him."

The color left Wesley's face, and his shoulders slumped as he closed his eyes.

"Oh, no. This'll crush Xavier."

I nodded and reached into my purse for a notepad. "And Xavier is your stepson, correct?"

"Yeah," said Wesley, nodding. "Thomas is his father." He paused. "Was his father."

I flipped through pages until I found the notes I had taken after interviewing Tara.

"Was Xavier close with his father?"

"Yeah," said Wesley. "Thomas was a good dad. He lived for that boy. He went to his basketball games, he picked him up from school, he talked to Xavier's teachers and made sure Xavier did his homework..."

His voice trailed off. So much for Tara's assertion that the guy was never around and played little role in their son's life.

"Sounds like he visited a lot," I said.

Wesley shrugged. "Tara and I have full custody, but Thomas came over three or four times a week to see him. He was such a good dad, we encouraged it."

I furrowed my brow. "He drove all the way from Arkansas that often?"

"No. He's got a house in town," he said. "Arkansas is just his hunting cabin."

I nodded, hoping to circle back to that house in a moment.

"You said you've met him," I said. "Did he ever have problems with anybody? Did he, maybe, have a girlfriend?"

"Not that I know of," he said. "We only had full custody because he flew a helicopter in the Army and lived overseas until two years ago. If he had asked for joint custody, we would have worked it out and set something up."

I nodded and jotted that down.

"Where's your wife today?"

"Work," he said. "She's a visiting nurse with the Missouri Rural Healthcare Network. She visits shut-ins and people who can't make it to a traditional health-care setting."

"When will she be back?" I asked. "I need to ask her a few questions."

He straightened.

"I'm not sure," he said. "She had an emergency at work. Usually that means she'll be gone for a few days to help with a new baby or to help someone pass."

Wesley may have thought well of Tara's ex-husband, but they had divorced for a reason. I doubted she'd kill her ex, flee, and leave her baby and son to make a run for it, but I also didn't buy her story of a sudden emergency at work.

"Can I get in touch with her?"

He brought a hand to his mouth and thought.

"If she's providing hospice care, she won't have her phone on," he said. "For emergencies, you can contact Dr. Peltier. He's her boss, so he'll know where she is."

I wrote the name down and nodded before looking up.

"Do you have Thomas Becker's address in town, by chance?"

"Sure. I'll get it," he said. I crossed my arms and waited for him to leave and then return with his cell phone. He read off an address in the town of St. Augustine, which I wrote down. "What do I tell Xavier about his dad?"

I blinked to give myself a moment to think.

"The truth," I said. "Somebody killed Mr. Becker, and we don't know why yet. The police are working on the case, though, and we'll do our best to find his murderer. If he has anything to tell me, I'd love to talk to him when he's comfortable."

He furrowed his brow and took a step back.

"He's a kid. Why do you need to talk to him?"

"He's a teenager who was close to his father," I said. "He'd know if his dad had a girlfriend. Xavier will have seen a different side of him than you and Tara."

"That makes sense, I guess," said Wesley. "I'll break the news to Tara when she comes home. We'll tell Xavier together. This won't be on TV, will it?"

"It hasn't hit the news yet, but it's only a matter of time," I said. "Tell Xavier earlier rather than later."

He said he would. I thanked him for his time and walked back to my cruiser with more questions bouncing around my head than answers. Tara Madison had not only misled me, she had also held things back from her husband and son. I didn't know what that meant, but it wasn't looking good for her.

I got into my cruiser and called Trisha to let her know I was driving to Thomas Becker's home in town. With the guy dead, I didn't expect to run into problems, but I'd rather let somebody know where I was going than not. The drive took about ten minutes. Becker lived about a mile from my station in a two-story, Federalist-style red-brick house. It wasn't a jewel in downtown St. Augustine, but it was a pretty house. With a couple hundred thousand dollars and a good contractor, it could have been gorgeous.

I parked on the street out front and knocked on the door. As I expected, nobody answered. Only the living had privacy rights, so I didn't need to get a warrant to search his house. I took a lock pick set from my purse and knelt before his deadbolt. After three or four minutes, I had the door open.

Becker's front door opened to a long hallway that led to the rear of the house. An old wooden stairway led to the second floor, while a cased entryway led to a drawing room on my right. Two rifles—one looked like an AR-15, but I didn't recognize the other—leaned against the wall beside the front door.

"Sheriff's Department," I called. "Anybody in here?"

Nobody answered, so I called again, this time louder. Again, nothing stirred. I didn't want anybody to see the guns from the street while I walked through the house, so I shut the front door and called out again. For the third time, only silence greeted me. It was time to get to work.

I snapped pictures of the entryway, including the firearms, with my cell phone before walking to the drawing room. He had a pair of matching sofas facing each other in the center of the room. Between them sat a coffee table that held four Glock pistols. A locked display case on the far wall held about thirty rifles of various sorts, another half dozen pistols, and four shotguns. It was an awful lot of firepower for one person. I snapped pictures of everything before leaving the room and continuing down the front hallway to the kitchen.

Becker didn't keep guns in the kitchen, but I found a laminated federal firearms license on the fridge. The probate court would turn those firearms over to Becker's heirs, but in the meantime, they would be a tempting target for thieves. I called my station and asked Trisha to send me a pair of officers who could take the guns and catalog them for safe-keeping.

I took a staircase in the kitchen to the basement and found Becker's workshop and about another hundred rifles in racks. It would take us hours to catalog all these.

The second floor held three bedrooms, one of which had a LeBron James poster on the door and dirty T-shirts, jeans, underwear, and socks strewn about the floor. I guessed it was Xavier's room. Becker didn't keep guns on the second floor, but I found a lot of pictures hung on the wall outside the bedrooms. Some of them had Thomas and Xavier, but time had faded others so that the colors were washed out and flat. In the older pictures, a teenage version of Thomas Becker often posed with two other young men.

The house gave me less than I had hoped for. I'd be glad to get the guns somewhere safe, but Becker hadn't died for them. If somebody wanted to rob him, they would have shot him, broken into his house, and cleared the place out. They wouldn't have tied him up and cut off his fingers.

I paused in the second-floor hallway as I looked at those pictures. People killed each other for all kinds of reasons, but in general, motives rarely varied. Pride, greed, and jealousy...the three sparks Dante believed set hearts all over the world ablaze. A jealous boyfriend shoots his girlfriend for cheating on him, an asshole shoots a stranger for cutting him off in traffic, a bank robber with an itchy finger shoots a teller for packing the money too slowly. In most cases, I found hints to the potential motive in the shooter's or victim's home. Here, I had nothing.

I swept the house again, hoping to find something interesting. Becker kept pictures and mementos on the second floor, but nothing worth killing over. The first floor had guns but nothing that pointed to a motive. As I searched the basement once more, though, I found a crumpled piece of paper in the trash can. I wouldn't have noticed had the trash held anything else.

It was a receipt from a company called Midwest Aviation of Cahokia, Illinois. According to the receipt, a man named Jeff Kellogg rented a helicopter from them for eighteen hours of flight time at a cost of almost twelve thousand dollars. Becker had flown helicopters in the Army, so maybe Kellogg had hired him to fly around.

I took the receipt to my car and slipped it into a clear plastic evidence bag. Once I got back to my station, I'd fill out the paperwork to explain what I had found and where I had found it, but for now, I dialed Midwest Aviation's number on my cell phone. Before I could enter the whole thing, though, my phone buzzed with an incoming call. It was my station.

"Trisha, hey," I said. "I'm in Thomas Becker's house. What can I do for you?"

"Marcus Washington just brought in Jennifer Corkern. I thought you'd like to know."

It was Jay Pischke's girlfriend. Good. I had hoped to talk to her.

"Great," I said. "Get her in a booth and make her comfortable. I'll be there as soon as I can. Did you send officers my way?"

"They should be there any moment."

"Okay, thanks," I said. "I'll see you soon."

My search team arrived about ten minutes later. They weren't happy to see the house because they knew they'd be there for a while, but they got to work cataloging and sorting Becker's weapon collection with minimal grumbling. Hopefully Becker had a will and a lawyer who could pick the guns up soon because they would take up a lot of room in our evidence vault. Our evidence techs could worry about that, though.

I had the girlfriend of a murder victim to interview.

# Chapter 22

Tara Madison's heart thumped against her rib cage, but the baby in her arms hardly moved. Thick, dark woods surrounded her in every direction. Twenty-four hours ago, her biggest worry had been whether her son would get a speaking part in the high school's annual Christmas play. Now, she had death on her mind, and it chilled her to the bone.

She rubbed Scarlett's back. After Detective Court came to her house yesterday, Andy and Shane had forced her into their pickup and driven her to their family compound deep in the St. Augustine County backwoods. She didn't know how many acres the Weavers owned, but their nearest neighbor lived miles away. Unfortunately, even if she reached their house, they were just as likely to shoot her for trespassing as they were to help. She and Scarlett were on their own.

A tremble passed through Tara's legs and into her back. She hadn't slept in more than twenty-four hours. Instead, she had been biding her time and waiting for an opportunity. Then it happened. Shane went to buy a couple jugs of water while Andy stayed to guard her. Fortunately, Andy was an idiot. Once Shane left, he switched from drinking beer to cheap vodka. After six shots, he passed out on the sofa in one of the compound's mobile homes, giving her a chance.

She rubbed Scarlett's back and stepped carefully over the soft, loose soil.

"We're going to be okay, honey."

The baby didn't respond, but she was alive. That was all that mattered. In high school, Tara, Thomas, Shane, and Andy—and whatever idiot girls Shane and Andy could persuade to come along—used to go to the Weavers' compound to get drunk. The Weavers had added a barn and mobile homes to the property since the days in which she and Thomas had fooled around after school, but the cabin still stood. Seeing it again in these circumstances hadn't been pleasant.

Every ten feet, she stopped and checked her phone. Andy and Shane hadn't even tried to take it from her because they knew she couldn't get a signal at the compound. They hadn't anticipated her sneaking off and running to the hills, where the elevation had given her a single, stable bar, though. There had only been one problem: She couldn't call the police.

Even if the police rescued her and saved Scarlett, Shane and Andy knew St. Augustine County better than anyone alive. They'd fight back, and then they'd disappear. The police might try to protect her for a while, but they couldn't be there all the time. Nor could they watch everybody in her family. It might take weeks or even months, but when she least expected it, they'd strike.

Everyone Tara had ever loved lived within twenty miles of her home. For years, that had been a source of strength. If she had needed an emergency babysitter, she could call her sisters or her aunts or even her grandmother. If Xavier needed someone to talk to, he could call his uncles or his grandfather. If she needed a hug, her mom was a phone call and a five-minute car ride away. Tara's roots ran deep in St. Augustine County. Shane and Andy Weaver could follow those roots right to her heart.

They wouldn't hurt Xavier, but they'd kill her husband without hesitation. They might even kill Joshua. In their minds, that'd be justice. Her baby in exchange for the baby she stole from them. And if they couldn't kill her immediate family, they'd kill her mom and dad or her siblings or her cousins or her aunts and uncles. Until she could figure this out, she and her family were living on borrowed time. It made her feel sick.

Around her, the woods were alive with birds and small animals. Instead of calling the police, she had called a colleague, a doctor. He could, at the very least, examine Scarlett and tell her whether her fears were founded. Once she got back to the compound with a specific diagnosis, maybe she could even persuade Andy and Shane to let her go. More importantly, maybe Dr. Peltier could tell her how to treat Scarlett to keep her alive.

CHRIS CULVER

This whole situation came down to time: The longer she could draw this out, the more time she had to think and plan. She had to keep her family alive, and she had to keep this baby alive. Nothing else mattered to her.

The dense forest canopy allowed little light to reach the ground, limiting undergrowth and making the hike easy. After about fifteen minutes of walking, she reached a gravel road. A few minutes after that, she heard the sound of a car's tires crunching on stones. Her heart pounded as she hurried off the side of the road to hide behind a silver maple tree.

The car appeared like a mirage with the sun glinting on its front window. It was a black Ford Fiesta hatchback. Tara closed her eyes and felt her chest loosen some.

*Thank you, God.*

The car slowed to a stop as she stepped out of the woods. Dr. Ezekiel Peltier rolled down his window.

"Hey, Tara," he said. "I got your call. What's going on?"

"Thanks for coming, doc," she said. "I need you to check out this baby. I'm worried about her."

He motioned for Tara to step back as he pulled his car to the side of the road. Once he had parked, he met her near the trunk lid.

"I'll check her out, but if you're worried about her, she needs to come into the clinic," he said. "I don't even have a thermometer with me."

"She's not running a temperature," said Tara, feeling the trunk to make sure it wasn't hot. She set her down but kept both hands on her sides to prevent her from rolling. Then she dove into the story she had been preparing. "She's about a week old, maybe less. Her mom is fifteen, and her dad's sixteen. Both sides of the family are long-term clients. They had a home birth. Both of them are so exhausted they're asleep. They think I'm babysitting right now. They don't want to bring her into the hospital, but I think she needs help."

The doctor opened his back door and pulled out a bag.

"What symptoms are you seeing?"

"Mild cyanosis, and her breath is shallow and fast. She doesn't move around as much as I'd expect from an infant, either."

The doctor nodded and pulled a stethoscope from his bag. "How's she eating?"

"Poorly," said Tara. "Her parents have her on infant formula, but she doesn't eat as much as she should. She doesn't cry a lot, either."

Dr. Peltier put a hand on her forehead.

"She doesn't feel warm, so that's something," he said before pressing the stethoscope's chest piece to the baby's skin. Scarlett opened her eyes and kicked but then fell back asleep. Tara held her breath. The doctor listened for a few moments and then moved his hand. Then he did it again. After two or three minutes, he removed the headset from his ears. "We need to get her to a hospital and get imaging studies done. It sounds like she's got a heart valve defect."

Tara swore under her breath, but she nodded. It explained the lethargy, the fussiness, and the color of her skin.

"What can we do for her here?"

"Nothing," said the doctor. "We'll talk to her parents and see whether they'll let us take her to the hospital. If they refuse, we'll get the state involved. Missouri has mandatory infant screening procedures to take care of kids like this. If she's got a heart defect, she could die. The quicker we move, the better. So where are mom and dad now?"

Tara picked up the baby and held her to her chest as she shook her head.

"You can't see them," she said, thinking. "They live off the grid in the deep woods with four generations of the family in the same house. If a stranger shows up on their doorstep and says he plans to take the baby, we're both going to get shot."

Dr. Peltier lowered his chin and furrowed his brow.

"Is she safe at home?"

"She's as safe at home as she would be anywhere else," Tara said. "Her family loves her, but it'll take work to persuade them to take her to the hospital."

He nodded. "Make sure they understand their daughter would receive comprehensive, free medical care through the Missouri HealthNet for Kids Program. They wouldn't have to pay for anything."

"I'll let them know," said Tara, adjusting the baby she rested on her hip. "I'll call you as soon as I can persuade them."

"If you don't, I'll come back with a court order and a social worker," he said. "I don't want to do that, but if this little girl's life is in danger, I won't hesitate."

"I understand," said Tara.

"Good," said the doctor. He softened his voice. "Are you okay here?"

Instead of telling him the truth, she swallowed and then nodded.

"I'm worried about her, but I'm fine."

Dr. Peltier reached forward to squeeze the baby's toes.

"Does she have a name yet?"

"Scarlett."

"It's a pretty name," said the doctor, smiling at the little girl.

"I'll call you as soon as I can," she said. "If Scarlett gets worse, I'll call 911 and have an ambulance take her to the ER at St. John's."

The doctor nodded and put his stethoscope in his pocket.

"I'll be waiting for your call."

She nodded and cradled the baby. The doctor drove away a few minutes later. Tara pulled Scarlett from her chest and looked at her tiny face. She was a beautiful little girl who didn't deserve to be in the ugly world in which she lived.

She cradled the baby against her chest. Tears came to her eyes unbidden as she walked back to the cabin. As if sensing where they were going, Scarlett cried. Tara rubbed her back and shushed her, hoping it would help her settle. That calmed the baby, but it didn't improve their situation. For now, she could only deal with one problem at a time. She had to keep Scarlett alive until she could figure out how to survive long term.

Unfortunately, that'd be easier said than done.

# Chapter 23

I parked on the street about two blocks from my station, grabbed the evidence bag with the receipt from Midwest Aviation, and hurried inside. When I got there, Sergeant Bob Reitz was in the second-floor conference room with Trisha. Both were drinking coffee and talking. They nodded hello as I walked into the room.

"I hear you found Jennifer Corkern," I said.

Bob smiled a little and nodded. "Lovely woman. I stopped by the QuikTrip out by Walmart for a soda, and I saw her in line to check out. When I asked whether she was Jennifer Corkern, she whirled around, threw her coffee at me, and ran. Before she could leave the building, the clerk hit the alarm, which locked the doors. I arrested her for second-degree assault on a law enforcement officer."

If that were true, we had her on a class-C felony, which would net her somewhere between three and ten years in prison. I could use that.

"Coffee didn't burn you, did it?"

"No. She hit me in the shoulder and arm. She tried to hurt me, though. That's clear."

"It is," I said, nodding. "Why'd she run?"

He closed his eyes and shook his head. "No clue. I patted her down, but she didn't have anything illegal on her. She may have had something in her car, but I didn't have cause to touch it. Nobody has an open warrant against her, either. I think she saw me and panicked."

We had picked her up for solicitation several times, so she had a record. This assault would be her first violent offense, though, so our prosecutor would look to make her a deal. She'd sit in jail for a while, but she wouldn't go to prison. A cooperative judge might even order her to receive addiction services along the way.

"Thank you for picking her up," I said. "I'd buy you a cup of coffee as a thank you, but I bet you've had enough coffee today."

"Sure have," he said, nodding and smiling. "Good luck with the interview. If you need me, I'll be at my desk."

I thanked him again, and he nodded and left the room. Before leaving, I asked Trisha how her day was going. She had no complaints, which was nice to hear. Our holding cells were in the basement, but I didn't want to interview Jennifer down there, so I escorted her to my office, wheeled Reuben's office chair beside my desk, and had her sit down.

Jennifer was twenty-four, four years younger than me, but her tired eyes made her look older. She sized me up from her chair and then crossed her arms.

"I hear you've been looking for me."

"I hear you've been throwing coffee at my colleagues," I said. "That wasn't a good idea."

She shrugged and looked away from me. "He looked thirsty."

I nodded and reached into my purse for my phone, which I used to record our conversation.

"This is Detective Joe Court," I said, speaking into my phone. "I'm sitting in my office with Ms. Jennifer Corkern. For the record, Ms. Corkern is under arrest for assault on Sergeant Bob Reitz. Are you comfortable, Ms. Corkern? If you'd like, I can get you some water or something to eat."

She looked at me and then to my phone.

"I'm fine."

"Like I said, you're under arrest. You have the right to remain silent, so you don't have to talk to me. If you talk, though, I can use anything you tell me against you in court. If you'd like, you can have an attorney present whenever I question you. If you can't afford a lawyer, the court can provide one to you free of charge. Does that all make sense?"

"I've heard it before."

I nodded and smiled. "Do you understand what it means?"

She nodded. "Yeah."

"Are you willing to talk on the record?"

She shrugged. "What do you want to talk about?"

"Jay Pischke and Reuben Terepocki," I said. "If you answer my questions, I'll talk to the prosecutor about reducing the charges against you. At the moment, you're facing ten years in prison for assault. I'm guessing you'd rather not spend the next ten years in a cage."

She scoffed. "I threw coffee at him. It wasn't even hot."

"It's still assault on a law enforcement officer," I said. "Had the coffee been hotter, you'd be looking at fifteen years."

She shook her head.

"I didn't know he was a cop."

"He was in uniform, Jennifer," I said, lowering my voice. "Arguing about your assault won't get you anywhere. You want to help yourself, you'll answer every question I have. Do you understand?"

She sighed and rolled her eyes. "Fine. What do you want to know?"

"Do you have a baby?"

She furrowed her brow. "No, I don't have a baby. What kind of stupid question is that?"

"You understand Jay Pischke is dead, right?" I asked. She straightened and nodded. When she spoke, her voice was softer than it had been a moment earlier.

"Yeah. You folks killed him."

I nodded. "One of our officers shot him. I'm trying to discover why. You can help me out by answering my questions. At the home in which we found Jay, we found camping supplies, guns, ammunition, and supplies to make meth. We also found diapers, a crib, wipes, formula, and even a few toys. Why would Jay have baby stuff if he didn't have a baby?"

She threw up her hands. "I don't know. Sometimes people give him stuff. He sells it."

"Good. So I don't need to worry about a missing baby," I said. "Do you know Reuben Terepocki?"

She looked away and crossed her arms.

"Maybe I know him, maybe I don't," she said. "What do I get out of talking?"

"We've got you dead to rights on a very serious assault charge," I said, leaning forward. "If you talk, we might get that assault charge knocked down to a lesser offense. If you help me enough, maybe we could even make it disappear."

"You people have arrested me before. Either you give me something in writing spelling out what I get for answering your questions, or I shut up right now."

I leaned back and crossed my arms. "To make a deal, I've got to bring in the prosecutor. He's an important guy, though, and he'll be mad if I waste his time. You've got to give me something I can give to him."

She considered me for a moment. Then she raised her eyebrows and leaned forward.

"I can tell you shit about Jay that not even his mom knows. I can tell you where he grew his weed."

"That's not what I'm interested in at the moment. I need information on Reuben Terepocki. Do you know him or not?"

She leaned back and sighed. "Yeah, I know him. Everybody who works for Vic knows him."

I nodded. "So you work for Vic Conroy?"

She didn't respond for a moment. Then she nodded and looked down.

"I used to dance for him."

"I heard he fired you."

She shrugged but said nothing.

"Why does every girl who works for Vic Conroy know Reuben?"

"'Cause he's a good customer," she said. "Man's got needs, doesn't he?"

I lowered my chin. "Are you implying that Reuben picked up and slept with girls who worked for Vic Conroy?"

She smiled. "You call your boss and get me a deal, and I'll say whatever you want me to say."

I straightened and sighed. "That's not how this works. I need the truth. Did you or anyone you have sexual relations with Reuben Terepocki for money?"

She kept the smile on her face but said nothing.

"How did Jay know Reuben? I heard they got into a fight. Was it over you?"

She ran the fingers of her left hand across her lips as if she were zipping them shut.

"If you don't answer my questions, I'll send you to prison," I said. "You have a lengthy arrest record. I'll push hard to make sure you get the maximum sentence allowed under the law."

She crossed her arms. "You do what you have to do."

I held her gaze for a few moments, but she didn't waver. Strong-arming her wasn't working. I needed a new tactic.

"You lived with Jay, right?"

She hesitated, but then nodded.

"How long did you live together?"

She thought. "About a year, off and on. Why?"

"After a year, you guys were almost married. In my mind, that means some of his stuff is now yours."

She blinked a few times. "What are you getting at?"

"Your boyfriend had a lot of money when he died," I said. "Like ten grand cash. He threw it around like it was nothing, too. He bought people drinks at Tommy B's."

She drew in a breath and nodded. "Jay was generous to those he loved. He wanted to split that money with me, you know. He said it was ours."

I was getting somewhere, so I leaned forward.

"Obviously, you can't have that money in jail. If you co-operated with me, though, and if you apologized to Sergeant Reitz and told him the coffee was an accident, I bet you could walk out of here a rich woman."

She narrowed her eyes. "By apologize, you mean you want me to give him a blow job or something?"

"No," I said, shaking my head. "You tell him you're sorry, and then you answer every one of my questions. I'll see what we can do about losing the paperwork for your arrest."

"And the money?"

I drew in a breath. "I'll make sure your claim is part of the record."

She thought for a moment before nodding. "Deal."

That got the wheels started. I escorted her to Bob's office, where she apologized for spilling coffee on him. He nodded and told her he appreciated the apology. Then I kicked her out of the office and told him what I was doing. Bob agreed to cooperate if it got her talking. Plus, letting her walk saved him about two hours' worth of paperwork and earned him a few favors from me. Everybody won.

After the apology, I marched her back to my office and sat her down.

"Before we can discuss Jay's money, I need to know where it came from," I said. "If he got it for selling drugs or something like that, it's evidence. If he got it for doing a job, we'll release it as part of his estate. You'll get your share then. So you know where he got it?"

"My man worked," she said, raising her eyebrows and lowering her chin. "He worked hard for his money, and he earned every cent he had."

"Great," I said. "Vic Conroy seems like a generous boss, but Jay didn't earn ten grand cash working the door at Club Serenity. Where'd he get it?"

"He was working a job for Tommy Pepper. I don't know what he was doing."

I nodded and narrowed my gaze at her. "And who's Tommy Pepper?"

"Just some guy Jay went to high school with," she said. She paused. "Maybe his last name wasn't Pepper. It was definitely Tommy, though. May have been Tommy Piper or Tommy Pecker. Or something like that. He hired Jay for a job and gave him ten grand."

I blinked a few times and looked down at my desk.

"Could Tommy Pepper have been Thomas Becker?"

"Becker," she said, throwing her head back and lifting her arms. "That's it. Tommy Becker. They went to high school together, but he, like, joined the Army or something. He hasn't been back long."

My heart beat faster. I tried not to let my excitement show, but I leaned forward anyway.

"What kind of job was this?"

She shrugged. "I don't know. Tommy gave Jay a big wad of money, and Jay's been buying shit around town for the past two weeks."

That explained the supplies in the meth lab, but it opened up a whole lot of other questions.

"Let's go back to Reuben Terepocki," I said. "What do you know about him?"

"Not much," she said, her voice low. "I hear the guy's lonely, though. He likes a little tug and a hug sometimes."

I blinked and lowered my chin. "To be clear, you're saying Reuben Terepocki has paid you for sex acts."

"Not me but other girls," she said. "I'm out of that business."

We talked for another half hour, but with every question, her answers got shorter and shorter. She claimed she didn't know what Thomas Becker hired Jay Pischke for, how much he paid him, or who worked with him on the job. When I stopped to take notes, she straightened and narrowed her eyes.

"I'm not getting that money, am I?"

I shook my head. "No, but you get to walk home instead of spending the next decade in prison. That's got to count for something."

"I'm done talking."

"That's fine," I said. I escorted her out of the building and then stopped by Bob Reitz's office again to make sure he was okay with letting her go. He said he was. After that, I went back to my office and plopped down in my chair.

Jennifer had given me both far more than I had hoped for and far less. I didn't know why Reuben killed Jay Pischke, but a common thread ran through both of my cases. That meant Reuben became my prime suspect in both murders.

This could get ugly.

# Chapter 24

When I got the call about Jennifer Corkern, I had just found a receipt in Thomas Becker's house from Midwest Aviation. Corkern hadn't given me many details about anything, but she did—in her own way—let me know something important: Thomas Becker was the key to both of my murders. Becker had access to cash, he employed Jay Pischke, and now both men were dead. I was getting somewhere.

I got the phone number for Midwest Aviation from the receipt and called on my office phone. The extension rang three or four times before a tired-sounding male voice answered.

"Midwest Aviation. What do you need?"

"Hey, I'm Detective Mary Joe Court with the St. Augustine County Sheriff's Department in St. Augustine, Missouri. How you doing today?"

"I've been better. What can I do for you, Detective?"

I leaned back in my chair. "I'm working a homicide, and I found a receipt with your company's name on it in my victim's trash can."

"Okay," he said. "What do you need?"

"Information," I said, tucking a stray hair behind my ear as I leaned forward to look at my evidence. "According to my receipt, a man named Jeff Kellogg rented a helicopter from you. If I'm right, Mr. Kellogg may have been one of the last persons to see my victim alive. I was hoping you could give me Mr. Kellogg's contact information."

The guy went silent for a moment.

"I don't know who you are, but don't call me again."

I squeezed my phone tight and forced my voice to stay calm and controlled.

"I'm a detective with the St. Augustine County Sheriff's Department in St. Augustine, Missouri. I'm asking you for information. If you don't want to give me that information, I'll get a court order. I will then come to your office with about a dozen officers, and we will tear your building apart. We might even confiscate computers. All I need is Mr. Kellogg's phone number. Can you give me that or not?"

Again, he went silent. I held my breath and felt a tickle of anger build in my throat. Then he laughed. I furrowed my brow.

"Something funny, sir?"

"Do you watch the news, Detective?" he asked.

I blinked, unsure what he was getting at. "Sometimes."

"You ought to watch the news more often," he said. "I can't help you. Good luck."

He hung up before I could say anything else. I stared at the receiver, unsure what had just happened.

"Dick."

I slammed the phone down and stood. Midwest Aviation wanted to do this the hard way; I could work with that. Sheriff Delgado wasn't in his office, so I went by the conference room, where I found Trisha typing something. She looked up at me and smiled.

"Hey," I said. "You know where the boss is?"

"If he's not in his office, he may be with Shaun Deveraux."

Deveraux was the prosecutor. He and Delgado met several times a week to go over cases, so it made sense.

"I just had the weirdest conversation," I said. "I'm working a homicide, and my victim is a former helicopter pilot. He had a receipt from an aviation company in his trash can, so I called the company up and asked whether they could give me a potential witness's contact information. The guy who answered the phone told me I should watch the news."

Trisha paused. Then she straightened and covered her mouth.

"He's right. You should watch the news," she said. "Are you sure your victim was a helicopter pilot?"

"Yeah. He was a pilot in the Army."

Trisha closed her eyes.

"Oh, Joe, you just walked into a shit storm."

"What's going on?"

"Three days ago, a group of people abducted a little girl from a hospital in St. Louis right after her mom gave birth to her. There was a big shootout in the hospital's front lobby. Seven people died, including the kid's father. They flew the girl away in a helicopter. The rest of the bad guys slipped away in a stolen ambulance. It looked like an action movie. It's been all over the news."

I covered my mouth as my mind went to work. Pieces of my puzzle fit together for the first time. Pischke was the logistics man for a kidnapping. He might have even been involved in the abduction. Thomas Becker hired him to set up a safe house, so Pischke bought weapons, ammunition, food, water, infant formula, baby wipes, diapers, a crib, and everything else they'd need to keep a newborn healthy and safe. Unfortunately for Pischke—and for Thomas Becker—Reuben showed up at the house before they could put it to use.

My theory fit the little evidence I had collected, but it didn't explain why any of this was happening. I didn't need to answer the *why* questions, though. I had bigger concerns, including a missing newborn.

"Thanks, Trisha," I said. "Looks like I've got work to do."

She wished me luck, and I jogged back down the hall to my office. I knew a fair number of detectives in St. Louis, but I didn't know who they'd assign to a case this big, so I called the main switchboard and asked the operator to forward my call to the liaison officer. He answered on the third ring.

"Hey," I said once somebody picked up the phone. "My name is Mary Joe Court, and I'm a detective with the St. Augustine County Sheriff's Department. I'm working a pair of murders in St. Augustine County. One of my victims was a helicopter pilot, and I've got good reason to think he was involved in an abduction in St. Louis."

The officer went silent.

"What do you want me to do?"

I paused, thinking that was obvious.

"Transfer me to the detective or administrator in charge of that case. I've got information pertinent to his investigation."

"Not going to happen, honey," he said. "You're the third person to call in the past hour about that case. We've got a good team on it. Don't you worry. We'll get these guys."

My lips curled into a tight, annoyed smile.

"I'm working a homicide, and I've found the man who piloted the helicopter used in your abduction case. Please transfer me to the detective in charge of that case so we can share information."

He sighed.

"Fine. Tell me what you've got. I'll call the major case squad myself and relay your contact information. If they find your information pertinent, they will call you. They're a busy team, and that's the best I can do."

"You said the major case squad is working this?"

He hesitated. "They are."

I hung up before he could say anything else. Then I dialed the first number in my address book. My mom picked up before her phone finished ringing once.

"Mom," I said. "It's your favorite daughter. You got a minute?"

"I've always got time for you, Audrey."

I smiled. "Funny, Mom. I'm working a case in St. Augustine that's connected to a case in St. Louis, but I can't get anywhere with the liaison. You know who runs the major case squad?"

"Jesse Leffelman. He's a lieutenant, and he works in the intelligence unit. I don't have his desk number, but I can give you his cell."

"That'd be great," I said. "Thank you."

After a moment, she recited a number. Then she paused. "What kind of case are you working?"

"A murder. I've got a dead guy who rented a helicopter from Midwest Aviation in Cahokia, Illinois. I hear they're looking for somebody like that in St. Louis."

She whistled. "Looks like you've stepped into something. Take care, Joe. That case involves some dangerous people."

I looked down at my desk and smiled.

"I'm always careful, Mom."

"I know you're careful," she said. "And you're a good cop. I'm not telling you this as your mom, though. I'm telling you this as a retired police captain. The people who abducted that little girl have significant training, and they will not hesitate to use it. We've already got seven bodies down. You need to be careful."

"I promise I will," I said.

She wished me luck and said she loved me. She also reminded me to take care of Roy. Then she hung up. After that, I called Lieutenant Leffelman. I had never met him, but I introduced myself and said I got his number from my mother, Captain Julia Green. Even though she was retired, Mom's name still opened doors better than any key I owned. He listened to everything I had to say and then paused.

"Thanks for your call, Detective. Secure Mr. Becker's house. I'll be down there with a team to help search. Meanwhile, talk to your boss. I'll have somebody from my department call so we can set up a formal information-sharing agreement. I appreciate your work on this."

He hung up before I could respond. I grabbed my purse and cell phone and headed out the door. Lieutenant Leffelman had about as much authority to order me around as my dog did, but I wanted to be at Becker's house when he arrived anyway. Traffic was a little heavier than it had been earlier, but it only took me a few minutes to get there.

Officers Emily Hayes and Gary Faulk stepped out of the house when they saw my cruiser park in front. I nodded to them both.

"Hey, Joe," said Emily. "Your victim sure liked his guns, didn't he?"

"He's got an FFL license, so he was probably a dealer," I said. "You find anything interesting?"

"One hundred and thirty-four rifles, thirty-nine pistols, nine shotguns, and thousands of rounds of ammunition," said Gary. "There are also three safes in the basement we couldn't get into."

I whistled, glad we had gotten there before anybody broke in. If someone had stolen anything, Becker's insurance company would have repaid his heirs, but that wouldn't have taken those guns off the street. In the wrong hands, a tactical rifle could hurt a lot of people. I hoped Becker's family would sell the weapons to people who loved spending time at the rifle range instead of people with bad intentions.

"We've got a change of plans," I said. "Turns out this case is a lot bigger than I expected. Keep cataloging the guns, but don't take any back to our station. Some bad guys might have used them in a major felony in St. Louis. We've got St. Louis County detectives on their way. They'll take some of these and test them."

Emily drew in a slow breath and then nodded, her eyes distant.

"What do you want us to do with the guns we already transported back to the station?"

"We'll make them available to the detectives from St. Louis. If they want them, they can pick them up themselves."

210

"You're the boss," said Emily. She and Gary both returned to the house a moment later. I called Sheriff Delgado's cell phone.

"George, it's Joe Court," I said. "I'm at a house west of our station, and I need some help. I've got a witness who told me Jay Pischke worked for Thomas Becker. I've also got evidence tying Thomas Becker to an abduction and multiple homicides in St. Louis. St. Louis County is sending detectives now. This case is turning complex."

Delgado swore and asked for the address, which I gave him.

"I'm on my way," he said. He sighed. "You found anything tying Reuben to Becker's murder?"

The question made a sour taste appear in the back of my mouth.

"Not yet, but we know Reuben shot Pischke, and we know Pischke worked for Becker. We also know Becker was up to his eyeballs in shit. I can't prove anything yet, but it's a live possibility. Reuben could have killed them both."

Delgado swore again. "I hope you're wrong."

"Me, too. I'll see you soon."

# Chapter 25

Delgado arrived at Becker's house a few minutes after my call. When he saw all the guns, he swore under his breath and looked at me.

"I'm glad you got here before the scavengers," he said. "Did he even have an alarm system?"

"No," I said, shaking my head. "In addition to the guns on display, he has multiple gun safes in the basement. We can't open them."

Delgado swore again. "All right. I'll handle this. The detectives from St. Louis will have questions for you, so keep your phone on. Go work your case. Becker's connected to something big in St. Louis, but he's still a murder victim here. Find out who killed him. We'll figure everything else out as we go."

I nodded. "Thanks, boss."

He grunted, and I walked to my cruiser and sat down to think. Thomas Becker likely died because of his involvement in the abduction in St. Louis. Whether his partners killed him or whether Reuben killed him, I couldn't yet say, but the St. Louis detectives would figure it out. That left me with Jay Pischke.

I used the laptop in my cruiser to remind myself of his arrest record. Then I looked up the arrest record of his girlfriend, Jennifer Corkern. I spent about twenty minutes diving through my department's files and found the names of seven people Jennifer and Jay both associated with. That was a start.

I started my car and drove to the first address, an apartment building about eight blocks from Thomas Becker's house. A young woman answered the door. A tie held her straight, brunette hair in a loose bun behind her head, while her tanned skin seemed to glow in the late afternoon sunshine. Her name was Leah Trentino, and we had arrested her once for solicitation. A lawyer Vic Conroy kept on retainer bailed her out.

"Yeah?" she asked, blinking. She wore a white shirt and flannel pajama pants imprinted with clouds. It was late in the day, but she had probably worked the entire night previous.

"Sorry if I woke you up," I said, reaching to my belt so I could show her my badge. "I'm Detective Joe Court with the St. Augustine County Sheriff's Department. Can I talk to you for a few minutes?"

She blinked again and then focused on me. When she spoke, I caught the sunlight glinting off a diamond stud in her nose.

"Sure, I guess," she said, taking a step back and motioning for me to go inside. I stepped into a small but comfortable living room. A pair of oversized and fluffy brown sofas faced a television, while a pass-through window in the far wall opened into the kitchen. There were candles on almost every flat surface.

She plopped down onto one couch. I sat on the edge a few feet from her and took a notepad from my purse.

"I hear you were friends with Jennifer Corkern and Jay Pischke."

Her lips parted into a tight smile.

"Yeah, I love Jenn," she said. "And everybody loved Stink. He was one of the good ones. Hearing he died broke my heart."

"I'm sorry for your loss," I said, lowering my voice. "As you've probably heard, a police officer shot Mr. Pischke. I'm investigating the circumstances of that shooting. Have you heard the name Reuben Terepocki before?"

Her back went straight, and her face lightened at least two shades. She crossed her arms and tucked her hands in her armpits like she was giving herself a hug.

"No."

I blinked a few times and leaned forward.

"Nothing you tell me will make it back to him," I said. "You can trust me. I'm just trying to figure out what happened."

She shrugged but wouldn't look at me.

"I don't know Reuben," she said.

"Are you sure about that?"

Her lips moved, but no sound came out for a moment. Then she cleared her throat.

"If you have more questions, talk to my lawyer."

I lowered my chin.

"If you're scared, I can keep you safe. That's my job. You need to talk to me, though. Has someone threatened you?"

She licked her lips and then shook her head.

"Can you please leave, Detective?"

I said nothing for almost a minute. When she looked at me, I reached into my purse for a business card.

"Call me if you change your mind about Detective Terepocki," I said. "Or if you just want to talk. You can also have your lawyer call me. We can do this formally if you'd prefer."

She didn't reach for my card, so I put it on the arm of the sofa and stood up. The moment I left the apartment, she shut the door and engaged three separate deadbolts. Outside, the sun was growing low in the sky, sending long shadows across the street. I didn't know what Reuben had done to that young woman, but clearly he had done something. The moment I mentioned his name, she almost trembled. She didn't deserve that.

I got in my car and drove to the second address, a house out in the county. The homeowner had a white paneled van with the name of a local painting contractor in the driveway. We had arrested him twice in the past two years. Once, we had charged him with driving while intoxicated. His second arrest had been for trespassing, but the prosecutor dropped all charges against him.

I knocked on the door and introduced myself. He told me he wasn't interested in talking and shut the door in my face. That could have gone better.

The next three addresses went about the same, but as I drove to my sixth address, my phone rang. Had the caller been almost anyone else, I would have sent it to voicemail. As it was, I pulled onto the side of the road and answered.

"Reuben," I said. "Didn't expect to hear from you. Is your attorney with you?"

"It's just me, Joe," he said. "I hear you're visiting some of our county's upstanding citizens and asking about me."

"Yeah," I said. "It's funny how they all know you."

"If they didn't, I'd be a shitty cop."

"I'll reserve judgment on that," I said. "What do you want?"

"A little conversation," he said. "Where are you?"

"If you want to talk, you can meet me at our station."

"Not the station," he said. "It's got to be somewhere neutral."

Reuben had at least fifty pounds on me. If he wanted to hurt me, it'd be hard to stop him. He wouldn't try anything in public, though.

"Meet me by Rise and Grind," I said. "They'll be closed, but they have tables on the sidewalk. We can talk there."

"Good. I'll see you there."

I told him I was on my way. He wouldn't admit he had murdered Pischke, but every conversation we had was an opportunity for him to incriminate himself accidentally. As long as I gave him a rope and the opportunity, he'd hang himself eventually.

The sun was setting by the time I reached Rise and Grind. Reuben sat at a black, wrought-iron table on the sidewalk. He nodded a greeting as I parked.

"I'm here," I said, pulling out a chair opposite him. Before sitting, I took out my cell phone, turned on an app to record our conversation, and set it on the table between us. "I'm recording our conversation. You know the drill. If you agree to talk, I'll use what you tell me against you in court. You've got an attorney, so you're good there. You know your rights. What do you want?"

He considered. "You kind of half-assed that Miranda warning. If I admit something, do you think it'll stand up in court?"

"You're not under arrest. You called for a meeting, you drove out here, and you can leave whenever you want. This is a noncustodial interview. I don't need to give a Miranda warning. What do you want?"

"I want to find out what you think you're doing," he said, crossing his arms. "Going around town like you are, you're scaring people."

"I'm not the person they're afraid of," I said, lowering my arms so that my hand rested on the grip of my firearm. "Who called you?"

"A little birdie," he said. "You don't need to know."

"You can tell your little birdie I was just doing my job," I said. "As for you, I don't know what you're doing. If you're trying to intimidate me, though, stop. I don't respond well to intimidation attempts. It makes me think you're hiding something. Are you hiding something, Mr. Terepocki?"

"Detective Terepocki," he said. "The title matters."

"You should get used to being called mister," I said. "While I've got you, maybe you can answer a few things. Do you know Thomas Becker? Jay Pischke worked for him."

He shook his head. "Nope."

"Becker's dead," I said. "Somebody cut off his fingers and set him on fire. Hell of a way to go. Where were you two nights ago?"

"Am I a suspect in every murder in St. Augustine County now?" he asked, almost grinning.

"Only those I can connect to Mr. Pischke," I said. "You killed Pischke. Maybe you killed his business partner, too."

"I didn't kill Becker. Two nights ago, I was at home."

"Anybody with you?" I asked. "I hear you like prostitutes. Maybe you had one around."

His lip flattened, and his eyes went black and mean. I wrapped my fingers around my pistol's grip.

"Who told you that?"

"A little birdie whispered it into my ear," I said.

His upper lip twitched. He reminded me of a dog getting ready to growl.

"You don't know what the hell you're talking about."

"Then enlighten me," I said. "Clear this up right now. How did you know Jay Pischke, and why did you beat him up? The more I dig into this case, the uglier it gets. I want to believe you're innocent, and I'm willing to give you the benefit of my doubt, but you're not making this easy."

He crossed his arms and leaned back. "It sounds like you've already got your mind made up. You think I'm the bad guy in this."

"You shot a guy," I said.

"I killed a guy who first pulled a piece and fired at me," he said. "You seem to have forgotten that. Let me give you a warning, though: your colleagues know what happened. I protected myself, and you're jamming me up for it and treating me like I'm a criminal. People remember that kind of stuff."

"Thanks for the advice," I said. He grunted and walked toward his car. I watched him drive off and felt a rock grow in my stomach. Muscles all over my body tingled. I wanted to run, but I forced my back to stay straight until his car disappeared. Then, I closed my eyes and clenched my hands into fists.

I didn't know where this case was headed or what would happen to this town or my department. All I knew for certain was that nobody would win. This one would hurt.

# Chapter 26

Once Terepocki left, I drove to the final address on my list and found a well-maintained brick ranch-style home with a big front yard and a concrete walkway. A magnolia tree out front swayed in the evening breeze and cast a shadow across the home and lawn. Bright yellow mums in terra-cotta pots brightened the front porch, giving it a cheery feel. When I knocked on the front door, a woman a few years younger than me answered. She had blonde hair with brunette roots and enormous hoop-shaped earrings. Her yoga pants and tank top made her look trim and fit.

"Renee Swift?" I asked.

She crossed her arms and looked me up and down.

"Yeah?"

I pushed my jacket back to show her the badge on my belt.

"I'm Detective Mary Joe Court with the St. Augustine County Sheriff's Department. Can I talk to you for a few minutes?"

She considered before answering. "You can talk. I don't have to answer."

"Fair enough," I said. "I'm here to talk about Jennifer Corkern and Jay Pischke. Jay's dead. I'm trying to figure out what happened. I'm hoping you can answer a few questions. Do you know Reuben Terepocki?"

Her upper lip curled, and she looked away.

"By your reaction, I'd say you're familiar with him."

She drew in a slow breath before looking at me again. "You could say that. He's a pig. I wish he'd gotten shot instead of Jay."

I straightened and reached into my purse for a notepad.

"Okay. How do you know him?"

"I work at Club Serenity with Jenn and Stink." She paused. "Or at least I used to work with Jenn and Stink there. Jenn got fired, and Stink's dead."

"Okay," I said, nodding. "Have you seen Reuben at the club?"

She shook her head. "He's never been there when I danced. Instead, he hangs out in the parking lot of the Wayfair Motel. Sometimes girls go over there and sleep between shifts."

She and I both knew the dancers went to entertain clients they had picked up in the club, but I nodded anyway.

"Okay," I said. "I'm with you."

She tossed her hair over her shoulder and shook her head.

"Terepocki sits in the parking lot and waits for girls to come. Then he searches them and makes them sit in his car.

He'll pretend that he's arresting them for solicitation, but they weren't doing anything wrong."

I blinked. "Why would he do that?"

"Because he's looking for gullible girls," she said. "Vic protects us from creeps, but he can't stop everything. Sometimes, when a girl gets put in handcuffs, she panics. That's what Reuben's looking for. He tells them he'll let them go for a favor. I hear he usually just wants a blowjob, but sometimes he wants sex. If a girl says no, he tells her he'll arrest her for solicitation and for offering him drugs. He says he'll send them to prison."

I lowered my chin. "To clarify, they don't have drugs on them?"

"No. If you're shooting up or snorting something you shouldn't be, Vic fires you," she said. "That's one of his rules. These girls are just dancers. They go to the motel to sleep. Some of these girls are up all day with their kids, so they're tired between shifts. They need to sleep."

"Has he ever coerced you into having sex?"

"No," she said. "I don't leave the club between shifts. You make more money if you stick around and flirt with the customers. It makes them more interested in a private show."

"And nothing sexual happens in those private shows, right?" I asked, smiling. She laughed.

"You book a private show, you'll get your money's worth, but you won't get laid. You should come by. I'll show you a good time. You can bring your boyfriend if you've got one. Or your girlfriend."

I looked down to my notepad. "I appreciate the offer. How many dancers would you say Reuben's gone after?"

She shrugged. "Three or four I know about, but he and Vic worked out a deal. Now, Reuben gets free lap dances when he goes into the club, but nobody has to sleep with him."

I wrote a few notes to give myself a moment to think.

"You know Vic Conroy better than I do," I said. "Do you think he'd extend that protection to girls who didn't work for him?"

She narrowed her eyes. "What do you mean?"

"Jennifer Corkern used to dance for him," I said. "I suspect she still spends time at the Wayfair Motel. Would Vic protect her if Reuben approached her like he did the dancers?"

She blinked and then looked down. "I don't know what Vic would do, but Jay loved her. If he found out someone had hurt her, he'd go ballistic."

And now I had a potential motive. If Jay found out Reuben had coerced his girlfriend into sleeping with him, he might have attacked him. Vic Conroy and the other bouncers could break up a fight at the club, but they wouldn't be able to stop the feud outside the club's walls. If that were the case, Reuben could have shot Jay to prevent their fight from escalating.

224

The theory was ugly, but it fit the evidence. Now I had to prove it.

"Would the girls Reuben coerced into performing sex acts talk to me?"

She shrugged. "Sure. It won't be free, though."

"Would they talk for a favor?" I asked. "Sometimes it's helpful to know a cop."

She shook her head. "Every girl there knows at least one cop. You want a girl to talk, you've got to make it worth her while. Book a girl for a private dance. You can talk about anything you want in the back room."

I smiled despite the situation. "I'm not sure how lap dances would look on an expense report."

"You want information, you've got to pay for it," she said.

I sighed. She might have been right, but Delgado would explode if I went through with it. Then again, Conroy had said if I bought enough lap dances on a Sunday morning, I'd get brunch for free. Maybe I could list the expense as food. I'd figure it out. I thanked her for her time and then walked back to my cruiser. Before I could get very far, my phone buzzed with an incoming text message from Ian, my brother.

*Mom says you don't want to talk to me again.*

I sighed and texted him back.

*You don't need me.*

Even as I hit the button to send the message, I knew it was a mistake. My phone rang right away. I groaned and sat behind the wheel before answering.

"Hey," I said.

"Why do you hate me?"

I leaned my head back. "That's a little melodramatic, don't you think?"

"Why don't you want to talk to me, then?" he asked. "You're my sister. We're family."

"We've got the same biological mother," I said. "Technically, I'm your sister, but there's a lot more to being a family than sharing genes."

"Okay, fine," he said. "Why don't you want to be my sister?"

I leaned my head forward so that my chin hit my chest. Then I sighed.

"It has nothing to do with you," I said. "If you got to know me, you'd realize you don't want me in your life. I'm a mess. And I'm busy all the time. I don't even have time to call my mom."

"But you're still my sister," he said.

"Biologically, yeah," I said, nodding. "Why do you even want a sister? Your mom and dad love you, you've got a great house, you've got a girlfriend, you've got college to look forward to...you've got everything you need. If you add me to the mix, I'm just going to complicate a good thing."

"But you're my sister."

I rolled my eyes.

"Yeah. I'm your sister. We've established that."

"That's why I want you in my life," he said. "You're my family."

I thought of Audrey and Dylan and my mom and dad—my adoptive family. When I first met them, I didn't know what to think about them. Dylan and Audrey were in elementary school, so they were easy to like. It took time for me to build a relationship with my mom and dad, but now that I had them in my life, I didn't want to live without them. I loved them.

"Family takes time," I said. "We don't even know each other."

Ian went quiet. When he spoke again, his voice was soft.

"That's an excuse. I think you're scared. That's why you don't want me in your life."

"Don't go there, Ian."

"No, that's exactly where I'm going. That's it, isn't it? You're so scared of being hurt that you can't care about anybody but yourself."

I swallowed hard but kept my temper under control.

"Stop, Ian. You don't even know me. This is inappropriate."

He snorted.

"I can't believe that's it. You're scared. That's pathetic. No wonder you live alone."

I squeezed my free hand into a fist. Then I held my breath so I wouldn't call him an asshole.

"Are you going to say anything?" he asked, his voice smug.

I blinked and forced myself to draw in a slow breath.

"What do you dream of doing with your life, Ian?"

He paused.

"What do you mean?"

"If you could do anything, what would you do?" I asked. "Would you become a teacher? Would you write poems? Would you play baseball? What do you want to do with your life?"

He considered. "I want to work in artificial intelligence. Why?"

I forced a measure of calm into my voice I didn't truly feel.

"When I was fifteen—your age—I wanted to get in a car and drive and never stop. I thought if I got far enough away from my life, I could start over. I'd forget what it felt like to sleep in the back of an SUV beside a woman who didn't care if I froze, that I'd forget what it felt like to beg for food from restaurants at closing so I could eat, that'd I'd forget my foster father had drugged and raped me on his sofa.

"You know what I've learned since then? You can't run from your past. It's stupid to even try. The best I can hope for is to forget everything. That's why I don't want you in my life. It has nothing to do with you, and it has nothing to do with being afraid. I just don't want to hear about Erin Court anymore. She poisoned everything she touched. You love her because you didn't know her. Trust me. If she had lived, you'd hate her as much as I do."

He paused for almost thirty seconds.

"Mom never hurt anybody. Why do you keep lying about her?"

"I'm not lying," I said. "You're a nice kid, but don't call me again. And stop looking into Erin Court. It's for your own good."

He started to say something, but I hung up. Within seconds, my phone beeped with an incoming text message.

*BITCH.*

I turned the phone off and tossed it to the seat beside me. My stomach felt as if it were full of rocks, and my throat felt tight. I hadn't wanted to hurt him, but he needed to understand why I couldn't be his sister. This was for the best, even if it made my stomach turn.

I stayed on the side of the road for almost ten minutes, replaying the conversation in my head. Maybe I could have handled parts of it more diplomatically, but I wouldn't have changed what I said. He had needed to hear every word. After a few minutes, my radio sputtered as a uniformed officer requested assistance searching a vehicle for drugs. The noise broke me from my maudlin thoughts. I looked over my shoulder to make sure the road was clear and then merged onto the street. I had a murderer to catch.

# Chapter 27

Tara didn't have a thermometer, but she didn't need one to know Scarlett had a fever. The cabin's incandescent lighting cast everything in a pale yellow shade, so she couldn't tell what the little girl's skin looked like. Her breath, though, was labored, and she felt warm. Joshua had needed to nurse at least every two hours in his first week, but she had to wake Scarlett up every three hours, and even then, the little girl ate very little. This was a problem.

She, Shane, and Andy sat in the living room of a mobile home beside the Weavers' old cabin. Despite being told that the baby had a fever, a sign of a potential systemic infection, Shane and Andy seemed unconcerned. They suggested Tara give her some Tylenol. That might have been a good idea if she were four or five, but Scarlett was a newborn. Her immune system wouldn't mature for another two to three months.

"She's sick," said Tara. "She needs help."

Shane rolled his eyes but didn't look at her. Andy reached for the remote and lowered the volume on the TV, allowing her to hear the dull roar of the generator outside.

"I'm tired of hearing you talk," he said. "You're here to take care of Scarlett. She's only got to live another couple of days until her granddaddy gives us our money. Then she's his problem. No more complaints. That clear?"

Tara nodded and stood. "Yeah. It's clear. I'll take her to the cabin and feed her there."

That got Shane's attention. He leaned forward.

"No, you are not," he said. "You want to feed her, you can feed her here where we can see you. Besides, she doesn't look hungry."

"That's the problem," said Tara. "She should be. It's been four hours since she last ate. She should be screaming, but she's asleep."

Andy waved her off. "Let her sleep, then. If she's sick, she needs the rest."

"It doesn't work like that with newborns," said Tara, her voice sharp. "Her immune system isn't mature yet. She can't fight off an infection on her own. She needs to see a doctor."

Shane looked at the television again. "That ain't our problem."

"You won't get your money if she's dead," said Tara. "That's what we're talking about here. Without antibiotics, she could go septic. If that happens, her organs could fail. Then she'd die. Do you want to murder a newborn?"

Andy looked at his brother. "Maybe Tara could take her to that free clinic in St. Louis. We'll tell them it's Tara's baby. Once they give her the drugs, we can run."

Tara shook her head. "We can't just take her and run. She needs fluids and IV antibiotics. We can't give them to her here. This is over. Thomas is dead. We need to think about exit strategies before somebody else dies."

Andy opened his mouth, but Shane spoke before his brother could say anything.

"This little girl's our meal ticket," he said. "She dies, I'll put a bullet in your head. Since you like her so much, we'll bury you beside her."

Tara's heart beat faster.

"Unless you let me take her to the hospital, you might as well shoot me now."

Andy looked at her with cold, black eyes.

"The more you talk, the more likely that'll happen. We're already negotiating with her grandpa. We've got him so scared, he'll give us everything he owns. That means you need to keep her alive. Figure out how."

Tara nodded. "Then I'm going to the cabin. I'll try breast-feeding her. My milk will have antibodies in it that might help her."

"The less we hear about your breast milk, the better," said Andy, waving her off. She looked at Shane. He rolled his eyes once more before standing.

"I'll walk you over. Wouldn't want you to get lost in the dark."

She had been walking around these hills since she was fifteen years old. Shane and Andy knew the local landscape better than her, but navigating wouldn't be a problem for her. She hugged the baby to her chest and stepped into the night. The evening had cooled to the low fifties. A breeze blew through the deep woods around them, sending a chill down her spine.

"Walk," said Shane. "You know where the cabin is."

So she walked. Her feet dug into the thick gravel walkway. Scarlett stirred in her arms, and then her eyes fluttered open. She probably felt cold.

"It's okay, sweetheart," Tara whispered. "I've got you."

"Less talking, more walking," said Shane. Tara looked over her shoulder and gave him a disgusted look.

"Shut up, idiot," she said.

"Your husband let you talk to him like that?" asked Shane. "I guarantee you Thomas wouldn't."

"Thomas and I were kids when we got married," she said. "I grew up since then. Why didn't you?"

He mimicked her voice and repeated what she had just said. She clenched her jaw. In the dark, Tara couldn't tell the Weavers' cabin from their barn, so she let Shane walk in front. When they reached the cabin, Tara turned to him.

"Before all this is through, I hope Scarlett's father kills you."

"Not going to happen," said Shane, fishing his keys out of his pocket. He unlocked the cabin's front door. "Your ex-husband's buddies shot him in the back while he was pushing his wife in a wheelchair. I saw it from the helicopter. It was cold-blooded."

"Then I hope her grandfather kills you," she said, carrying the baby past him and into the cabin. A thick timber wall separated the interior into a public space and a bedroom in the back. The cast-iron wood-burning stove was cold, and the room was dark. Nobody spent much time here at night anymore, so the Weavers hadn't connected it to the generator.

"How long will this take?"

"It depends on Scarlett," said Tara.

Shane considered before nodding. "I'll come back in two hours. There's wood by the stove and matches on the mantel. You should be able to find paper somewhere. If you get cold, light a fire. If you burn down Papaw's cabin, though, I'll burn down your house with your husband inside. *Capiche*?"

She narrowed her eyes. "I get it. And nobody says *capiche* anymore. It makes you sound like a moron."

His eyes traveled down her body before focusing on her face again. "If you weren't pretty in high school, Thomas wouldn't have even talked to you. You know that?"

"Yeah, I know," she said, nodding. "That's why I divorced him. He was an asshole."

He shook his head but said nothing as he left the building. The moment he shut the front door, the deadbolt hit home with a thud. Where most deadbolts had a knob on the inside that allowed a homeowner to lock and unlock it, this one needed a key. That was okay with her. Thomas had shown her the cabin's second exit in high school.

Before leaving, she went to the back bedroom and pulled her cell phone from her pocket. It gave her enough light to see what she was doing. She sat on the bed, lifted her shirt, and woke up Scarlett. The baby whimpered and cried, so Tara tickled her feet until her eyes opened wide. Then she held her to her breast.

It felt wrong, but if nursing kept this little girl alive a little longer, she'd put up with some awkwardness. Scarlett ate little, but at least she ate something. Afterwards, Tara covered herself and held the baby against her chest.

"I'll get you out of here. I promise," she whispered. "Don't you worry."

She had been fifteen the first time she and Thomas had visited that cabin. Shane and Andy were months younger than her, but they had been two years behind her in school. While Shane and Andy went off to shoot a .22 at old liquor bottles, she and Thomas had hooked up in the cabin's bedroom. Afterwards, he showed her the trap door beneath the bed. It led to a basement in which Shane's grandfather had stored his moonshine and the cabin's secondary exit.

She pushed the bed and threadbare rug aside to reveal the cutout in the floor. Within moments, she walked down the narrow steps, clutching Scarlett in one hand and her phone in the other. The tunnel was narrower than she remembered, but that was okay. She crawled on her hands and knees down a stone-lined tunnel for about a hundred yards before coming across a wooden door.

She pushed it open and crawled onto the side of a grass-covered hill. Scarlett whimpered, but she didn't cry. Tara held her breath and looked back toward the mobile home in which Shane and Andy were watching TV. The lights were on, and the diesel generator hummed, but she couldn't see anybody. She rubbed Scarlett's back and tried to control her breath.

"Okay, baby, here we go," she whispered. Instead of sprinting, she crouched low and jogged forward, hoping she'd look like a deer or other wild animal darting through the woods. She had thought about running toward the road, but there was no guarantee her phone would work there, and as far in the country as they were, passersby were rare. Instead, she ran toward the biggest hill on the property, the one she had called Dr. Peltier from yesterday.

A well-packed trail wound from the Weavers' compound and around the hill to the top, but she didn't dare take that and risk being seen. Instead, she climbed straight up. The moon illuminated small trees and plants she could use as hand holds, but it did little to help her avoid the loose dirt. Twice, she almost slipped down, but she held on to Scarlett anyway. The little girl whimpered and cried some, but probably more from cold than anything else. Every few feet, Tara would adjust and rub the girl's back.

After about fifteen minutes of climbing, she looked back toward the compound. Somebody was out with a flashlight. They must have known she had left. There was no going back now. She had to go forward.

"Come on, Tara," she said between ragged gasps. "You can do this."

She pushed herself ever higher and didn't stop even when her arms ached with strain, and her back screamed at her for a break. By the time she reached the top of the hill, she could barely lift her right arm to rub Scarlett's back. Dirt covered her face, hands, elbows, and knees. She fell to the ground and pulled her phone out but didn't turn it on yet. The moment she hit that power button, the phone would light up like a beacon. She needed to be ready.

So she sat there for a few moments, gathering her breath. The flashlight at the base of the hill had disappeared. Shane and Andy wouldn't stop looking for her until they found her, but they probably thought she had made a run for the road. For the moment, the threat was gone. She closed her eyes and patted the little girl's back before nodding.

"Okay, here we go," she said, opening her eyes once more and powering on her phone. She had one steady bar. "We'll make it."

Before, Tara had been too worried about what Shane and Andy would do to her family if she called the police. Now, her worry had shifted to Scarlett. Everyone in her family had firearms, and the police would protect them as well as they could. Her family at least had a chance. Without help, Scarlett didn't. Tara dialed 911 and held her breath.

"St. Augustine Sheriff's Department. What's your emergency?"

She could have cried with relief.

"I need help. I'm out on—"

Before she could finish speaking, she felt the barrel of a pistol pressed to the back of her head. Her breath caught in her throat as someone leaned over her and whispered into her ear.

"Thought you'd come here. Give me your phone. You say one more word, I'll blow the back of your head off."

Tara closed her eyes as tears streamed down her cheeks.

"Please don't do this, Shane," she whispered. "Let us go. Please."

"You there, miss?" asked the dispatcher. Shane wrenched the phone from her hand and turned it off. Then he threw it like a frisbee down the hill.

"I trusted you," he said. "That ends now."

"Scarlett will die if we don't do something," she said. "You won't get your money."

"If I don't get my money, you don't get to live," he said. "Now follow the trail and try to enjoy your walk. You ain't going outside again for a while."

# Chapter 28

I got to work the next morning at ten to eight. Over the years, my department had experimented with dozens of schedules for our uniformed patrol officers, all of which someone had designed to minimize overtime. When Delgado had become sheriff, he mixed things up again. We now had six overlapping, eight-hour shifts a day. It seemed complicated, but it ensured that we had officers on the street at all times, and it minimized the commotion during shift changes. It was one of Delgado's better ideas, and I happened to walk in when one of those shifts was just coming out.

Few people smiled as I held the door. Officer Dave Skelton came last. Skelton had been born and raised in St. Augustine and knew the county better than almost anybody. He wore a clean blue sweater and jeans, but dirt streaked his neck, and bits of broken leaves clung to his hair. He nodded when he saw me.

"Morning, Joe," he said.

"Hey, Dave," I said. "I thought you were working the day shift."

Skelton grunted. "Sheriff called me in early this morning. We got a 911 call from a woman who said she needed help. Before she could say where she was, she hung up. Jason tracked the phone out to a spot by Cotter's Creek, but we never found her or her phone. I think it was a prank."

I didn't know where Cotter's Creek was, but if going there meant Skelton came back with dirt on his neck and leaves in his hair, it wasn't accessible by car.

"At least you got overtime."

He grunted again. "Yeah. At least I've got that. Have a good one."

"You, too," I said. As Skelton walked toward the parking lot, I took the stairs to the second floor, where I got a cup of coffee and checked my email. Sheriff Delgado must have read some of the reports I had written because he'd sent me an email at seven this morning asking me to stop by his office as soon as I got in to talk about a few things.

I grabbed my coffee and walked. Delgado's door was open, but I knocked anyway and waited for him to call me in. The sheriff sat at the conference table with his back to the window, while the St. Augustine County prosecutor, Shaun Deveraux, sat across from him with his back to the door.

"Morning, gentlemen," I said.

"Glad you're here, Joe," said Delgado, waving me over to the table and gesturing to the chair beside Deveraux. "Have a seat. I want to talk about your investigation into Reuben so we can figure out our next moves. Start by filling in Mr. Deveraux on your findings."

I nodded, pulled out the chair, and started talking. Deveraux took notes, while Delgado crossed his arms and listened. The prosecutor seemed especially interested in the discrepancies between the physical evidence found at the crime scene and Terepocki's story about the shooting. When I finished, Deveraux wrote notes for a few moments and then looked up at me.

"This is disturbing," he said. Then he paused and sighed. "The law gives police officers wide latitude to use their professional judgment in deadly force situations, so if I prosecute Terepocki for murder with what you've got, I'll lose."

I crossed my arms and nodded. It was disappointing but expected.

"What about the sex crimes? I've talked to a lot of young women who work at Club Serenity. Most of them don't admit to knowing Reuben, but I think they're lying. Last night, I visited a woman named Renee Swift. She said Reuben hangs out in the parking lot of the Wayfair Motel and coerces dancers from Club Serenity into committing sex acts."

Deveraux drew in a breath and narrowed his eyes at me.

"Do you have corroborating evidence or other witnesses?"

"Not yet."

He nodded and looked to his notes. "Do you think we can honey trap him?"

I cocked my head to the side. "You mean, you want to use another young woman as bait and record him propositioning her?"

Deveraux nodded. "If you can do that, I'll arrest him."

I shook my head.

"We'd need Vic Conroy's cooperation to get a girl, and I doubt he'd give it. He'd be too worried about implicating himself in prostitution."

"That's a problem," said Deveraux. He went silent and then turned to his notes. "Tell me about Thomas Becker, then. We know Terepocki shot Pischke, and we know Pischke worked for Becker. Do we have any direct connection between Becker and Detective Terepocki?"

"No," I said.

Deveraux looked to Delgado.

"Do we know where Detective Terepocki was at the time of Thomas Becker's murder?"

"He says he was home," said Delgado. "He lives alone, though, so we have no way to verify that."

Deveraux sighed.

"We can't charge him in Jay Pischke's shooting with what we've got. Detective Terepocki's lawyer will argue that his recollection was faulty in his initial interview. He'll give us a revised statement, and that'll be that.

"To charge him with murder or manslaughter, I need evidence or a witness who says Detective Terepocki drove to that house intending to commit a crime. Without that prior intent, he'll argue that he went to the house on police business. His badge gives him a lot of protection."

I forced a smile to my lips so I wouldn't scowl.

"What about the sex stuff?" I asked.

"You've got innuendo, but you don't have evidence," he said. "Find something."

I clenched my jaw as warmth spread from my chest to my face and back. Deveraux may not have said it aloud, but he might as well have told me I had just wasted several days. He was just doing his job, but I couldn't help but feel annoyed at him anyway. I balled my hands into fists and then forced my annoyance down as I looked to my boss.

"Where are we on Thomas Becker's death?"

"It's moving along," said Delgado. "He was definitely involved with the abduction in St. Louis. It took resources to pull off a job like that, and the police in St. Louis are following the money. They'll figure out their case. You focus on Reuben. Put this asshole in prison."

That was easier said than done. My investigation into Jay Pischke's shooting wasn't a lost cause yet, but it was close. Unless Reuben told somebody he wanted to kill Pischke, he'd skate on that charge. I still might be able to get him for sex crimes, though.

I went back to my desk and searched Club Serenity's website to get a list of its dancers and their schedules. The website only gave me stage names and headshots, but we had arrested about half the dancers at the club for solicitation. I compared the headshots on the website with mug shots in our database, and I put together a list of ten dancers with records for prostitution.

Over the next three hours, I drove all over the county and interviewed six different people. Several of the dancers denied that they worked at Club Serenity and then shut their doors in my face when I asked about Reuben, while others simply told me they weren't interested in answering questions. The final dancer I questioned acknowledged that she worked at the club but denied ever stepping foot inside the Wayfair Motel. It was a complete waste of a morning.

When I got back to my station, I sat down at my desk to write a report of my morning activities when I noticed a sticky note on my phone asking me to call Darlene with our crime lab. My mouth held a sour taste, and the muscles of my jaw felt tense from clenching my teeth, but I picked up the phone anyway and dialed. Darlene answered on the third ring.

"Hey, it's Joe Court," I said. "I got your message, so I'm calling you back. What's up?"

"Hey," she said. "Sorry to interrupt your day, but I thought you'd want to hear this. I've got Jay Pischke's cell phone in an evidence bag. It's been ringing all morning."

I furrowed my brow. "The battery's still working?"

"Nobody's used it for a while. I guess it's been on standby."

I pulled a notepad from my desk. "Who's calling?"

Darlene said nothing, but a plastic bag crinkled from her end.

"You got a pen?" she asked. I said I did, so she read off a ten-digit phone number, which I wrote down.

"I got it," I said. "Thanks, Darlene."

"Good luck, Joe," she said. "If you need anything, let me know."

I thanked her and then hung up before calling this new number. It wasn't local, and I hadn't recognized the area code. The phone rang twice before someone answered. A dull roar filled the line.

"Yeah?"

It was a man's voice, but I had a hard time hearing him over the noise.

"Hey," I said. "This is Detective Joe Court with the St. Augustine County Sheriff's Department in St. Augustine, Missouri. I hear you've been trying to get in touch with Jay Pischke."

"Yeah, but I've already left the area. He needs to pick up his shipment at the freight terminal in St. Charles. He's missed his delivery window."

"Mr. Pischke's dead, so nobody will pick up his shipment. If you're making a delivery, I need your name and your cargo manifest."

The man went quiet for a moment.

"I'm Frank, and I work with FedEx freight. If you need more information, you'll have to talk to my supervisor."

My shoulders sank just a little.

"What were you delivering to Mr. Pischke?" I asked, trying to mask my disappointment.

"I'm not sure," he said. "Manifest just said it was office supplies."

"Well, like I said, Mr. Pischke's dead, so nobody'll pick it up. Did you touch anything at the house when you tried to make your delivery?"

He paused. "There wasn't a house at the delivery address. As best I could tell, it was just a drop-off point in the woods."

I furrowed my brow. "And where was this?"

He read off an address. I wrote it down, thanked him for his time, and then hung up. I didn't recognize the address, so I looked it up on Google Maps. The address was smack dab in the middle of nowhere. I wouldn't have thought anything of it had I not run into Dave Skelton on my way into work. A creek ran alongside the area's only road. A woman in distress called from there last night. That wasn't a coincidence.

I had a lead.

# Chapter 29

I called the boss to let him know where I was going. Then I got in my cruiser and drove. Trees covered the landscape like a carpet, and the road snaked across hills and valleys, making the drive feel almost like a roller coaster. After fifteen minutes, I turned onto a gravel road and followed Cotter's Creek until I came across a concrete parking pad on which two pickup trucks had parked. I parked behind them and wrote down their license plate information. Unfortunately, the hills blocked my cruiser's internet connection, preventing me from connecting to the license bureau's database.

The air outside my car was quiet and still, but the woods were alive with birds and small animals. I had spent several years on patrol in St. Augustine County before becoming a detective, so I had visited a lot of people in places like this. Some of them had wanted to live off the grid and grow their own food, while others simply wanted to get away from society. A few lived out there because they had something illegal to hide.

I grabbed a bulletproof vest from my trunk and pulled back the receiver on my pistol to chamber a round. A wooden bridge crossed Cotter's Creek near the parking pad and led to a well-trodden pass between two steep hills. I couldn't see a house or settlement, but Pischke wouldn't have ordered a delivery to the middle of nowhere without reason.

I whistled a song I had heard on the radio that morning and followed the trail about a quarter of a mile through woods so deep little sunlight penetrated the forest canopy. Goose bumps formed up and down my arms, and a chill traveled down my spine. Eventually, I emerged from the woods in a clearing nestled at the base of a tree-covered hill. A windmill between a pair of silver mobile homes turned in the fall breeze. Thick power cables ran from a generator between the mobile homes to ports on their sides. Nobody came out to greet me.

"St. Augustine County Sheriff's Department," I called. "Anybody home?"

About half a minute after I yelled, the door on one of the mobile homes opened, and a man stepped out. He was thin but not skinny. Tattoos crisscrossed his forearms, while a thick brown beard covered his chin. His hair was unkempt and wild, but his clothes looked clean. He carried a rifle with a black composite stock and scope against his shoulder as if he were going hunting.

"What do you want?"

I stepped forward. He didn't take the rifle from his shoulder and point it at me, which was a good sign.

"I'm Detective Joe Court," I said. "Are you the property owner?"

He considered me for a moment and then nodded. "I guess I am. My brother and me."

"Is he around?"

"Sleeping," he said. "What do you want?"

"Like I said, I'm Detective Joe Court," I said, bringing my right hand across my body to get a notepad from the inner pocket of my jacket. The man in front of me tensed. "I'm just reaching for a notepad in my jacket. That okay with you?"

He considered me and then nodded, so I took out a notepad.

"What's your name?" I asked.

"Andy."

"You got a last name, Andy?"

He narrowed his eyes before shifting his weight from one foot to another.

"Weaver."

"Andy Weaver," I said, writing that down. "Great. I'm here because I'm working the shooting death of a man named Jay Pischke. People called him Stinky Jay. You know him?"

He blinked a few times and then put a hand on the butt of his rifle.

"I met him at the bowling alley once, I think."

"Does your brother know him?"

Andy shrugged. "Couldn't say."

"Before he died, Mr. Pischke sent a freight delivery here. You know why he'd do that?"

Andy shrugged again.

"Maybe he liked me more than I thought."

"Maybe he did," I said, nodding. "Last night, a woman called my station for help, but she hung up before giving her address. We traced the phone out to a spot around here. Did you hear a commotion yesterday?"

He frowned and then tilted his head to the side as if he were thinking.

"Nah," he said. "It's been quiet."

"Can I look around?"

He crossed his arms. "Knock yourself out, but stay away from the trailers. Like I said, my brother's sleeping."

I wanted to ask whether his brother was sleeping in both of them, but I didn't want to put him off or upset him. Despite his willingness to let me search, I didn't like this guy. He creeped me out.

"I won't be long," I said, nodding and forcing a smile to my lips.

He grunted and spat on the ground but said nothing. The compound had two trailers, an old cabin, and a big barn. Hard-packed soil stretched from one side of the clearing to the other, allowing little vegetation to grow. During the spring, rain would have flowed down the nearby hills, turning the bowl-shaped clearing into a pond, while our winter ice storms would have rendered the pass to the property hazardous. Andy and his brother must have had a home elsewhere.

I kept an eye on him and then crossed toward the timber-framed barn. Inside, tobacco hung from the second-story trusses. There wasn't enough to sell, so they had likely planted it for personal use. An old tractor rusted in one corner, while a workbench with a metal-working vise sat opposite. It was just an old barn; an architectural salvage firm would pay top dollar for the wood, but it didn't help me at all.

The cabin had a futon and wood stove in the front room and a full-sized bed in the back bedroom. No one was inside, but I found footprints in the dust. When I opened the door to leave, I found Andy standing on the front step as if he were going inside. I stopped short and dropped my hand toward my weapon but didn't draw it. He stumbled back a step.

"Sorry," he mumbled. "I was seeing if you had found what you needed to find."

"Yeah," I said. "We're good. Your brother up yet?"

"Nope," said Andy. "He had a late night. He'll be in bed all day."

"I see," I said. "A woman's been here recently. Where is she now?"

For a split second, Andy's breath caught in his throat. "What woman?"

I crossed my arms and tilted my head to the side.

"There are footprints from a woman's shoe inside," I said. "I'd like to talk to her."

He thought for a moment. "Ain't no women here. You should go along now."

I furrowed my brow and stepped forward. Andy stepped back.

"Do you or your brother wear women's shoes?"

He shook his head.

"No. That's sick."

"Who made the footprints?"

He shrugged. "I don't know. Maybe my brother brought somebody by. I'll ask him."

"Please do," I said, reaching into the inside pocket of my jacket for a stack of business cards. I handed him one. "Call me when your brother wakes up."

He took my card and nodded.

"Will do."

I thanked him for his time and walked back through the woods to my cruiser. As I drove back to town, I kept glancing at my phone until I got a solitary but solid bar. Then I pulled over. My mom had called while I was out hiking, but she hadn't left a message. I hadn't talked to her much since she dropped off Roy, so she was probably calling to make sure he was okay.

I flipped through my phone's address book until I found Delgado's cell number. He answered on the second ring.

"Hey, boss," I said. "I just visited the farm of Shane and Andy Weaver. Jay Pischke had a big delivery sent their way, but Andy claims he and Pischke barely knew one another. I walked around their barn and cabin but found nothing. I'm guessing they've got pot growing somewhere, though."

Delgado grunted. "They out by Cotter's Creek?"

"Yeah," I said. "You know the area?"

He grunted again. "Yep. Those boys aren't growing anything; they're distilling it. I bet they're moonshiners. They set up by the creek and use its water to cool their condenser. If you want more information about them, Dave Skelton's the man to ask. He might even know them."

My shoulders relaxed some, and I nodded.

"That makes sense, but it doesn't tell me why Pischke sent a package to himself there."

"I can't help you there," said Delgado. "You thought Pischke was setting up a safe house for Thomas Becker. Maybe that was his backup location."

"If that's the case, the Weavers are involved in a much bigger crime than moonshining."

"That's for you to figure out, Detective. Good luck."

I thanked him and then hung up a moment later. I tossed my phone to the seat beside me, but before I could put the car into gear, it beeped with an incoming text message. It was from my mom.

*Call me when you can.*

I sighed and scratched my eyebrow. Mom knew I was at work, so she wouldn't have asked me to call unless this was important. I dialed her number and leaned my head back.

"Hey, Mom," I said. "It's Joe."

"Hey," she said, drawing the syllable out in her soft, mother's voice. "You got a minute?"

I sat straighter. "Yeah. What's wrong?"

She paused. "It's your brother."

"Dylan?" I asked, furrowing my brow. "He okay?"

"Not that brother," she said before sighing. "Do you remember Lacey Rayner?"

Lacey was Erin Court's best friend, and growing up, I had called her Aunt Lacey. I stayed with her when Erin was too busy or too drunk to take care of me. Aunt Lacey would brush my hair and read me stories and put me to bed. We lost touch after I entered the foster care system, but I had called her about six months ago. When I was a little girl, I had loved her, and she had loved me. As an adult, I still loved her, but regret and neglect had made our relationship complicated.

"I remember her," I said, my voice soft. "What's wrong?"

"Are you sitting down?"

"Yeah," I said, nodding. "What's wrong?"

Mom paused. "I'm sorry, but she died recently."

I blinked, sure I had misheard her.

"What happened?"

Mom hesitated. "It's a murder."

I closed my eyes and shook my head again.

"No," I said. "That's not right. She's a solid citizen. She lives in Creve Coeur, she pays her taxes, she's got a job...nobody would have any reason to kill her."

"I'm sorry, honey," said Mom. "The police think it was a home invasion that went wrong."

My throat tightened hard, and my eyes grew wet. I choked all that down. Now wasn't the time to grieve.

"Okay," I said, drawing in a deep breath. "You said you were calling about my brother. Is he okay?"

"He found the body and called it in. The Creve Coeur police have him in their station. He's not a suspect, but they want to interview him. He refused to give them his mom and dad's phone number and instead said to call you. A detective sitting in on the interview knew me and knew you were my daughter, so she called me. I'm calling you."

"Okay," I said, nodding. "Tell them I'll call his mom. Also tell them I'm on my way. I'll be there in an hour."

"I know he's Erin's son, but you don't need to go out there," she said. "You don't owe him anything."

"I'm not going for Ian," I said. "I'm going for Lacey. Thanks for calling. I'll talk to you soon."

I tossed the phone beside me and put my cruiser in gear. I didn't know what I'd find in St. Louis, but somebody I had loved was dead. Staying put wasn't an option.

# Chapter 30

Tara huddled in the dark with Scarlett against her chest. The baby had improved since being breastfed, but she wasn't out of danger yet. Still, Tara welcomed any improvement. Scarlett felt warm, and she slept more than most infants, but she was easier to wake. She still should have been in the hospital, but at least she was hydrated now. That shifted Tara's worry from the baby to the man sitting across from her in the trailer's living room.

Since her escape attempt, Andy and Shane had taken shifts watching her. They even made her keep the bathroom door open. Tara didn't know how she'd get out of this, but as long as she was alive, she'd keep trying. Never in her life had she hated anyone as much as she hated Andy and Shane. After everything that had happened to her, that hot, black hatred was the only thing keeping her going.

That, and the baby in her arms.

Scarlett fussed and kicked as her eyes popped open. Tara stroked her back and smiled at her.

"She's hungry," said Shane, a hint of a smile on his lips. "Better feed her."

"You're disgusting," said Tara, glancing up. Shane's smile broadened, but he said nothing. It had been almost three hours since she last fed Scarlett. At home, Tara had a shroud she could wear that covered her chest and gave her privacy to nurse her own baby. Here, she had nothing. Shane wanted it like that. He wanted her to feel embarrassed and afraid. He got off on it.

Tara kept her expression neutral as she slipped her shirt and bra off her shoulder to nurse the baby. Shane leaned back and laced his fingers behind his head. They were sitting in the darkened living room of his trailer. Detective Joe Court had just left the compound, but even when she was searching, Tara hadn't dared scream. If she had, Shane would have killed her and the baby, and Andy would have killed the detective.

As long as Tara and the baby lived, they could escape. She had to get home to her husband and kids.

"Never get tired of seeing you take your shirt off," said Shane.

"You should try porn," said Tara. "It's even better."

Shane grinned but said nothing. After about ten minutes at Tara's breast, Scarlett slowed down and drifted back to sleep. Tara squeezed her toes to wake her up and then covered herself and grabbed a burp cloth as she held the baby on her shoulder and patted her back.

"How much is this girl worth to you?" asked Tara. Once the baby burped, Tara wiped her face and chin and switched her to her other breast. She still felt awkward breastfeeding a stranger's baby, but it kept Scarlett alive. That was worth it.

"Ten million cash," said Shane. "Why? You think you deserve some of that?"

"If I keep Scarlett alive, I'd say so," she said. "Besides, I'm your partner's ex-wife."

Shane considered for a moment and then leaned forward so that his elbows rested on his knees. He pointed toward the trailer's door.

"That cop came because you tried to escape," he said. "You don't deserve shit."

She looked at the baby. "My son would never forgive you if you killed me."

"As much as I like Xavier, I like my money a whole lot more. I can handle rejection."

"You won't get your money if Scarlett dies," she said. "Please let me take her to the hospital. I'll do whatever you want. I know you wanted me in high school. You can have me now. I'll do things with you I don't even do with my husband. Just let me take Scarlett to the hospital. Please. If you have an ounce of decency in you, let me go."

His eyes traveled to her legs and then settled on her chest before he looked at her face again.

"I always was jealous of Thomas in high school," he said. "You were something else back then."

"I'm something else now, too," she said. "I've learned a lot since then. Your brother doesn't have to know. We can have our fun, and then Scarlett and I will leave. You can tell him the baby and I escaped. Come on. Haven't you always wondered why Thomas walked around with a smile on his face when we were together?"

Scarlett fussed and then cried. Tara bounced her on her knee, hoping to calm her. Shane's eyes traveled down her body once more, sending disgusted chills down her spine. If this was what it took to escape, though, she'd pay the price. She slipped her top off her shoulder again, exposing her breast.

"You said you enjoyed watching," she said, winking. "How about you come over here?"

Shane shook his head and sighed.

"If I still wanted you, I would have taken you already," he said. "Thanks for the show, but no thanks. You got old, honey. Now put a boob in that kid's mouth and shut her up. We're here for the long haul."

*** 

I didn't know Creve Coeur well, but the police station was easy enough to get to. I took I-64 west through the city, exited on Ballas Road, and then headed north past a hospital, a synagogue, and a Catholic boys' high school. Trees lined the street, and many of the houses I passed were large and sat on impressive, well-landscaped lots.

The police station looked more like a high school than it did a law enforcement outpost. The lot it occupied sloped downward, and the station's architect had used that hill in his design instead of trying to fight it by leveling the landscape. I wouldn't have called it pretty, but it was a nice building. It blended into its natural surroundings rather than dominating them. I rarely saw that kind of thoughtful design in law enforcement facilities.

I parked my cruiser in the lot out front and went to the front desk, where I flashed my badge to a uniformed officer and introduced myself. He led me to an office at the rear of the station. A detective sat behind the desk. She had shoulder-length brown hair and oval-shaped glasses, and she wore a sky-blue cardigan over a white shirt. When she saw me, she held up a finger and typed for another moment before standing and holding out her hand.

"Grace Marshall," she said. "You must be Joe Court. I know your mom."

I smiled and shook her hand. "Everybody seems to know Julia. So you've got a body, huh?"

She nodded and raised her eyebrows before gesturing to a chair in front of her desk. I sat down, and so did she.

"Yeah," she said. "The victim is Lacey Rayner. She's a fifty-one-year-old single, white female. She's the homeowner, and she's lived at her residence for at least fifteen years. Her neighbors described her as kind and quiet. She never had problems with anybody, and no one has called us to her house. Her record's clean. She doesn't even have parking tickets. As best we can tell, she doesn't have a boyfriend or significant other. She attended services at Holy Cross Lutheran Church and made a living writing romance novels. She's got boxes and boxes of her books in the basement."

I nodded. "I didn't know she wrote romance novels."

Detective Marshall reached for a notepad on her desk. "So you knew her?"

I nodded. "Once. It's complicated. She was my biological mother's best friend, so I spent a lot of time with her when I was young. Then, my biological mother overdosed on heroin multiple times, and the courts deemed her unfit to raise me. A judge put me in the foster care system. Lacey and I lost touch. We've been picking things up lately, though."

"When did you talk to her last?"

I drew in a breath and thought. "Maybe three weeks ago. We had coffee at a Starbucks in Frontenac."

"She seem okay?"

I shrugged. "It was an awkward meeting, so it's hard to say."

"What'd you talk about?"

I leaned back. "Our lives. I told her about my job, my house, and Ian. She listened and asked questions."

"Was she scared or worried about anything?"

I shook my head. "Not at all."

Detective Marshall nodded and tapped the back of her pen on her notepad.

"What can you tell me about Ian?"

I tilted my head to the side. "Not a lot to tell. He's fifteen, he's bright, and he lives with his mom and dad in St. Charles. As best I could tell, he's never been in real trouble, he gets along with his parents and teachers, and he's got a lot of friends."

"How'd he know Ms. Rayner?"

"She was his babysitter before his biological mother died," I said. I paused and looked at the table. "Erin Court, our biological mother, was murdered. I've tried to persuade him to stop, but he's been looking into that. He may have visited Ms. Rayner to talk about his mom."

Detective Marshall raised an eyebrow but said nothing.

"It's complicated," I said. "Erin Court's murder is unsolved, but we've found some new leads. The original investigating officer thought her murder was a robbery that had gone wrong, but since then, we've found she had more money at her time of death than she should have. We don't know where she got the money, but she could have worked in a criminal enterprise that went bad. Detective Mathias Blatch is working her case now. He works out of the South County precinct on Sappington Barracks Road in Mehlville. I can get you his phone number if you want it."

"I'll look him up," she said, nodding and considering me. "Anything else I should know about Ms. Rayner?"

I considered and then drew in a breath.

THE MAN IN THE METH LAB

"When she was younger, she and my mother were both high-end prostitutes. I don't know whether they worked for anyone or if they were independent, but they both had long client lists. Erin Court, my biological mother, did a lot of drugs. Lacey was always clean, though."

Detective Marshall crossed her arms.

"Seems like there's more to my victim than I expected."

"That was a long time ago. She's a civilian now."

Marshall nodded and stood. I did likewise.

"Still, you've given me a lot to look into. Ian asked for you earlier. You want to say hello?"

"Is he alone?"

She shook her head. "No. His parents are with him."

"Then no," I said. "He's good."

She hesitated.

"He asked for you, though."

"Only because he thought he'd get in trouble for calling his mom and dad," I said. "He's okay. I'll head back to St. Augustine. I'm working two different murders, and I don't have time to stick around here."

She hesitated again.

"If that's how you want to play this. Do you have a card in case I need to get in touch with you?"

"Of course," I said, reaching into my purse. We swapped business cards, and then she escorted me out of the building. Between the two different murder cases I was investigating, I had enough work for four detectives. Ian's mom and dad would take care of him. He'd be just fine. He didn't need me, and I had shit to do. I didn't have time to babysit.

# Chapter 31

I drove back to St. Augustine, knowing I had a long night ahead of me. To send Reuben to prison, I needed witnesses willing to testify that he had coerced them into having sex with him. That meant I had to talk to some strippers.

Before going home, I went by my bank and withdrew three hundred dollars from the ATM. Then I went to my house, fed and pet my dog, and changed into a pair of dark jeans and a white T-shirt before heading to Club Serenity. The bouncer took one look at me and waved me through the door without asking for the cover charge. I didn't know what to make of that, but it saved me ten bucks.

Inside, the lights were low, but the music was so loud it felt like a slap to my chest. Young, scantily clad women carried drink trays and danced on stage. In the far corner, young men played video games while naked girls sat on their laps and cheered and occasionally whispered into their ears. A woman who looked as if she were in her early twenties danced on stage. The men whooped and hollered and drank, but nobody tried to reach for her or their waitresses. They knew the rules.

The crowd parted in front of me as I walked toward the bar. A lot of male eyes landed and stayed on me, but nobody tried to grab me. That was nice. They probably thought I was a dancer. The bartender knew better. He was thirty or thirty-five, and he wore a black T-shirt that stretched taut over a well-muscled physique.

"What can I do for you, Detective?"

If he knew I was a detective, Vic Conroy had probably shown my picture to his staff.

"Is Renee Swift in tonight?"

He looked at a schedule tacked to the wall behind the bar.

"She's set to dance in about an hour on the main stage, but she might be available for a private show beforehand."

That was why I brought the cash. Everything cost money in Club Serenity—a dancer's time, most of all.

"How would I find her?"

He picked up a phone beneath the bar. "Stay here. I'll make sure she finds you."

I thanked him and then turned to watch the crowd. The club goers were mostly male, but there were a few women, too. Almost everyone was having a good time. About ten minutes after I sat down, a young woman in a string bikini walked toward me with a tray on her shoulder. She smiled at me, and it didn't look fake. She was a good actress, which probably served her well.

"Mr. Conroy says hello," she said, placing a cheeseburger on the bar beside me. "On the house."

Before I could thank her, she had turned to take drink orders from a table of men in business suits. I looked at the burger, and the bartender placed a glass of water and silverware wrapped in a napkin beside me.

"Renee's running late, but she'll be in," he said, almost yelling so I could hear him over the music. "Vic must like you. He doesn't give away food often."

"I can't accept free food," I said, reaching for my purse. I put a ten on the bar.

The bartender slid the cash off the countertop and added it to a roll he kept in a pocket on his apron before nodding.

"You need ketchup, let me know."

I thanked him and ate my burger. The last time I saw Vic Conroy, he'd said his chef made the best burger in town, and he hadn't been lying. Unfortunately, that burger was the highlight of my night.

Renee Swift came in for her shift without time to spare, so I didn't get to talk to her before it was her turn on stage. Almost an hour and a half after I arrived in the club, I got a moment with her in one of the club's VIP rooms. It was quiet enough that we could talk. For fifty bucks, she gave the names of five young women who might have spent time with Reuben Terepocki.

I talked to all five women, but only one acknowledged knowing Reuben, and even then, she said she only knew him in passing because he had purchased lap dances from her. She gave me another girl's name, though: Shelby McAllen.

Shelby used to dance at the club, but nobody had seen her for almost two weeks. She disappeared without even telling anyone she was leaving. When asked about her, Vic Conroy told his employees not to bring her up again. She said Shelby and Reuben had been close. I didn't know what that meant, but I'd find out.

I left the club at three in the morning and drove home. As soon as I let Roy out of the dog run in the backyard, he bowed in front of me.

"It's too late to play, sweetheart," I said, scratching his ear. He didn't understand, obviously, but he followed me inside, where I crashed on my bed and fell asleep almost instantly. Unfortunately, my cell rang just hours later at a little before nine in the morning. The sun was bright, but I felt even more tired than I had when I closed my eyes.

I groaned and grabbed the phone from my end table.

"Yeah?" I asked, clearing my throat.

"Joe, it's Trisha. I need you at the station. We've got two people here who need to file a missing person report."

I swore under my breath.

"I had a late night," I said. "Do we have someone who can take their statement for me?"

"Sorry, honey," said Trisha. "With Reuben out, you're it. That's the job. For what it's worth, Sheriff Delgado is forming a new hiring committee. We'll bring in new detectives, but it's not going to be easy after what you've done to Reuben."

I sat straighter.

"What does that mean?"

Trisha paused for almost thirty seconds, so I repeated my question. Then she sighed.

"I love you, honey," she said. "You know that, right?"

"You're a friend, yeah," I said. "What do you think I've done to Reuben?"

"I've seen dozens of people come and go in our department. My time here is almost over. I've got, maybe, five more years in me. Your time's just starting. You need to think about that."

"What's on your mind?" I asked, my tone sharp.

"People are talking about you, and they're not saying nice things. You built up a lot of good will on the Apostate case a few months back, but your investigation into Reuben is wearing thin on people."

I swung my legs off my bed and paced my bedroom.

"I'm working a case, Trisha. That's it."

"I get that," she said. "I'm just telling you what people are saying. You're a great detective, but Reuben's a good detective, too. He's not been here long, but he's closed tough cases. People think you don't like sharing the spotlight. They think you're playing politics."

My mouth popped open to respond, but I didn't know what to say. Then I blinked and drew in a breath.

"Do you think I'm playing politics?"

"I'm just repeating what I've heard."

My face felt hot, and I clenched my jaw tight.

"I'm not playing politics. I'm following the evidence and doing my job."

"If you could share some of that evidence, it might help us understand what you're doing," she said. "Just think about that."

"No," I said, shaking my head. "This is an active case. I'm not releasing information until I can make an arrest. I won't smear a man's name just to improve my position within my department. Then I would be playing politics."

Trisha hesitated. "You've got to do what you think is best."

"I am," I said. "Thanks, Trisha. I'll see you at work."

I hung up before she could say anything else. Then I tossed my phone onto the bed. I wanted to scream, but instead, I sat beside the dog on my bed and petted his back. He put his head in my lap.

"At least you don't think I'm playing politics," I said. Roy cocked his head to the side and seemed to furrow his brow. I patted his back. "Come on, dude. I'll get you some breakfast."

I fed the dog and let him outside before showering and getting ready for the day. By the time I reached my station, every parking spot within two blocks of the front door had a car in it, which meant I ended up having to park near Rise and Grind, St. Augustine County's only coffee shop. That worked out well because I needed coffee.

When I got to the station, Delgado was in the second-floor conference room with Trisha. I nodded to them both.

"Morning," I said.

"I'm glad I caught you," said Delgado. "In your investigation into Thomas Becker's death, have you come across the name Lorenzo Molena?"

I shook my head.

"No," I said. "Why?"

"The St. Louis County police think he's the mastermind behind the abduction in St. Louis. He might even be Thomas Becker's killer, but we can't prove it yet."

I nodded and softened my voice.

"Any news on the little girl they abducted?"

Delgado shook his head. "No. The kidnappers haven't tried to make contact. We'll make an arrest, but I can't say we'll get that little girl back alive."

That put my squabble with Trisha that morning into prospective.

"Good luck," I said. "I hope you find Thomas Becker's murderer, but I hope you get the little girl even more."

The boss nodded and then told Trisha he'd check in with her later. Once he left, I looked to my friend.

"I'm sorry about earlier," I said. "I'm cranky in the morning."

"Yeah, I know," she said. "I shouldn't have said anything. It wasn't my place."

"No," I said, shaking my head. "You had my best interests at heart. That's all I can ask for in a friend. Now where's this couple who wants to file a missing person report?"

"Conference room B," she said, sliding a notepad toward her. "It's an older woman and her grandson. Xavier Becker and Eileen Madison. They're looking for Tara Madison. She's been gone for a couple of days."

I brought a hand to my face and rubbed my eyes before groaning.

"Something I said?"

"No," I said. "Tara Madison is Thomas Becker's ex-wife. I talked to her a couple of days ago and thought she was hiding something. If she's on the run, she might have killed her ex-husband. I may have let a murderer escape."

# Chapter 32

I left Trisha and hurried to the conference room. Eileen Madison was in her sixties, but she could have passed for her early fifties. Her wavy brunette hair framed an oval-shaped face, while her tasteful makeup accentuated her green eyes and high cheekbones, making her look like a wizened matriarch on a suburban sitcom. Xavier, her grandson, had short brown hair and green eyes. He looked sullen, which was understandable with his mother missing.

I walked into the room and sat across from them at our conference table. The overhead lights were off, but big picture windows allowed in enough light that we could see well. Before doing anything else, I took my notepad and cell phone from my purse and put both on the table.

"Okay," I said, running my thumb across my phone to start the app that would record our conversation. "I'm Detective Mary Joe Court with the St. Augustine County Sheriff's Department. As I understand it, you're here to file a missing person report on behalf of Tara Madison. Is that right?"

Eileen nodded. Her lips were straight and thin.

"That's right. I'm Eileen Madison. Tara is my daughter-in-law," she said, nodding toward Xavier. "This is my grandson Xavier Becker. He's Tara's son from her first marriage."

"Where's Wesley today?"

Eileen straightened and then cocked her head to the side.

"He's at home with Joshua, his baby," she said. "How do you know my son's name?"

I gave her the softest look I could muster.

"Full disclosure, your family has been on my radar since I learned of Thomas Becker's death. I've run background checks on everybody," I said, looking at Xavier. "I'm very sorry about your father."

He gave me a shallow nod but said nothing. His grandmother's expression hardened.

"Why were you investigating my family?"

"It's standard procedure in a homicide," I said. "If I don't clear the victim's former spouse of suspicion, a defense attorney could claim I missed an obvious alternative suspect when I make an arrest. It just makes things easier in court."

She stiffened a little.

"And did you clear my daughter-in-law?"

"I had some open questions, if I'm honest," I said. "I hope we can answer those today. When did you last see her, and what do you mean when you say she's missing?"

"She's not there," said Xavier. I smiled at him, hoping to encourage him to continue, but his grandma gave him a pained expression. He looked confused. "I mean that's why we think she's missing. She's not home."

"That makes perfect sense," I said. "When I talked to your stepdad, though, he thought she was at work. Is it possible she's still at work?"

Xavier looked to his grandma.

"My daughter-in-law works very hard, but she wouldn't have left her family this long. She has a newborn at home."

"I've heard him," I said. "He's got quite a set of lungs."

I said it to lighten the mood, but Mrs. Madison lowered her chin.

"How could you have heard him?"

I didn't know what she was getting at, so I hesitated before speaking.

"I stopped by the house to interview Tara after learning she had once been married to Thomas Becker. While Mrs. Madison and I spoke, her baby cried."

Mrs. Madison tapped her index finger on the table.

"This was during the day?"

I nodded. "I don't remember the exact time, but yeah. Why?"

"Because my grandson is in daycare during the day," she said. "Every day. His mother and father work, so there's no one home to watch him."

It felt as if the world stopped moving. Thomas Becker and his friends abducted an infant. Now I knew where they had taken her.

275

"When was Tara last seen?"

"Four days ago," said Mrs. Madison. "My son, Wesley, saw her before he went to work. He dropped off Joshua at daycare."

I looked to Xavier.

"Where were you?"

"Going to school," he said. "I take the bus."

This was a problem. It meant I might have been the last person to see Tara before she disappeared with the baby. She hadn't abducted that baby on her own, though. She had help. I focused on Xavier.

"Has your mom had any visitors lately?" I asked. "Or has she, maybe, gotten a lot of phone calls lately? Or did your biological father come by more often than usual?"

Xavier said nothing.

"What are you implying about my daughter-in-law?" asked Mrs. Madison.

"I'm not implying anything," I said. "I'm trying to figure out where she might be. Those who associated with her recently can help. Has anyone been to the house lately?"

Xavier said nothing. I held my eyes on him until he glanced up. Then he looked away.

"Something you want to tell me, Xavier?" I asked.

He blinked.

"Dad doesn't come by," he said. "He and Wesley don't get along well."

"I see," I said, nodding. "How about other people? Did any of her co-workers come by the house lately?"

He shook his head.

"Friends?" I asked. "You're not in trouble."

Again, he shook his head. I sighed and looked to Mrs. Madison.

"Can I speak to Xavier alone for a minute?" I asked.

She crossed her arms. "Xavier's my grandson. I'm not leaving."

I gritted my teeth but ignored her and focused on Xavier.

"Do you have something to tell me, Xavier?" I asked. "Something you can't say in front of your grandma?"

He said nothing.

"We're all on the same side, Xavier," I said. "I'm trying to find your mom. I can't do that unless people answer my questions. Does your mom have a boyfriend?"

Mrs. Madison scoffed, but Xavier shook his head.

"Does she have visitors that your stepdad doesn't know about?"

He said nothing. The kid had already shown he could answer a question, so I knew he was holding back. I looked at Mrs. Madison again.

"How about you get a cup of coffee?" I asked. "There's a machine in our break room. Our dispatcher can help you find it."

She straightened and drew in a breath. "I'm staying right here."

I looked at her and allowed just a hint of ice into my voice.

"Let me rephrase. Get a cup of coffee. If you're uncomfortable with me talking to your grandson alone, I can bring in a social worker. He knows more than he's letting on, but he's afraid of saying that in front of you." I softened my voice. "Your daughter-in-law needs help. This is the best chance of getting it."

She looked to Xavier.

"Are you all right with this, honey?"

The kid nodded. She swallowed and stood.

"I'll get coffee," she said. She looked to her grandson. "If you need anything, I'll be near. You've got your cell phone. Text me or call me."

"I will," he said. She hesitated and then turned to leave. Once she shut the door, I looked at Xavier.

"You're not in trouble," I said. "Who's been coming to visit when your dad's away at work?"

His lips moved, and he said something, but I couldn't hear it. I waited a few seconds.

"You can write it down if you can't say it."

He looked up. His eyes were bloodshot. I gave him a moment to compose himself.

"Uncle Shane. I wasn't supposed to be there. I was supposed to be in school, but I skipped and played video games in the basement. He had a baby with him. Mom didn't know I was there. She was supposed to be at work."

I furrowed my brow. "Do you skip school often?"

He shrugged. "School's not important. Dad said as long as I graduated, I could join the Army like he did. I wanted to fly helicopters."

Following in his father's footsteps made sense, I guess.

"Was the baby your cousin?" I asked.

He shook his head. "No. Uncle Shane brought it by, but he doesn't have a kid. Neither does Uncle Andy."

I lowered my chin.

"When you say Shane and Andy, are you talking about Shane and Andy Weaver?" I asked.

He nodded. "Dad grew up with them. They were his friends. Mom never liked them, but we used to go hunting and shooting and stuff. They aren't really my uncles. I just say they are. Uncle Shane brought the baby to the house, and Mom was pissed. I don't know what was going on, but they left together. That was on Tuesday."

Another piece now fit into my puzzle. Thomas Becker, Shane Weaver, and Andy Weaver abducted a baby from a hospital in St. Louis. Before that, though, Thomas hired Jay Pischke to set up a safe house in St. Augustine. Unfortunately, Reuben Terepocki shot Jay Pischke before they could put that safe house to use.

Somebody then killed Thomas. Maybe it was Shane and Andy, maybe it was someone else. Either way, they didn't know what to do, so they went to Tara Madison, Thomas's ex-wife. She was a nurse with experience caring for infants. I didn't know how involved she was in this caper, but she played a role. Shane, Tara, and Andy took the baby to the Weavers' compound in the woods. The partnership then went sour. Tara fled and called 911, but before she could give our dispatcher any information, she hung up.

The theory had a lot of conjecture, but it fit the evidence.

"Do your mom and Shane get along well?" I asked.

He hesitated and then shook his head. "She thinks Shane and Andy are idiots and says I shouldn't be impressed by them. They're nice, though. They're teaching me how to be a man."

"And how do they do that?"

"You know," he said, shrugging. "We go hunting. They taught me how to make traps and read a trail to track deer. And they told me about history. A man can't know where he's going if he doesn't know where his family's been. That matters. You've got to honor your ancestors."

I nodded.

"Were they in the Army with your father?"

He nodded. "Yeah, but they didn't fly helicopters. Shane was a Ranger, but Andy was just in the infantry."

Either way, they had the training to steal a little girl from the hospital and ride off in a helicopter. More than that, they had the training to hold that compound of theirs indefinitely, given the terrain. I stood.

"You stay here. I'll find your grandma. People will need to talk to you. You're not in trouble. In fact, you've helped me out a lot."

He nodded. "Are Shane and Andy in trouble?"

I hesitated and then drew in a breath before nodding.

"Yeah. They did something wrong. I think they've got your mom."

He swallowed and nodded but said nothing.

"I'll be right back," I said, standing and hurrying toward the door. His grandmother sat on a bench in the hallway. I didn't give her details, but I told her my interview was done and that other officers would need to see her grandson soon. Then I ran to Sheriff Delgado's office. I knocked but opened the door before he could respond. The boss was on the phone, and he raised his eyebrow when he saw me.

"I think Scarlett Nolan is in St. Augustine County with Tara Madison. She's the ex-wife of Thomas Becker, and she's on a compound owned by Shane and Andy Weaver. Both Shane and Andy are ex-Army, and both were very good friends of Thomas Becker. I don't know who killed Thomas, but they're armed and dangerous."

Delgado stared at me for a moment but then focused on his phone call again.

"Jane, let me call you back. I've got something I need to take care of," he said. He hung up his phone and looked at me. "Tell me what you've got."

# Chapter 33

I walked Delgado through my investigation and conclusions. When I finished, he leaned back and crossed his arms.

"If I showed you a video, you think you could identify Shane or Andy?"

"I've only met Andy, but yeah."

Delgado nodded and leaned forward to use his computer. After a few moments, he turned his monitor so we could both see it.

"The St. Louis police haven't released the video to the public, but the hospital had security cameras everywhere. This is the helicopter pad during the shooting. Tell me if you recognize anybody."

I nodded, and he started the clip. Most surveillance video was fuzzy and unusable, but this was clear and stable. A helicopter sat on a landing pad with its main rotor spinning. Nothing else moved for about fifteen seconds, but then, its rear door slid open, and a man stepped out. He wore a blue flight suit with the sleeves rolled up past his elbows, exposing tattoos on his forearms. A thick brown beard covered his past.

"That's Andy Weaver," I said.

Delgado nodded. "Keep watching."

I nodded but said nothing. A moment after the door slid up, a middle-aged man carrying a baby ran onto the screen. He was fit, and he had olive-colored skin and black hair. My mom would have said he was handsome, but his eyes looked cruel. Delgado paused the video.

"This is Lorenzo Molena," he said. "He spent twenty years in the Army and retired as a lieutenant colonel two years ago. The rest of his crew served with him."

"That include Andy Weaver?" I asked.

Delgado shook his head. "No, but it includes Thomas Becker."

"Okay," I said. "Play the video."

Delgado clicked, and the video started up again. We couldn't hear what they said, but Lorenzo and Andy spoke for a moment. Then Lorenzo turned and ran. He didn't see Andy pull a firearm from behind him. Before Lorenzo could make it off the tarmac, Andy shot him twice in the back. After that, a second person jumped out of the helicopter. He and Andy shared the same blocky face shape and hook-shaped nose, so it was probably Shane.

The two men ran toward Lorenzo's prone body and rolled him over. Shane grabbed the baby from Lorenzo's hands, and Andy fired twice at his chest. Lorenzo's body rocked with each blow. Then Andy ran toward the helicopter. I covered my mouth with my hand.

"Jeez," I said. Delgado nodded toward the screen.

"There's more," he said. I nodded and kept my eyes on the monitor. Lorenzo lay still for a few moments, but then he rolled over. I expected blood to puddle beneath him, but none did.

"He must have a vest," I said.

"That was our guess," said Delgado.

For a second, it looked as if Lorenzo was trying to push himself up, but then he collapsed on the ground. A moment later, a man and woman entered the field of view and dragged Lorenzo away. Delgado paused the video.

"We're not a hundred percent sure what happened out there, but we think Thomas Becker double-crossed his boss and took the baby. If you're right, his buddies Shane and Andy helped."

I nodded and let it sink in.

"I thought Tara Madison, Becker's ex-wife, had killed him. This makes me think it was Lorenzo Molena and his crew. They caught up to Becker, cut off his fingers one by one to get him to talk, and then lit him on fire. Bad way to go."

Delgado leaned back. "Live by the sword, die by the sword."

"Do you know where Molena is now?"

Delgado shook his head. "Not a clue. Best we can tell, he's disappeared from the face of the earth. We think the woman who pulled him off the helicopter pad was Laura Singleton. She was an MP and did her training at Fort Leonard Wood. We believe the man was Captain Josh Knight. He served under Lorenzo in Iraq. There were multiple fatalities within the hospital, but we don't know who was an innocent by-stander, who was part of the victim's security team, and who worked for Lorenzo Molena."

"Won't the Nolan family be able to tell you who their people are?"

Delgado sighed and closed his eyes. "They could if they were cooperating with the investigation, but they're not. The missing girl's grandfather runs some kind of private security and intelligence firm. He's worth several billion dollars and thinks he can do a better job finding his grand-daughter than we can."

With that kind of money and the resources it could provide, he might be right. It was beside the point, though.

"We need to get the girl before she gets hurt."

"I agree," said Delgado, already picking up his phone. "Stick around. Since you've been out to the Weavers' compound, we'll need your help."

Things moved quickly after that. Delgado called Lieutenant Jesse Leffelman with the St. Louis County police, and I went into the conference room to talk to Xavier and his grandmother again. I was clear and honest with them both. Tara Madison, Xavier's mom, was likely with Andy and Shane Weaver. We didn't know what was going on, but we suspected she was in danger. We also suspected she was caring for an infant abducted from St. Louis. Our job was to put together a plan to rescue her, and Xavier could help with that.

I stayed in the conference room for about an hour. Xavier had spent a lot of time on the property with his uncles and father, so he knew the area well. He even drew me sketches and showed me where they had dug tunnels between the various buildings and secret storehouses in which their ancestors had kept moonshine. Xavier didn't know what they kept in those storehouses now, but he knew they still existed.

After meeting with him, I walked to Delgado's office. The sheriff, Lieutenant Leffelman, and Major Bryan Hilden with the State Highway Patrol stood around the conference table, looking at a laptop. When I walked in, Delgado nodded.

"Gentlemen, this is Detective Joe Court," he said. "She's working the case with me. What have you got, Joe?"

I put the sketches Xavier had drawn on the table.

"We can't force our way into the compound," I said. "It would be stupid."

Hilden straightened and looked to the drawings.

"Why would it be stupid?"

"These guys have spent years preparing for an assault," I said. "I talked to Xavier Becker. He's spent a lot of time on the property with his uncles. They're nuts. They wanted to get on a TV show called *Apocalypse Survivors*, so they've hardened their entire compound. They've got tunnels, guns, traps, and hardened positions from which they can shoot behind cover throughout the compound. We'd take a lot of casualties."

Leffelman put his coffee on the table beside the laptop and crossed his arms.

"My department's tactical operations unit has a Bearcat. Its armor can withstand being shot by a .50-caliber rifle. Unless they've got artillery, nothing they have can go through that. It'll give us a mobile platform from which we could return fire and stay safe."

"If we could get it there, it could work," I said, glancing at him as I leafed through some of Xavier's drawings. "How big is it?"

"Pretty damn big. I'll save you a seat," said Leffelman. The other men chuckled a little, but I ignored them and pulled a drawing to the top.

"The compound itself is about an acre and a half and is located on a ridge overlooking a wooded valley," I said. "It has a barn, a cabin, and two mobile homes. A trail winds through the woods from the mobile homes to a parking pad about a quarter of a mile away. Unfortunately, that trail passes between a pair of limestone ridges about a hundred yards from the mobile home. There's no way around it. It will force us to walk in a single-file line without cover. They'd pick us off one by one."

CHRIS CULVER

"If they've got mobile homes on the property, there's got to be another way onto the compound," said Leffelman. "We just have to find it."

I directed their attention to a drawing Xavier had made.

"True," I said. "The mobile homes have been there for twenty years, and twenty years ago, they had a driveway. According to Xavier, it was several miles long and dumped you onto some railroad tracks. Shane Weaver told him that his grandfather and father had brought the mobile homes to the property by dragging them behind an old excavator. Since then, they've planted trees over that driveway and dug holes with the excavator. Even if we could follow the same route, we'd crash into a hole in the ground and get stuck."

Major Hilden crossed his arms and considered me.

"So if we go in the front door, we'll get shot. If we try to go in the back door, we'll fall in a hole."

"And get shot," I said. "Shane and Andy grew up in these woods. They know every tree and trail, and their grandfather taught them to build the traps he saw during the Vietnam War. If we go in there, we'll find holes in the ground full of sharpened spikes, we'll find trip wires connected to deadfalls that will drop spiked tree limbs on us, and we'll find improvised explosives. Once we get to the compound, we'll find two armed former soldiers—one of whom was a Ranger with extensive combat experience—in hardened positions. No one will win."

Delgado narrowed his eyes at me. "How do we get in there, then?"

"We don't," I said. He raised his eyebrows at me but said nothing. Leffelman looked to Major Hilden as if I were crazy. I drew in a breath. "Send me in alone. This can't end with a fight. It needs to end with a negotiation. I've met Andy Weaver. He won't trust me, but at least he knows I didn't shoot at him when I had the chance earlier. I can bring a satellite phone to him so we can talk to each other. If I'm lucky, he'll let me see Scarlett so I can make sure she's okay and has everything she needs."

"So your plan is to lay siege to the property," said Hilden.

I nodded. "Yeah. We'll wait them out. It'll take resources, but nobody has to die."

Nobody said anything for a moment. Then Delgado cleared his throat.

"Joe's seen the property and met the people involved," he said. "If she thinks this is the best plan, it is."

He didn't often say nice things about me, so I straightened and nodded my thanks to him. Major Hilden sighed.

"We need a contingency plan in case the baby's not well," he said.

"Agreed," I said. "If Scarlett's sick, I say we go in with the Bearcat through the woods. It's risky, but it might be worth the risk to save her. If she's well, though, negotiation's our best strategy."

The room went silent again. Then Lieutenant Leffelman sighed.

"So is this the plan?" he asked.

I looked to Major Hilden and Delgado. Both men nodded, so I drew in a breath.

"I need to call somebody before we leave," I said.

Delgado nodded. "You do what you've got to do, Joe. We'll finalize things here."

I nodded and left the room. As I walked back to my office, I pulled out my phone to call my mom. My stomach churned, and my chest felt tight, but I couldn't let my nerves stop me. This was too important. Mom answered on the third ring.

"Hey, Mom," I said, blinking. "I'm going to do something stupid at work, but it might save a baby's life. I wanted to hear a friendly voice before I left."

# Chapter 34

No bulletproof vest was actually bullet proof. If Andy or Shane shot me with a .50-caliber rifle, the round would punch right through my vest and into my heart and lungs. Meager protection was better than no protection at all, but I wished I had something more substantial.

Half an hour after leaving my station, my feet sunk into the mud of the trail. Despite the temperature dipping into the upper fifties at night, mosquitoes still buzzed around during the day. I swatted one from my neck and wished I had put on some bug spray. We hadn't known what I'd run into at the Weavers' compound or what they might need, so I wore a heavy canvas backpack holding premixed infant formula, diapers, baby wipes, an Iridium Extreme satellite phone, and a gallon of water. A Glock 17 weighed down the holster strapped to my thigh.

I looked over my shoulder one last time. Sheriff Delgado, Lieutenant Leffelman, and Major Hilden stood on the concrete parking pad near the trailhead while technicians from St. Louis County piloted their department's massive drone from the back of a mobile command vehicle on the road. The drone had twelve rotors and could carry up to a hundred and ten pounds for forty-five minutes. Today, its payload included an infrared camera system and a radio relay that would allow our team to communicate even deep in the hills.

Besides the drone, I had twelve officers in tactical gear watching my back from various positions in the woods. Hopefully the Weavers weren't stupid enough to shoot at me.

Delgado nodded at me and mouthed "good luck." I nodded my thanks and turned around to walk as my radio crackled to life.

"Can you hear me, Detective Court?"

I didn't recognize the technician's voice, but that didn't matter. I reached into my pocket for my walkie-talkie.

"Yep. You're coming through."

"Good. We've got the drone at five hundred feet. With our current payload, we've got forty minutes of flight time remaining. I'll let you know if we see movement ahead of you."

I keyed my walkie-talkie's microphone.

"Understood. Thank you."

I put my radio back in my pocket and continued walking. The Weavers lived on a picturesque piece of property, but if Xavier Becker was right, they had studded it with lethal traps. With that knowledge, every muscle in my body felt tight and ready to spring. I had already walked the trail once and knew it was clear, but every step our team members made in the woods could have been their last. They'd be as careful as they could, but they were putting their lives in danger for me.

After five minutes, my radio crackled once more.

"Joe, we've got movement from the compound. You'll have company momentarily."

As I opened my mouth to respond, I heard the deep thumping noise of a helicopter's rotor somewhere distant, but I couldn't see the aircraft through the trees. St. Augustine County was a hundred and fifty miles from the nearest army base and sixty miles from St. Louis. Helicopters didn't fly here to check the traffic. More than likely, there was a medical emergency somewhere.

"Are Andy and Shane both coming, or is it just one of them?"

"Just one."

I nodded. "Understood. Thanks for the heads up."

I walked again, but with every step, the sound of the helicopter grew louder and louder. It should have just flown right over me, but it hadn't. It was slowing down. I pulled out my radio.

"Who's in the helicopter?"

I waited a moment. The tree line had already thinned, which meant I was only a couple hundred yards from the Weavers' compound. If they had a rifle with a decent scope, they could shoot me before I even knew where they were.

"We're working on that. Standby."

I stopped walking and shook my head.

"If Andy and Shane think that's us, it'll spook them. They'll shoot me instead of talking."

Again, it took the radio operator a moment to reply. The helicopter had come so close to the trees above me that I had to press my radio against my ear to hear anything.

"It's not one of ours," said the technician.

I opened my mouth to respond, but then I heard a scuffle over the radio and Sheriff Delgado's voice came through.

"The helicopter is beneath our drone, and it's dropping rappelling ropes. I'm pulling my team back. Get to cover, Detective. We've got unknown contacts moving in."

***

Tara felt almost proud as Scarlett kicked her feet in the air. The baby's breath was still fast, and she didn't eat well, but breast milk had done her well. Feeding the little girl had done Tara well, too. She missed her boys, but she knew Wesley would take care of them. Nothing about her situation was normal or fine, but feeding and taking care of Scarlett had grounded her. It had given her a purpose and reason to keep going. This little girl depended on her. As long as Tara could breathe, she'd keep her safe. That was her promise.

She put a finger on Scarlett's palm and then smiled as the little girl wrapped her fingers around it. It was just what should have happened.

"Time to play on your tummy," she said in a singsong voice. Scarlett didn't respond, but that didn't stop Tara from turning her over. The baby squirmed and fussed. For a moment, her back flexed as she tried to lift her head. "It's okay, sweetheart. You're doing well."

"She's not doing shit," said Shane from the couch.

"She's a newborn. This is how they exercise," said Tara, not taking her eyes from the baby. Scarlett's face had already grown red, and she had closed her eyes. She'd scream soon, but until then Tara would keep her on her belly. "As long as she's with me, I'll do the same for her I'd do for my own kids. I'm taking care of her."

Shane scoffed. "Better you than me."

She couldn't agree with that more. Scarlett's soft whimpers turned to full-throated screams within moments, so Tara picked her up and put her on her shoulder so she could rub her back.

"It's okay, sweetie," she whispered. "You did well."

This time, Shane said nothing. A beer sat on a rickety end table beside him. Tara and Scarlett were on the ground. Scarlett hadn't eaten well earlier, so Tara's breasts still felt full. She'd have to pump, but she'd put it off as long as she could. She was tired of her breasts being Shane's afternoon entertainment.

She looked at him and then stood to carry the baby to the Pack 'n Play they were using as a crib.

"When does Scarlett get to go home?"

Shane narrowed his eyes. "You worry about keeping her alive. Andy and I will worry about taking her home."

His voice sounded angrier than normal. Tara swallowed hard.

"Her family isn't cooperating, are they?" she asked. "You're trying to ransom her, but they're not willing to pay."

Shane took a big swig of beer and then pointed to her with his index finger.

"You know what your problem is?" he asked. Tara said nothing, knowing he'd tell her no matter what she said. "You don't know your place. Women like you never do."

Had his opinion meant anything to her, she might have tried to argue with him. Instead, she nodded.

"Okay."

"Okay?" he asked, screwing up his face. "What does that mean?"

"I don't know, Shane," she said, shaking her head and shrugging. "What do you think it means?"

He took another swig of beer.

"If you didn't have to take care of that baby, I'd put your lights out."

"Let us go," she said. "If Scarlett's family isn't willing to negotiate, she's more trouble to you than she's worth. Let me take her. We'll go to the hospital, and I'll say a family I work with brought me her. We can say they found her alongside the road or something. I'm a rural health-care worker. The police will believe me."

He snickered. "And I'm sure you'd forget all about me and Andy."

"If you forget all about me, I might," she said. "You and your brother could go down to Mexico. You could make a good living there as security guards."

He put his beer down and leaned forward.

"I ain't interested in making a living," he said. "I'm here to get rich."

She nodded, but before she could say anything, the trailer door opened. Andy walked in.

"Get your rifle, bro," he said. "That lady detective's walking down the trail. She's got a backpack."

"She alone?" asked Shane.

"So far."

Shane nodded and looked to Tara. "You scream, you and the baby die."

"I know the drill," said Tara. "And I've heard your threats. I'll keep Scarlett quiet."

"You'd better," said Andy. He turned and left the trailer. Shane stayed inside and stared at her. Then he finished his beer and tilted the empty bottle toward her.

"You want one?"

"No, thank you," she said.

"Your loss," he said, standing and walking toward the kitchen. Then, he stopped and cocked his head to the side and looked at her. "You hear that?"

"I don't hear anything."

He blinked but said nothing. Then he narrowed his eyes.

"Almost sounds like a helicopter."

Tara sat straighter, sizing the opportunity. It was probably an air ambulance or a rich guy going home to St. Louis, but she could use this all the same.

"I bet it's the police coming to rescue me. Better say your prayers, Shane."

Shane grunted and then walked to the back bedroom, where he picked up a black assault rifle from his bed.

"You try to escape, I'll shoot you in the back."

"Sure," said Tara. Shane looked torn for a moment, but then he ripped the door open and stepped outside.

"Andy, we've got incoming," he shouted. He slammed the trailer door and locked the latch outside, sealing her in. Tara rubbed Scarlett's back to keep her calm, already hurrying toward the bathroom. She had thought staying was her best chance to stay alive and to keep her family alive, but now she knew that if she stayed, she was dead. In the bathroom, she grabbed a towel and wrapped it around her left fist. Andy and Shane thought they were smart for nailing their windows shut, but they hadn't put up bars. This was her chance.

She went to the bedroom, stood on the bed, and punched the glass as hard as she could. The window broke but not cleanly. She hit it a second and then a third time, clearing the shards of glass from the windowpane. Then she unwound the towel from her hand.

The sound of the helicopter grew louder and louder. She stuck her head out the window. She couldn't see her captors, but their barn was twenty yards away. If she could reach it, she could run out the back to the woods. Then she could double back and head toward the parking pad near the road. She could make it. She looked down at the baby, who was already falling asleep.

"We're getting out of here, Scarlett. You hold tight."

Then she heard the first gunshot.

# Chapter 35

I didn't know what Delgado meant by unknown contacts, but it didn't matter. I shot my eyes around the woods. The ground around me looked undisturbed, but the Weavers could have dug it up months or years ago and allowed the vegetation to grow right over any traps they'd set. I didn't have any cover at all on the trail.

I tiptoed west to a big silver maple tree with a trunk big enough to give me some cover. The thwap of the helicopter's blades cutting through the air drowned out any noise around me. My heart thumped against my chest. Xavier didn't know what traps his uncles had setup, but he had emphasized how dangerous they were. By the time I reached the tree, the helicopter hovered two or three hundred yards away.

"Boss, what's going on?"

My radio crackled.

"We don't know," said Delgado. "We're trying to get the drone close enough to the helicopter to see its registration number, but they've got a door gunner who keeps pointing a weapon at us as soon as we fly close."

I furrowed my brow.

"What kind of helicopter has a door gunner?"

"It's a Black Hawk. The Army uses them."

I closed my eyes and shook my head. "Why is it here, then?"

"We're working on that, Joe. You just stay behind cover. Most of our team is back at the parking pad. Everybody's safe. You're the one we're worried about, so we've got you on camera. We'll keep watching as long as we can."

I nodded. "They find any traps out here, or was Xavier exaggerating?"

"Kid wasn't kidding," said Delgado. "We found about a dozen holes full of punji sticks. Would have killed you if you had fallen on them."

I drew in a breath and nodded. "So I can't run back through the woods."

"Stay put."

The moment Delgado finished speaking, a gunshot rang out. It was close. I pressed my back hard against the tree and held my breath, every muscle in my body tense. No shots more followed, but men shouted.

"What's going on?"

Delgado hesitated. "One of the Weavers shot at the helicopter. It banked hard, and somebody fell out the door. Guys are rappelling out now. This is about to get ugly."

The moment he finished speaking, more gunshots rang out. They were slow at first, but then it sounded as if we were at a firing range. The helicopter lifted from the ground, and the treetops calmed. Occasionally, a round would zip through the woods around me and thwack into the ground. Every muscle in my body told me to run, but I couldn't. Though they weren't aiming at me, the gunfire had pinned me down. My lungs felt tight, and I squeezed the walkie-talkie until my knuckles turned white.

"What do I do here, George?"

I waited half a minute, but he didn't respond. I repeated the question. Then my radio crackled. Somebody might have said something, but I couldn't hear it over the sound of something heavy crashing into a tree above me. It was the drone, and it slammed into a walnut tree hard enough to shake the whole thing. Then it ricocheted against another tree before slamming into the ground with a deep thump. My radio went dead.

I took a breath. Since I didn't need the walkie-talkie anymore, I tossed it to the ground and unholstered my firearm. I didn't know who was in the helicopter or what their intentions were, which meant I needed to be prepared for hostility if they came toward me.

The gunfire stayed steady for almost five minutes. Men shouted, but I didn't know what they said. Then, the world quieted. I crept around the tree, but I couldn't see the compound through the forest. I did, though, see somebody hurrying down the trail. She was stooped, and she carried something in her arms. Every few feet, she looked behind her.

It was Tara Madison, and she had the baby.

I wanted to call out to her, but a rifle cracked before I could. The round slammed into a tree somewhere to my left. I couldn't recognize the shooter from my position, but he was about a hundred yards away. If I'd had a rifle, I could have hit him easily. If I fired my pistol at a hundred yards, though, the round would drop a good foot before it hit the target, and even the slightest breeze could blow it to the left or right.

The shooter's rifle cracked again. This time, he didn't miss. The round slammed into Tara's back with a puff of blood. She stumbled and fell forward but braced the baby. The little girl screamed, and the rifleman fired again. The round hit the dirt near her feet. Tara crawled forward. My heart thudded against my rib cage. I held my breath, hoping to slow it down, as I dropped to a knee and lined up my shot.

The guy with the rifle fired again. This time, the round hit Tara in the lower back, or maybe her rear end. She and the baby both would die unless I did something. I held my breath as I took the slack from my trigger. My heartbeat slowed; I counted, adjusting my aim so I'd at least have a chance of hitting him.

Then I squeezed the trigger.

I missed, but the guy with the rifle dove to the ground and then scurried toward a nearby tree trunk for cover. I fired again. The round hit the tree in a shower of bark. My shot was dialed in, but a pool of blood had already spread beneath Tara. Without a radio, I couldn't even call this in.

"Can you hear me, Tara?"

She turned her head toward me. Her face was pale. Her lips moved, but no sound came out. She was dying, and I couldn't hear the baby. She should have been crying. I darted my eyes around, but I was alone.

"George!" I shouted. "I'm pinned down and need help now."

"Stay down."

I didn't recognize the voice, but it wasn't Sheriff Delgado. A moment later, six tactical police officers in black gear sprinted up the trail from the parking pad. The bad guy with the rifle opened fire, forcing the tactical team to scatter to the trees for cover. The point man looked as if he had gotten hit, but I couldn't tell. He had a whole team behind him, though, so his health wasn't my immediate concern.

I waited until the bad guy ducked behind his tree to reload. Then I holstered my firearm.

"I'm coming out. Don't shoot me," I yelled, already running toward Tara. This time, I didn't bother stepping gingerly. I didn't care about the traps. I just ran. Tara didn't move, but she looked alive. The baby in her arms cried. I reached beneath her for the newborn. The little girl struggled and cried, tearing at my heartstrings. With the baby in one arm, I grabbed Tara's shirt with the other and pulled her off the trail, hoping I could get behind a tree before the shooting started again.

Then I felt the round hit me in the back.

Pain exploded across my rib cage and into my side. I dropped to my knees, unable to draw in a breath. Then another round hit me, this one between my shoulder blades. I fell forward, gasping. I wrapped my arms around the baby to protect her. My lungs wouldn't inflate. Round after round whizzed past me as my team returned fire.

Unfortunately, everybody had guns, and the Weavers knew how to use them. While our tactical team had extensive training, they were police officers first and foremost. When they started their days, they were patrol officers and detectives. Tactical work wasn't their specialty. The Weavers understood controlled violence, and we had stepped into their homes.

They used our team's gunfire to pinpoint their locations and returned fire in controlled, three-shot bursts. One of our guys went down. Then a second fell. I saw it as it happened. Both looked as if they wore bulletproof vests, but rounds still could have broken through. As the rest of the team fell back, Andy Weaver sprinted through the woods toward me. I reached for my weapon and felt muscles, tendons, and skin all over my body scream in pain. I was hurt, but I ignored it and lifted my pistol to shoot.

Weaver was too fast, though. He stomped on my hand just as I began to squeeze the trigger. My weapon dropped, and he kicked me in the face, causing my vision to flash white. Hot, salty blood filled my mouth. Everything hurt so much I could barely process what was happening until I felt him tug at my arms.

He was trying to get the baby.

I tried to fight him and claw at his hands and arms, but my body wouldn't listen to my brain. The little girl cried as he wrenched her from my grip. I grabbed his ankle, but he kicked free. Then he stomped on my chest and sprinted away. I couldn't breathe or move.

Moments later, the trees around me shook, and the helicopter that had started this mess flew overhead. Within seconds, it disappeared. I heard nothing. I couldn't even hear the baby crying.

"Joe!"

It was Sheriff Delgado. I lifted my head and tried to sit up, but it hurt so much I dropped back to the ground.

"We're here. We need help."

Within seconds, I found an entire tactical team hovering around me.

"We've got casualties," shouted one of the team members. "Get the back brace. We need ambulances."

Before I could say anything, one of the tactical team members unbuckled my vest and pulled it away from my chest.

"Rounds didn't go through your vest, so you're not bleeding," he said. "Can you move?"

I tried sitting up again. It felt like someone had just stabbed me, so I leaned back down.

"I'm hurt, but I can breathe," I said. "Check on Tara."

"We're already carrying her away," he said, feeling along my rib cage. As he prodded, I gasped. "That hurt?"

"Yes."

"Good news is that your ribs don't feel broken, and nothing's penetrated your skin," he said. "Our first ambulance is taking Tara to the ER, but a second ambulance is coming for you."

I shook my head and tried to sit up again. The tactical officer held me to the ground.

"Don't move," he said. "You're just going to make it hurt worse. You could have a spinal injury."

I nodded and closed my eyes. "What happened, and where are the Weavers?"

He looked around and shook his head. "I don't have a clue."

# Chapter 36

I didn't think I had injured my spine, but six officers from the Highway Patrol carried me out of the woods on a back brace anyway. It felt excessive. My ribs and back ached, but my vest had stopped both rounds from penetrating my skin. I'd take some Tylenol and be just fine.

At least that was what I thought until the ambulance pulled onto the gravel road.

The paramedics had strapped me onto a padded gurney, but every bump and jostle brought pained tears to my eyes. The EMT sitting with me in the back offered me narcotic pain relievers, but I told him no. After what had happened, somebody would need to interview me, and I didn't want to feel inebriated. More than that, though, I didn't want the drugs to dull my temper.

Feeling Andy Weaver rip that little girl from my hands had stoked in me something I hadn't felt in a very long time. Scarlett was innocent. She couldn't even lift her head on her own yet. Nothing in Heaven or Hell would keep me from finding her.

We reached the hospital about twenty painful minutes later. The doctors knew I was coming, so they ushered me into a private room for an exam. The moment I pulled my shirt off, the nurse nodded and walked around me. Then she opened the linen closet to expose the mirror attached to its door. I flinched as I saw the purple welts on my ribs and the bruise on my cheek. I looked as if I had been in a car accident.

After feeling my ribs and asking about what had happened, she covered me with a warm blanket and told me to lie down. The doctor came in about fifteen minutes later and checked out my side and back. He also flashed a light in my eyes and asked if I were dizzy or disoriented. He was checking for a concussion, which I didn't think I had. The last time I had a concussion, my ears had rung, I had felt nauseated and dizzy, and I couldn't remember what had happened to me. Physically, I felt as if I had run into a wall at full speed, but mentally, I felt fine.

The doctors didn't think I had any broken ribs, but they warned me there could have been fractures they couldn't see on the X-rays. If I felt short of breath or if my pain got worse, they told me, I should come back to the hospital. They also told me to take it easy for at least a week. I doubted that would happen, but I thanked them anyway.

Two hours after the ambulance brought me through the front door, Trisha Marshall, our dispatcher, drove me back to the station so I could pick up my car. I needed to write a report, but I hurt too much to sit down for that long.

Instead, I drove home. Roy wagged his tail and licked my hands and then my face as soon as he saw me, which was nice. I ran a hand along his back. He expected to go for a walk, but climbing the stairs to my porch hurt too much for me to even consider it. I needed a break for the night, so I let Roy run around in the backyard, while I went inside, downed some ibuprofen, drew a bath, and soaked until the water turned lukewarm.

The dog and I sat on the couch together afterward. He put his head in my lap, and I petted him as I called my mom. Even as Mom and I spoke, I found my mind drifting back to Scarlett Nolan. Negotiation had been our best shot of getting her back. Now, we didn't know where she was; we didn't know her condition; we didn't even know who had her anymore. For all we knew, Andy and Shane had passed her off to someone else. Or they might have even killed her.

I had blown it. It was as simple as that. I couldn't control that helicopter or the men it carried, but I had her in my arms. Then Andy Weaver had taken her from me. Because of me, because I wasn't strong enough or smart enough to fight Andy off, Scarlett could die. Hell, for all I knew, Tara Madison had died on my watch, too.

I should have brought a rifle with me. I was certified with an M4 carbine. If I had carried one with me, I could have shot Andy Weaver's balls off at five hundred yards. When we were planning this, Delgado even suggested I carry a rifle, too. He said I could sling it over my shoulder along with the backpack, but I thought it would look too aggressive. I thought Andy and Shane would see the rifle and assume I was there to fight, rather than listen to what I had to say.

That's what bothered me the most, I think. This wasn't a failure of ability: It was a failure of judgment. I screwed up, and the bad guys got away. They took a baby because of me.

Mom and I spoke for about half an hour, but whenever she tried to steer the conversation to my day, I steered it back elsewhere. She knew something had happened, but I didn't tell her what. She didn't need to hear how I had screwed up.

Once I hung up with Mom, I hobbled to the kitchen and got a bottle of vodka out of the freezer. I poured myself a stiff drink and carried it back to the couch. When Roy saw me, his tail thumped against a throw pillow, and I petted his back.

"I'm glad you're here, sweetheart," I said, scratching behind his ear. "I've had a shitty day. I need a friend."

\*\*\*

I got to work at eight the next morning. As had become usual in the past couple of weeks, trucks and trailers full of construction equipment and tools filled the parking lot, so I had to park about a block away. With every step I took, my back and sides ached. A pair of construction workers gave me sideways glances as I walked past them—probably because of the bruise on my cheek—but neither said anything. When I got inside, I went straight to the second-floor conference room. Trisha was just getting set up for the day, but she smiled when she saw me.

"Hey, Joe," she said, giving me the same soft voice my mother had when I spoke to her last night. "How are you feeling?"

"Better than yesterday," I said. "Where's the boss?"

"In his office with Shaun Deveraux. There are two other men with them. They came in with Deveraux. Delgado told me to send you up when you came in."

The prosecutor wouldn't have brought people to the sheriff's office without good reason, so I thanked her and walked. Yesterday, I had nearly gasped with every step. I felt better already, but I took a few more minutes than usual to cross the building and reach Delgado's office.

As Trisha had said, Shaun Deveraux was inside with the sheriff. They sat across from two older men in dark suits at the conference table near the far window. When I opened the door, Delgado nodded and waved me over.

"Morning, Joe," he said. "Come on in. We'll get started now."

The sheriff pulled out a seat beside him, so I sat down. Shaun Deveraux smiled at me.

"How are you feeling, Detective?"

"I've been better."

Deveraux looked to the strangers.

"One of the Weavers shot Detective Court multiple times yesterday. Thankfully, her bulletproof vest prevented the rounds from killing her."

I looked at Deveraux's guests with fresh eyes. The one on the left wore a black suit, crisp white shirt, and black tie. He could have been a lawyer. The man on the right wore a tailored charcoal gray suit jacket, white shirt, and green tie. Several days' worth of stubble covered his chin, leaving him with a rugged look that contrasted with his straight teeth. He was handsome, but he had the black eyes of a snake. He looked like an actor typecast to play the villain in an action movie.

"I'm glad you're still alive, miss," he said.

"And who are you?"

"Gerald Nolan," he said, his voice as flat and cold as his eyes. "I appreciate that you were trying to help my granddaughter yesterday."

I nodded and laced my fingers together before leaning forward.

"I'm very sorry I wasn't able to save her," I said. "Before we continue, remind me what you do for a living, Mr. Nolan."

"I manage a small private security firm."

"It's more like a private army you rent out, isn't it?" I asked. "That's what I hear."

He blinked but said nothing.

"Do you have helicopters, Mr. Nolan?"

This time, the man in the black suit beside him spoke.

"We're here as a courtesy at the request of Mr. Deveraux. If you have questions about Mr. Nolan's business, please ask them in a more appropriate venue."

"Did you order the helicopter out there yesterday?" asked Delgado.

"We never intended to interfere with a police investigation," said Nolan.

I lowered my chin. "You didn't answer the sheriff's question."

This time, neither Nolan nor his lawyer answered. I looked to Deveraux.

"What are we charging him with?"

"We're still figuring that out," said Deveraux. "The situation's complex. The helicopter and its crew flew away before we could find out who they were. Unfortunately, they flew so low the airport in St. Louis couldn't track them on radar. There aren't many Black Hawk helicopters in civilian hands, though. Correct me if I'm wrong, but Nolan Systems owns a training facility near the Mark Twain National Forest, right? That's fifty miles from here."

Nolan looked to his attorney, sighed, and then stood.

"I'm not interested in answering your questions. My granddaughter has a congenital heart defect. Without surgery, she will die. That's why she was leaving the hospital the day she was abducted. We were taking her to the Texas Children's Hospital in Houston because they have the best pediatric cardiology department in the country. I lost my wife to cancer many years ago, and I lost my son to the people who abducted his daughter. Scarlett is the only family I have left. There's nothing I wouldn't do to save her life. Please stay out of my way."

He and the lawyer started to leave, so I looked to Deveraux and then Delgado.

"We're letting them go?" I whispered.

Delgado waited until they left the room to speak.

"We don't have enough to charge him with anything at the moment."

"And even if we did," said Deveraux, cutting in, "we don't have the resources to prosecute him. I've got two lawyers and a paralegal in my office. His company has an entire firm's worth of attorneys on staff. Even if we charged him with a crime, it would cost us millions to prosecute him."

I clenched my jaw and shook my head before speaking.

"I don't accept that," I said. "He's rich, but that doesn't mean he can do whatever the hell he wants and get away with it. I could have died yesterday. For all we know, his granddaughter's dead. That's on him. Is Tara Madison alive today?"

Delgado nodded. "They airlifted her to Barnes-Jewish Hospital in St. Louis yesterday. She was in surgery for almost five hours, but they stopped the bleeding and fished out the bullets from her back. As I understand it, her long-term prognosis is uncertain, but she's alive and stable for now."

"That's Gerald Nolan's fault," I said. "If his goons hadn't flown in, I could have negotiated her release."

"Maybe, but maybe not," said Delgado. "We can't change what happened. We can only deal with the future. We need to find his granddaughter. Any ideas how we do that?"

I swore under my breath before opening my mouth to answer.

"Not a one."

# Chapter 37

I shuffled to the break room for a cup of coffee to give myself a few minutes to think. Shane and Andy Weaver had Scarlett Nolan. Tara Madison might know where they'd go, but she'd be on so many painkillers she wouldn't be able to tell us anything. Not only that, her doctors wouldn't let me question her until she was stronger. Tara's son Xavier knew Shane and Andy pretty well. We'd talk to him, but I doubted he knew anything. To find Shane and Andy, we needed somebody involved in the crime.

I took my coffee and went back to Sheriff Delgado's office. He and Deveraux were still inside, but neither looked hopeful. The sheriff nodded as I sat at the conference table.

"We've got a manhunt," he said. "I've put out an APB to every law enforcement agency within five hundred miles. Every uniformed officer in the state has seen Shane and Andy Weaver's pictures. If these boys show up anywhere in Missouri, Tennessee, Arkansas, Kansas, or Illinois, we'll find them. I'll also call the US Marshals in Cape Girardeau. We'll use every resource we've got, but Shane and Andy are good old boys. They know these hills better than we do, and they've got a lot of friends willing to hide them. We'll find them, but it'll take time."

"Time's the one thing we don't have," I said. "Scarlett Nolan could die if we don't find these assholes. We need to be creative."

Delgado crossed his arms. "Sounds like you've got a bee in your bonnet."

"We need to talk to Reuben Terepocki. Becker hired Jay Pischke to set up a safe house for him to store the Nolan girl. Reuben shot him. He's the only guy we've got connected to this thing."

Delgado considered. "You think Reuben's involved in the abduction?"

"I don't know, but he's alive, and everyone else is dead or missing. I'll talk to him. You can talk to Shane and Andy's friends."

Deveraux sighed. "If he asks for a lawyer, you've got to back off."

"Last time I saw him, he threatened me. Something tells me he's not going to want witnesses for this conversation."

Both Deveraux and Delgado straightened.

"What did he say to you?" asked Deveraux.

"Nothing I could arrest him for," I said. "But it was a threat. This is personal for him, and I plan to use that."

"You want somebody to go with you?" asked Delgado.

"No. If anybody else goes with me, he'll clam up. He doesn't trust me, but he's pissed off enough to talk. I'm going to let him."

Neither Delgado nor Deveraux seemed convinced, but I didn't care. I knew what I could do. I'd find Scarlett even if I had to break every bone in Reuben's body to do it. The sheriff wished me luck and told me to call him if I ran into problems.

I got Reuben's address from Trisha and headed out. My former partner lived downtown in a two-story red brick Federalist row house with an exposed limestone foundation. Stone dentil molding accentuated the roofline, while brick arches above the windows contributed to the home's attractive facade.

I parked out front beside his car and took the steps to his small porch. The front door opened before I could even knock. Reuben wore dark jeans and an orange polo shirt. Several days' worth of stubble grew on his chin. He scowled, crossed his arms, and leaned against the doorframe.

"What do you want, Joe?"

"We need to talk."

He closed his eyes and sighed before taking a step back.

"Call my lawyer," he said, shutting his door. I put my foot in the jamb to stop him.

"I'm trying to find a little girl. She has a congenital heart defect and will die unless we find her. She was abducted from a hospital in St. Louis. The people who abducted her hired

Jay Pischke to set up a safe house for her. You shot him in that safe house. I need to know everything you know about Jay Pischke."

His face softened some.

"I heard you got shot yesterday. You sure you should be walking around?"

"My doctors told me to take it easy," I said. "This is me taking it easy. Did you know you were walking into a safe house when you went to visit Jay?"

"No."

"Good," I said, nodding. "Why'd you visit him? And please be honest. I'm not here to jam you up. I'm here to find information that could help me find a sick infant."

He held my gaze for a moment before looking down.

"Jay Pischke was a violent son of a bitch with a mean streak. I went to his house because I heard he had been flashing cash around town. Someone needed to keep an eye on him."

"Tell me about the fight at Club Serenity."

Reuben clenched his jaw tight enough that I could see the muscles work beneath his cheeks. Then he shook his head.

"Don't go there, Joe."

"It's on video. I know you got into a fight," I said. "What was it about?"

He brought his hands up to his face and rubbed his eyes. Then he sighed.

"It's personal and stupid."

I nodded. "If you don't want to talk about Pischke, tell me about Shelby McAllen."

For just a split second, he stopped breathing. Then his eyes flicked to mine. Reuben had interviewed thousands of people over the years. He knew how to disrupt my momentum in an interview and what to say to throw me off a line of inquiry. He couldn't hide that kind of reaction, though. I had gotten Shelby's name from a stripper at Club Serenity. She said Shelby and Reuben had been close. I didn't believe her at first, but now I knew she hadn't lied. Shelby had been important to him.

Reuben drew in a slow breath.

"How do you know that name?"

"One of her co-workers told me to ask about her," I said. "She said you liked her."

He considered me and then snickered.

"Liked her?" he asked, shaking his head. "I loved that girl with everything I had. She was my daughter."

My back straightened.

"Oh."

He smiled just a little.

"She would have liked you. Shelby didn't put up with bullshit, either."

A pit grew in my stomach. When I had heard Shelby's name for the first time and learned that she and Reuben were close, I thought I had found a piece of leverage I could use to pry more information out of him. His tone of voice told me I had stumbled on something profound.

"Where's your daughter now?"

When he looked up at me, I noticed that his eyes were bloodshot and his lip trembled.

"She died three weeks ago in St. Louis. It was a drug overdose."

The pit in my stomach grew.

"I'm sorry," I said. "I didn't know."

Neither of us spoke for almost thirty seconds. Then he stepped back and motioned for me to follow him. We walked down a hall to a dated but functional eat-in kitchen at the back of the house. He plopped down on a chair at a scarred oak table.

"You want some coffee?"

"Sure," I said. He nodded toward a coffee maker on the other side of the room. Mugs hung on a wooden rack. I poured two cups and walked back to the table to sit across from him. Then I reached into my purse and showed him the recording app on my cell phone. He nodded, so I hit the record button and set it on the table between us. "If I had known Shelby was your daughter, I wouldn't have brought her up. I'm sorry."

He waved away my concern.

"I was a shit father," he said. "Her mom and I broke up when she was a baby, so I didn't see her a lot when she was young. I was married to the job. You know what that's like."

I swallowed hard and nodded.

"I guess I do."

He grunted. "Yeah, well, when Shelby was seventeen, she got pregnant. She and her mom had a big fight, and her mom kicked her out. Shelby tried to live with me for a while, but I didn't know how to raise a pregnant teenager. She ran away two days before her eighteenth birthday. I tracked her down and found her at a friend's house. Then she ran away again, and I tracked her down again. After she gave birth and put the baby up for adoption, she ran away a third time."

He paused and looked at his coffee cup.

"She called some, so I knew she was alive, but she never told me where she was. I didn't try to find her. I figured she could handle things herself. Then she stopped calling."

I sipped my coffee. It was lukewarm, but that was okay. I didn't want coffee. I wanted to give him a moment.

"How'd she end up in St. Augustine?"

"I don't know," he said. "Her mom called me about a year ago and said Shelby was here and that she was struggling. I came to see her, and I found her working at Club Serenity. Conroy was pimping her out. She told me it was her choice, but that's not the life I wanted for my little girl. I was still her father."

"Is she why you moved here?"

He nodded. "I thought if I was close to her, I could help her. She was an adult, so I didn't want to interfere with her life, but I didn't stop being a dad because she grew up."

"And she was okay with that?"

"Not at first, but I think she accepted me," he said. "About a month ago, she told me she wanted to quit working for Conroy." He paused. "She wanted to go to college and become a nurse like her mom. When she told me that, I looked her right in the eye and said I'd make it happen. I lied right to my baby girl's face."

I wanted to check my phone and make sure it was recording this, but I didn't dare move.

"How did you lie to her?"

"I knew Conroy would never let her go. I tried talking to him. I even offered him money—ten grand cash. A week later, she died of a drug overdose in north St. Louis."

I softened my voice. "Could it be an accident? It's not uncommon to find young women in her position addicted to illegal drugs."

He ran a hand across his face and shook his head.

"My daughter didn't shoot heroin," he said. "Like I said, I was a shit father. I took hair samples from her comb and had Darlene run a hair follicle drug test. It wouldn't hold up in court, but I didn't care. Darlene didn't even find traces of THC. Shelby wasn't on anything. She wanted a new life. She wouldn't have driven to St. Louis to try heroin for the first time. Conroy killed my baby girl."

If that was true, I'd make sure he got a needle in his arm for it. We'd talk about that later, though.

"Tell me about Jay Pischke."

Reuben sighed and looked to the table.

"Pischke was Conroy's pit bull. When Conroy had a problem with somebody, or if a dancer stepped out of line, Pischke took care of it."

"Is that why you fought with him?"

Reuben shook his head. "No. I got into a fight with him because he wouldn't let me see Conroy. He thought I was there to punch his boss's ticket, but I wasn't. St. Louis police hadn't even told me she was dead yet. I figured Conroy might know where she was. Pischke took a swing at me, and I fought back."

I'd have to investigate to confirm the story, but I nodded anyway.

"Why did you visit Pischke at the meth lab?"

Reuben drew in a deep breath and let it out slowly before speaking. He wouldn't look me in the eye.

"A couple of days after Shelby died, I heard a rumor that Pischke was flashing around a lot of cash he got for doing a job. He killed my baby. That was his payment."

I closed my eyes and shook my head.

"You stupid bastard."

"Pischke was a murderer," he said. "He deserved it."

"That wasn't your call to make, and that money wasn't for killing your daughter," I said. I squeezed my jaw tight and counted to five. "Thomas Becker gave him that money to set up a safe house where he and his buddies could hide while trying to ransom Scarlett Nolan to her family. Pischke may have been bad news, but he didn't kill your daughter."

Reuben shook his head.

"You're wrong, Joe," he said. "He killed Shelby. He told me right before I shot him."

"Jesus, Reuben," I said. "You should have arrested him. Hell, you could have called me, and I would have arrested him. That's our job. We're not vigilantes."

"That's *your* job," he said. "Jay Pischke murdered my baby because she had the guts to refuse to sell herself and make his boss rich."

I covered my mouth with my hand and stared at him for a moment. If someone had hurt Audrey, my sister, I would have wanted to kill him, too. That didn't make it right, though. I closed my eyes and swallowed the lump in my throat.

"Reuben Terepocki, you're under arrest for the murder of Jay Pischke. I'm sorry."

Reuben's lips cracked into a thin smile. "Don't be sorry. Putting that motherfucker down was the only right choice I've ever made as a father. I did my job. You should be proud to do yours. Congratulations. You closed a murder."

I balled my hands into fists and gritted my teeth as I shook my head.

"I'm sorry Shelby's dead, but don't pretend this had anything to do with her," I said, feeling heat begin to spread through my chest and to my neck and face. "You murdered

Pischke because it made you feel good. Because of you, I might not be able to find an infant who was ripped from her mother's arms. I used to think you were a good detective. I even looked up to you. Now I'm ashamed of you.

"Stand up but keep your hands flat on the table, Mr. Terepocki. I'll pat you down for weapons, and I'll call in uniformed officers to take you to jail."

He narrowed his eyes.

"After that speech, you don't even have the guts to drive me downtown yourself? And you think I'm the shameful one? You've got a lot to learn, honey."

"Whatever I've got to learn, you're not the one to teach me," I said. "Now shut up. I've got more important things to worry about than you."

# Chapter 38

Officers Selena Martelle and Carrie Bowen picked up Reuben about five minutes after I called my station. I locked his door and followed them out a few minutes later. When I went to Reuben's house, I had hoped to find something that would help me find the Nolan baby. Instead, I had closed a homicide. I wished I had just called in sick that morning.

When I got to my station, I walked to Delgado's office to tell him what had happened and get an update on his search. While I was arresting Reuben, our uniformed officers had rounded up a couple of Shane and Andy's friends. Delgado and Sergeant Bob Reitz planned to talk to them. Bob was a good interviewer, and Delgado—despite his many faults—wasn't a slouch, either. They'd do fine.

I spent the rest of the day filling out paperwork and shoring up my investigation into Reuben. At four in the afternoon, I walked to the courthouse to see the prosecutor and present my findings. Deveraux listened and took notes. Then he congratulated me for taking a bad cop off the streets. It didn't feel like a day for congratulations, though; it felt like a day to get drunk.

At a little after five, I drove home. I felt sick to my stomach. Tara Madison had kept that baby alive, but now she was clinging to life in the hospital, my old partner was sitting in a jail cell awaiting an arraignment hearing, and I was at home without a clue of what to do next.

Roy greeted me as soon as I went to the backyard. His tail wagged so hard it looked like a propeller on his hindquarters, and he almost seemed to grin at me. I let him out of the dog run, scratched his ears, and knelt in front of him. He licked my face, so I pushed him back.

"Hey, boy," I said. "You want to get drunk with me?"

His tail wagged harder, so I scratched his cheek. As much as I wanted to forget my problems, I instead went to my room and changed into some leggings and a sports bra. I ran through the woods until my legs burned. The constant jostling made my ribs and back ache, but I forced myself to ignore it. I probably deserved some pain.

About halfway through my run, I stopped in the woods and leaned against a tree. My sweat had glued tiny particles of dust and dirt to my face, while my hair had trapped twigs and God only knew what else. My chest felt heavy but not from exertion. When I blinked, I almost had tears in my eyes. If I brought my arms to my chest, I could almost feel Scarlett squirming against me—just as she had when Andy took her from me.

My legs gave out, and I slid to the ground. I tried to hold it back, but my lower lip trembled. Death was part of my job. I didn't see it every day, but I saw it often enough that I thought I had become numb to it. Scarlett was a baby, though. Death shouldn't have known her. She should have been at home, wrapped up in a blanket and held in her mother's arms. Instead, she was being held hostage for money.

I stayed at that tree long enough for the sun to grow low and the shadows to grow long. I walked home in twilight. It was a beautiful night, but the gorgeous sunset had done little to ease the heartache I felt for a child I had barely even met.

When I reached the house, Roy bowed in front of me.

"You hungry?" I asked, my voice flat and devoid of emotion. "Come on. Let's go in."

I fed the dog and made sure he had some water. Then I took a long shower. I wanted to drink and keep going until I didn't care about the world anymore, but I needed to stay sober in case something happened in the night. As I put a frozen pizza in the oven for dinner, my phone rang. It was Mathias Blatch. I swallowed hard and answered.

"Hey," I said, my voice soft. "Everything okay?"

"Yeah. I'm calling about lunch."

It took me a moment to remember I had promised to take him out to lunch after leaving him alone at a diner in

Kirkwood at our last meeting. Then I closed my eyes and sighed softly.

"This isn't a great time," I said. "Can we talk about this later? I've had a bad day."

Mathias paused.

"You want to talk about it?" he asked. "I know a few things about rough days."

I almost told him I had a therapist and didn't need to talk. For some reason, though, when I opened my mouth to say that, something else entirely came out.

"Someone tried to kill me yesterday. I got shot twice, but my vest caught both rounds. That wasn't the worst part, though. I was holding a baby. We were trying to rescue her, but I lost her. I think she's dead now, and I can't stop thinking about her."

After that, I talked for almost ten minutes straight. At first, it was a little awkward, but Mathias listened intently and let me speak without interrupting. I told him about my failed negotiations with the Weavers, about Reuben Terepocki, and even about Ian.

Mathias had been a detective just as long as me. Even though he worked in a major metropolitan area, and I worked in the middle of nowhere, we saw the same kind of things at work. He understood what I meant when I said I was tired of the job. It was an overwhelming exhaustion that made me want to close my eyes and pretend the world was different than it actually was.

Once I finished speaking, Mathias drew in a slow breath. "I'm glad you're okay."

"Thank you," I said. Then I sighed. "I don't know what to do anymore. Do you ever think about quitting and leaving? I could write a letter of resignation tonight, hop in my car, and drive. The mountains, the beach, the woods. I could be anywhere but here."

"I'd be a fool if I didn't think about quitting every now and then," he said. "This job asks for a lot."

"Yeah," I said, nodding and raising my eyebrows while simultaneously wondering whether I had said too much.

"I'd miss you if you left," he said. "All your friends would miss you. Even Ian would miss you."

A tight smile came to my lips unbidden.

"You're sweet," I said. Then I sighed. "I don't know what the hell to do about Ian. I told him I didn't want to see him again. Does that make me an asshole?"

Mathias paused. "You made a hard decision."

I snickered and looked toward my oven as my timer began beeping.

"That's a diplomatic way of saying I screwed up," I said, standing to get my dinner. Again, Mathias paused as I pulled the pizza from my oven.

"My dad died when I was sixteen. He had colon cancer. Took us all by surprise."

"I'm sorry," I said. "I didn't know."

"I don't tell many people. At the time, I was mad at everything. Dad took everything that disease had with as much grace and dignity as he could muster. That pissed me off even more. I wanted him mad. I wanted him to scream and rage because he was going to leave me."

I didn't know what to say, so I said nothing.

"Before he died," said Mathias, "I yelled at him. I asked him why he wasn't fighting this and why he wasn't mad like I was. He told me we don't get to choose what life throws our way, but we do get to choose how we react to it. He chose to live his final months for me and my mom and my sister. So, for six months as he fought his cancer, I got to spend time with a kind and loving father instead of an angry, bitter one."

I nodded and licked my lips, unsure where he was going with this.

"I'm glad you got to be with him."

"Me, too," said Mathias. He paused. "I might be overstepping, but I care about you, so I'm just going to say this. You didn't get to choose what happened to you when you were young, but you don't need to let it dictate who you are now. You get to choose what role Ian plays in your life—if any. Don't let your past make that choice for you."

Heat came to my face, and the muscles of my back tightened. I almost told him to keep the pop psychology bullshit to himself, but instead, I gritted my teeth.

"That's good advice," I said, doing everything I could to keep my sudden anger from my voice. Mathias and I talked for a few more minutes, but the conversation seemed a little clipped after that. When I hung up, I pet Roy's cheek.

"At least you don't give me crappy advice," I said. The dog seemed nonplussed, but that was okay. I wasn't hungry after the conversation, so I poured myself a drink and went to the front porch to think. The Nolan family wasn't cooperating, the Weavers hadn't called to make demands of us, and every lead I had investigated led nowhere. Unless that changed soon, Scarlett would die—if she hadn't already. I ran my hand across Roy's back. I needed a break.

"Hey, buddy," I said. He raised his head. "You want to go for a walk?"

He shot to his feet, which made me smile just a little. Dogs were the best kind of friends. Simple, faithful, kind, obedient, and they knew when to leave well enough alone. When Mom dropped Roy off at the house, I hadn't known whether I was ready for a new dog. Already, though, Roy was more than just my dog. He had become a friend, and I could always use one of those.

I grabbed a flashlight by my back door.

"Let's walk, dude."

# Chapter 39

I got to work the next morning at a little before eight. As soon as I arrived, I grabbed coffee and then met Delgado and the rest of the morning shift in the second-floor conference room. The sheriff kept the roll-call meeting short, which I appreciated. A pair of pickup trucks had hit each other in the county, and someone stole an iPad from a young man's backpack at the library, but nobody had murdered or assaulted anyone else. That was a relief, at least. We didn't have the resources to pick up a murder or other serious felony.

After roll call, Delgado waved me toward him.

"Morning, boss," I said.

"Morning, Joe," he said. "How you feeling?"

"Better than I've been," I said. "What's the news this morning?"

He looked at his watch. "Reuben Terepocki has an arraignment hearing at nine. Shouldn't be any fireworks, but considering what he did, I don't expect the judge to grant bail."

"He doesn't deserve it," I said. Delgado nodded. We lapsed into silence, but then I cleared my throat. "Are we any closer to finding Scarlett than we were yesterday?"

"No," he said. "We talked to about two dozen people, but nobody's answering our questions. The Weaver family's been running moonshine through St. Augustine since Prohibition. They know how to hide."

At first, the comment made me clench my teeth and curse under my breath, but then something clicked.

"We can use that," I said, nodding slowly. "If the Weavers have been here that long, there'll be records with their names on it. Land grants, bills of sale, property deeds, arrest records, search warrant affidavits...we might even find newspaper stories that mention places where we arrested their ancestors."

Delgado furrowed his brow. "And that'll get us what?"

"A list of places they might be."

He straightened and then crossed his arms.

"It's a long shot."

"All we've got left are long shots," I said. He sighed and ran a hand across his head before nodding.

"The library has a lot of old county records, but I don't know how well organized they are. They'll also have old newspapers. If you want to research it, go ahead. Good luck."

"Thanks, boss," I said, knowing I'd need it.

I left the building and walked a block to St. Augustine County's public library. Like many buildings in St. Augustine, the library was old but well loved. At one time, it had been a single-story red brick building with a portico and columns out front, but in the eighties, the county had added a second story, demolished the portico, and painted the entire building a cream color. Now, it looked like an odd cube with ornate brickwork on the first floor but little ornamentation on the second. Nobody would call it pretty, but it filled a need in the community. I appreciated it and the people who worked inside.

I introduced myself to the reference librarian at the information desk and told her what I needed. She wished me luck before leading me to the archives room in the basement. The room was about forty feet by forty feet and full of filing cabinets, bookshelves, and dusty old books. The librarian looked around.

"We've got property records and maps in the far corner, and we've got records of court proceedings by the door. They're organized by date, but we've never created a catalog. Honestly, I don't know what else we've got down here. We've never had the funding to hire an archivist to go through everything."

I nodded, feeling my heart sink just a little.

"Are there old newspapers somewhere?"

"Other side of the building," she said. "We've got the original papers, but we've also run them through an OCR scanner so they're digital. If you're looking for somebody in particular, you look him or her up, and it'll call up every article we've got from about 1893 onward."

"Let's start with those."

She led me to a bank of computers and told me how to search the database. It didn't take long to find almost a dozen articles mentioning the Weavers. The oldest article was a brief obituary of Samuel Weaver, who died of tuberculosis at seventy-one. It described him as a lifelong resident of Missouri who had spent time in Taney County in the southwest before settling in St. Augustine to raise his family. Unfortunately, that article didn't mention specific locations. The most recent article was about a basketball game in which Andy Weaver had scored twelve points and four rebounds for the local high school.

I printed a couple of things out and then walked to the reference desk. The librarian smiled at me.

"Find what you need, Detective?"

"I'm not sure," I said. "You familiar with the term Bald Knobber?"

She blinked and drew in a breath. "They were a vigilante group in southern Missouri in the late nineteenth century. Why?"

"I read Samuel Weaver's obituary, and it described him as a lifelong Bald Knobber. Are they still around?"

She shook her head. "No, and they weren't in this part of the state. They hid way down south in the Ozark Mountains."

The Ozarks were closer to rolling hills than they were mountains, but they were picturesque. Xavier Becker had told me history had mattered to his uncles. If Shane and Andy's ancestors had hidden in those hills, they might have done the same thing. Not only that, Thomas Becker had an address in Rogers, Arkansas. It was a different state but the same part of the world.

"Would the Bald Knobbers have been in Rogers, Arkansas?"

She considered and then shook her head. "I've never been much of a historian, but I'm sure we've got a resource that can answer your question."

"If there's a *Bald Knobbers for Dummies* book, I'm all ears."

"We'll find something."

She and I spent the next twenty minutes looking for articles or books. The Bald Knobbers were a topic of local interest, so the library had dozens of books and movies. I grabbed what I could and read at a table in a quiet corner of the second floor.

According to what I could find, the Bald Knobbers started as an organization dedicated to preserving civil law in a lawless county. It was a war, in their eyes, between civilization and barbarism. As was often the case with vigilante groups, reality was more complex than they envisioned.

"I hear you're looking for Shane and Andy."

I had been so engrossed in my book I hadn't noticed the woman walking toward me. She was five-eight or five-nine and had brown hair with tight curls and high cheekbones. Her dark red lipstick contrasted with rather than accentuated her pale skin, but her bright green eyes still popped. She was pretty, but she looked tired.

I put my book down and nodded.

"Yeah. I'm looking for them. You are?"

"Brandi Joslin. Andy is my ex-husband."

I pushed back from the desk. "I didn't realize he had an ex-wife. How'd you find me here?"

She lowered her chin. "You ain't that hard to find. You've got a big name in a little county. People talk."

I crossed my arms and nodded. "I see. What can I do for you?"

"Andy and I aren't together anymore, but I don't want him hurt."

I forced myself to smile.

"That's understandable," I said. "If you want to help Andy, the best thing you can do is to call him and tell him to turn himself in. He can bring the baby with him. We'll make sure she's taken care of. Can you do that?"

She blinked and then shook her head.

"He won't have his cell phone," she said. "He thinks the government could track him with it. And even if I could talk to him, he'd never turn himself in. He'd rather go down fighting."

I cocked my head to the side. "Then we've got a problem. If he wants to go down fighting, he'll go down hard."

She drew in a slow breath.

"If I told you where he is, could you get him at night when he's not expecting you? That way, you wouldn't have to hurt him."

My heart beat a little faster, and I leaned forward.

"Where is he?"

She bit her bottom lip and rubbed her fingers together.

"When we were married, we applied to be on a TV show. *Apocalypse Survivors*. Andy wanted to start his own company that converted old shipping containers into cabins. He was real good with his hands. He thought the show could give him the publicity he needed to get his company off the ground."

I nodded. "I've heard he had some interest in that show."

She pushed a lock of hair behind her ear and nodded.

"We never got on the show, but we talked to the producers a bunch. They said we'd have a better shot of being featured if we had a bug-out location besides our place in St. Augustine. They thought it'd look good if we were prepared in case our place in St. Augustine was overrun."

"Where is it?"

She nodded. "Taney County. It's on his great-great-granddad's property. It's real cool, too. They've got two storage containers buried in the ground. When you're inside, it's like a luxury cabin, but you can't even see them from outside. They keep it stocked with food and water. That's where he'd go in an emergency."

She might have been right. If her description was correct, it'd be just as difficult to breach as their place in St. Augustine, but we could work with it. They'd have to come out to dump their chemical toilet if nothing else.

"Tell me about this property."

Brandi and I spent the next ten minutes together. Afterwards, I hurried to my car and called Delgado.

"George, it's Joe Court," I said. "I know where the Weavers are."

# Chapter 40

I hurried to my station and went to the sheriff's office. He was already on the phone with the US Marshal's office, so I sat and waited for him to finish his conversation. When he hung up, he looked at me and nodded.

"I've got the Highway Patrol, Taney County Sheriff's Department, and US Marshals on standby until we need them. Tell me what we've got."

I walked him through everything Brandi had told me as well as my research. When I finished, he crossed his arms and nodded.

"It's the best lead we've had," he said. "We'll go down, check the area out, and then put a plan together. That sound good with you?"

"I'll need somebody to take care of my dog, but yeah. That'll work."

"Get to it. We'll leave as soon as we can."

I walked to the conference room and found Trisha typing on her computer. She looked up and smiled. I told her what was going on, and she agreed to feed Roy if I had to stay overnight in southern Missouri. The dog hadn't met Trisha, but he was pretty laid back. He'd be okay.

After that, I met Delgado in his office. We left within minutes and drove four and a half hours in separate cars to the Taney County Sheriff's Department in Forsyth, Missouri. It was warmer there than it had been in St. Augustine, making me wish I had worn a short-sleeved shirt. The afternoon sun beat down on the blacktop outside the station, but we didn't stay outside long.

Delgado had already spoken to the Taney County sheriff on the phone, so he knew what was going on. He even wished us luck. After our brief discussion with him, Delgado and I climbed into his SUV and headed out.

The Weavers owned a wooded twenty-acre parcel off a gravel road near Lake Taneycomo. Thick forest grew near the road, but it thinned considerably closer to the shoreline. The property had an old log cabin, but the roof and one wall had collapsed. From the road, neither Delgado nor I could see evidence of buried storage containers, but we did find an old pickup truck in the woods nearby. It had a stolen license plate from a Honda Accord, but I had seen it before on the parking pad outside the Weavers' property in St. Augustine.

Delgado slowed but didn't stop as we drove past.

"They're here," he said. "We'll get a team together and hit 'em at dark. I'll camp out up the road and watch to make sure they don't leave. In the meantime, you call Taney County to send a deputy to pick you up and bring you to your car."

I nodded and reached into my purse for my phone. I had a solid two bars.

"Check your cell and make sure you get a connection," I said. "If not, you can borrow mine."

He nodded and checked and then drove about half a mile down the road before stopping. I called the sheriff's office and told the dispatcher what was going on. He sent a deputy my way. I waited about five minutes before a marked cruiser pulled up behind us. Then I looked to the sheriff.

"You okay with me going?"

He nodded. "I'll be fine here. Coordinate a plan with the sheriff and make sure he knows to use whatever resources are available. This is a big case, and he'll get credit for the bust. You've done good work on this, Detective. You should be proud of yourself. We're going to get that little girl tonight."

"I hope you're right," I said, opening my door. I paused. "And thanks."

He grunted, and I walked to the deputy's cruiser. I didn't like leaving Delgado there alone, but he had his phone and rifle in the back of his SUV. He should be fine. When the deputy and I got back to Forsyth, the Taney County sheriff, the chief deputy marshal from the Springfield US Marshals Office, and an officer from the Missouri Highway Patrol put together a plan to raid the property. I got pushed aside, but I didn't care. This was their world. Delgado and I would just sit on the sidelines.

After some discussion, they decided to hit the property at somewhere around five in the morning, reasoning that the men inside would be deep asleep by then. The team would run to the bunker's hidden doors, blow them open with a small shaped charge, and then throw in canisters of tear gas. The moment Shane and Andy came out, one team would arrest them while a second would put an exhaust fan over the entrance to suck out the tear gas. Paramedics with neonatal experience would then rush in for Scarlett. They'd have a helicopter waiting to take her to a children's hospital in Springdale, Arkansas.

The plan put Scarlett through a lot of risk, but the team thought it would give them the best chance to minimize their own casualties. I understood where they were coming from—no rescue would work if the rescuers died in the attempt—but it still filled me with unease.

At a little before six that evening, I called Sheriff Delgado to tell him what was going on and to warn him that a uniformed deputy in an unmarked cruiser was coming to relieve him. Then I went by a T.J. Maxx in Branson, a nearby tourist town, and bought some clothes before renting a cheap motel room. Finally, I called Trisha to make sure Roy was okay. He had shied away from her at first, but he had warmed up to her once she gave him food. I thanked her, ordered a pizza, and then flopped on the bed.

Before my pizza could arrive, my phone rang. It was Ian. I thought about hanging up on him, but he'd just call back. Instead, I closed my eyes and sighed before answering.

"Hey," I said. I thought he'd chew me out right away, but he said nothing for ten or fifteen seconds. "You there, Ian?"

"You were right," he said, his voice wavering.

"What was I right about?"

"Mom," he said. "I found some of her bank records. She was a junkie. You were right. I didn't believe you."

I softened my voice. "What'd you find?"

"Bank statements. Detective Marshall from Creve Coeur asked for them because she thought Mom and Aunt Lacey might have been involved in something together before Aunt Lacey died. She went to rehab, like, twice a year. That's why I stayed with Aunt Lacey so often when I was a kid. That's why someone killed her. She probably ripped off her drug dealer."

"I'm sorry," I said.

He ranted against Erin for a few minutes. Little of it made sense, but I didn't interrupt. He needed to get it out. When he finished, I could hear the tears in his voice.

"Say something," he said. "Tell me you were right, and I was wrong."

"I'm sorry, Ian," I said.

"I was so stupid," he said. "I thought she was the greatest person to walk the earth, but she didn't even love me enough to stay off drugs."

I shook my head and closed my eyes, preparing to do something I never thought I'd do.

"Read the bank statements again," I said. "Count how many times she went to rehab."

"Why?" asked Ian.

"Please just do it," I said. "Trust me."

He paused. "Nine."

"Nine times in how many years?"

"Four."

"Nine times in four years. Think about that," I said. "She tried to quit for you over and over even though she knew she'd fail. She didn't do that for me, and she didn't do it for herself. Addiction is a bitch. Erin's drug use had nothing to do with her love for you. It hurt every time she tried to stop using, and yet she kept doing it over and over. She did that for you. You don't know how lucky you are to have a mom who cared about you that much."

He said nothing for almost a minute.

"I miss her. I know I shouldn't, but I do."

"It's okay to miss her. She loved you, and you loved her. That doesn't need to stop just because she died."

"Why would somebody kill her?" he asked.

I blinked and shook my head and started to tell him I didn't know. Then I thought of my conversation with Mathias last night. We don't choose what life throws our way, but we choose how we react to it. As annoyed as hearing that had made me, Mathias was right. Ian didn't ask for what happened to him any more than I had asked for one of my foster fathers to rape me. I didn't like Erin Court, but her son—my brother—was an innocent kid thrust into a shitty situation. He deserved better than my scorn. He deserved a sister who gave a damn about him.

"I don't know why someone would kill her, but we'll find out."

He hesitated.

"You mean that?"

I nodded before I could even articulate my reasoning. Then, when I could articulate it, it seemed obvious.

"Yeah. We're family. I'm sorry I took this long to realize that."

We stayed on the phone another few minutes, but then the pizza delivery person knocked on my door. Ian wanted me to start looking into things right away, but I had other responsibilities at the moment. He seemed to understand that, which I appreciated. Before hanging up, I promised I'd call him as soon as I got home. He thanked me and wished me luck.

As I ate dinner, I thought about Erin. She had fought for her son. Maybe she didn't succeed, but she had tried to be a good mom to him. If she had tried to be good to him, I wondered whether she had tried to be good to me, too, and I just hadn't seen it. I'd probably never answer that, but considering that possibility beat hating her.

I set my alarm for four in the morning and went to bed at about nine. The bed springs hurt my back and sides, but I slept anyway and appreciated the break.

When my alarm rang, it was still dark outside. I dressed and then checked out of my room before driving to the sheriff's office. Thankfully, they had coffee in the lobby.

At a little before five, Taney County's sheriff projected a crude hand-drawn map of the Weavers' property onto a screen and started the briefing. We'd have twenty-four officers, two paramedics, one nurse, and nine vehicles. Since our department's insurance company would flip out if we went on this raid, though, Sheriff Delgado and I would stay with the paramedics and observe. After my last encounter with Andy and Shane Weaver, that was just fine with me.

We left in a convoy at ten after five and arrived at the Weavers' place with the horizon just turning a lighter shade of gray. It'd be at least another hour before the sun rose. The team split into four groups, each of which had a specific job. Delgado and I stayed with Sheriff Wright in his marked SUV. At the sheriff's word, the raid started, and twenty-four officers sprinted to their appointed places.

My nails bit into my palms, and I held my breath as the first group approached the tree that Brandi said marked the bunker's entrance.

*Let Scarlett be safe.*

I wasn't a religious person, but I repeated it in my mind as if it were a prayer. When they reached the tree, a US

Marshal stepped forward with a metal detector. He waved it over the ground, then stopped. Then the marshal stepped back, allowing two new men to step forward. They squatted and pulled the bunker's outer door open. Twigs, leaves, and other forest debris flew while two more team members ran forward. They knelt for maybe ten or fifteen seconds, and then both stood and motioned for everyone to get back.

The shaped charges ripped through the morning silence and echoed against the nearby trees. I couldn't imagine what it would have sounded like inside, but it was loud as hell from my position. The two men who had carried the explosives dropped in the gas grenades. They popped, and great, billowing clouds of vapor erupted from the hole in the ground. Those nearest the hole covered their mouths and eyes and stepped back.

I counted to five, expecting Shane and Andy to pop up any moment. They never did. Then I counted to ten and then thirty. Nobody moved. I looked to Delgado and Sheriff Wright.

"If that little girl's down there, the tear gas could kill her," I said. "Clear it and get her out."

Wright nodded and then spoke into his radio. The team in charge of the fan ran forward and placed it over the hole in the ground. An extension cord ran to an outlet on the paramedics' fire and rescue vehicle. We waited another thirty seconds as the air cleared, and then a breaching team climbed down. They shouted within seconds.

"We're clear!"

Wright, Delgado, and I crossed the property toward the bunker while uniformed officers climbed from the hole. We stopped near the tree.

"Bunker's empty," said an officer in a black tactical vest and carrying a black shotgun. "There are food wrappers in the trash and empty containers of infant formula on top of a cabinet. Somebody's been here, and they had a baby, but they're gone now."

Wright looked to Delgado.

"You think they spotted us while we did recon?"

Delgado shrugged. I swore under my breath and shot my eyes around the woods.

"Their compound in St. Augustine had multiple tunnels and escape routes. It stands to reason their bunker might, too. Get some flashlights and search the woods."

Wright considered and then looked toward his team.

"You heard the lady. Line up arm's width apart and search the woods."

I grabbed a flashlight from the sheriff's SUV and joined in the search, but it was fruitless until we reached the lakeshore, where we found a drainpipe big enough for a man to crouch in. A gate inside had been swung open, and footsteps led down to a spot on the lake, where it looked as if someone had dragged a boat through the wet sand.

Sheriff Wright and Delgado joined us on the beach. When Wright saw the drag marks, he called his dispatcher and requested that officers from their maritime unit get on the water to search. He thought we'd find them, but I wasn't so sure. They had already escaped twice. Now they knew we were close, and I couldn't help but think of Brandi Joslin's warning: Andy wouldn't turn himself in; he'd rather go down fighting.

It was only a matter of time before he and his brother realized they had nowhere else to go. They'd make their last stand, and no baby would survive that.

# Chapter 41

Sheriff Wright knew the local area, and he understood the capabilities and limitations of his own officers far better than Delgado and I did. He took over the search. Besides calling for dogs, he assigned officers to watch every major road in and out of the area, and he called in an Amber Alert on Scarlett Nolan. Every single person in a nine-county area who had opted into the state's emergency alert system would get a text message or email with Shane and Andy's pictures. Maybe we'd get lucky.

Delgado and I had little to do but sit around. He dozed in Sheriff Wright's SUV for a while, but then we hitched a ride with a uniformed officer back to Forsyth and our cars. Delgado had stayed up all last night, so he took a nap on a couch in the sheriff's office, while I went to breakfast at a diner near the station.

The diner's interior smelled like fried onions and potatoes. It made my mouth water. Landscape paintings adorned the dingy, nicotine-stained walls. The carpet was threadbare, but someone sat in nearly every seat in the place, which told me everything I needed to know about the food. A young woman in jeans and a blue T-shirt with the diner's name on the front grabbed a menu and led me to a table for two near the front window.

"Will anybody be joining you, or is it just you?"

"Just me," I said, forcing a smile to my face.

She nodded and poured me a glass of water.

"Can I get you anything right away?"

I hesitated and then showed her my badge.

"I'm here working a case," I said. "Did you, by chance, get an alert on your cell phone this morning?"

Her face fell as she nodded.

"The Amber Alert," she said. "It's sad. You find that little girl?"

"Not yet, but we're working on it," I said. "I'm glad you got the alert."

"Me, too," she said. "I was busing tables when it came through. Every cell phone in the building beeped at once. It was almost like a movie."

"Good," I said, nodding. "Thank you."

As I spoke to the hostess, a woman a few years older than my mom walked toward my table with a smile on her face. She wore an apron over her waist and the same blue T-shirt the hostess wore.

"What are you two chatting about?"

"This lady's a detective," said the hostess. "She's looking for that little girl who's missing."

"Oh," said the waitress, nodding with a thoughtful expression on her face. "I can't imagine what her parents are going through. I hope you find her. Anything we can do to help?"

"Keep your eyes open," I said. "The men who abducted her are armed and willing to shoot. If you see them, call 911. Don't try to follow them or stop them yourself."

The waitress nodded. "I'll pass the word around, and I'll get you some coffee. You look like you need it."

"I'd appreciate it more than you know. Thank you."

Both women nodded and left. I looked out the window to my right and watched the town wake up. An older man at a table near me turned and smiled.

"Did I overhear you say you were a detective?" he asked. I wasn't in the mood to talk, but I nodded anyway. He held out his hand for me to shake. "Dave Crawford. I'm retired, but I was the deputy sheriff here for twenty years. Sheriff Wright ain't a local, but he's a good cop. He'll do right by your case."

I shook his hand. "I'm Joe Court. The sheriff has been a big help so far."

"Glad to hear it. The good news is that we've got experience with missing persons around here. A lot of tourists come through here, and a couple times a year, somebody goes missing while hiking or boating. We usually find them. We'll find your missing girl, too, I bet."

I forced myself to smile. "I hope so."

Mr. Crawford and I spoke for a few minutes while I waited for my coffee and then a breakfast sandwich. I rarely liked talking to people I didn't know, but he was lively and even a little funny. When my sausage biscuit came, he joined me at my table and sipped his coffee. He was easygoing, so I didn't mind the company. After a few minutes, we lapsed into a comfortable silence. Then he leaned forward.

"Why'd your suspects come here to hide out? Why didn't they keep driving and head down to Louisiana or Texas? It's big country down there. Lots of places to hide."

I put my biscuit down and tilted my head to the side.

"Their family is from here, and they had some property along Lake Taneycomo," I said. "We checked the place out, but they disappeared. We think they got in a boat and rowed away. It was night, so we didn't even see them."

He grunted. "Boats make it hard. Lake's wide open, so you can see them a mile away during the day, but at nighttime, a canoe or kayak's just a dark mark on the water. It's like trying to find a black hole. These boys are smart."

I nodded and continued to eat my breakfast. Mr. Crawford drank his coffee. When I finished eating, I wiped my mouth with a napkin.

"You know any Bald Knobbers, Mr. Crawford?"

He gave me a bemused smile. "I may be old, Miss Court, but they were before my time."

I smiled. "Do you know anything about them?"

He sipped his coffee and nodded. "I've lived in Taney County for sixty-eight years. I would be remiss in my duties as a resident if I didn't know a little."

"Shane and Andy are the descendants of a Bald Knobber," I said. "They're proud of that. I'm worried that they're setting themselves up for a last stand. The Weavers will try to make their deaths symbolic of a bigger struggle. Did the Bald Knobbers have a clubhouse or meeting place in the county?"

Mr. Crawford considered me for a moment and then leaned back to talk to an even older man at the table beside ours.

"Hank, I know you've been listening. Where would a Taney County Bald Knobber make his last stand?"

The old man put down his fork.

"Captain Kinney disbanded the group peacefully in 1886, so they didn't have a last stand here in Taney County. They did their job and quit like honorable men. If they *were* gonna make a last stand, though, I bet they'd do it on Snapp's Bald. It'd mean something to 'em, because it was their first meeting site."

"And where is that?" I asked.

"Lots of people think it's by the Oak Grove School House off of Sunset Hill Road, but that ain't what Sam Snapp's family says. They say it's on Benjamin Place. To get there, you take Highway 76 east out of Branson and then Highway T north. Then hang a right at the storage place onto Guillian. That's how you know you're in the right area. You take

Guillian on to Benjamin, and you're there. Road's narrow, but it's real pretty up there. You'll have a nice view."

I grabbed a notebook from my purse and wrote the directions down. Then I put two twenties on my table.

"Thank you, gentlemen," I said, standing. "Breakfast is on me."

They tried to protest, but I was already out the diner's door. I got in my car and headed toward Branson. Along the way, I called my boss. He didn't answer, and his phone went to voicemail. He was probably asleep, so I called again. This time, the phone rang three times before he picked up with a sigh.

"What do you need, Joe?"

"I've got a tentative lead on the Weavers," I said. "It's at a place called Snapp's Bald. I'll check it out. If there's anything to it, I'll call you again. I wanted to keep you informed, though."

"You got any locals with you?"

I shook my head. "No. And I don't need a babysitter. I'll just drive up there and surveil the area. If I see anything, I'll call it in."

"Your safety is your priority," he said. "You see the Weavers, you lie low and call for backup. You can't help Scarlett if you're dead."

"Understood," I said, nodding. "I'll talk to you soon."

I hung up and tossed the phone beside me. Even early in the morning, traffic through Branson was thick. I followed

Mr. Crawford's directions through town and then onto Highway T. Hills rolled into the distance in every direction. The road rolled over the hills. Every time I went up, my engine struggled with the grade, but then on the way down, I didn't even have to use the gas to stay at sixty or seventy miles an hour. There were houses, but the forest grew so thickly the area looked like a nature preserve.

When I reached a storage business, I hung a right onto Guillian Drive. The road narrowed, and the pavement became rough. I wasn't far outside of town, but the area still felt isolated. If we had a medical emergency, it would take an ambulance at least fifteen or twenty minutes to get there. A medical helicopter would get there faster, but it wouldn't have anywhere to land.

Benjamin Place was a small cul-de-sac on top of a hill. The landscape undulated for miles around. It was pretty, and the nearby houses seemed to take full advantage of the view. I parked on the side of the road and called my boss to let him know I was there and that I planned to knock on some doors and see whether the neighbors had seen anyone unusual walking around.

As Sheriff Delgado and I spoke, a funny thing happened: I spotted a man walking a golden retriever alongside the road in my rearview mirror. At first, I thought nothing of him, but as he drew closer, I recognized him. My mouth dropped open, and I stopped listening to my boss.

"Joe? Are you there?"

360

I shook my head to break myself from my stupor. Then I lowered my voice.

"They're here," I said. "Shane Weaver's walking a dog beside the road. He'll go right past me."

"Get out of sight," said Delgado. "I'll tell Sheriff Wright to send some backup."

I ducked low in my seat, but that was too late. Shane dropped his leash and ran toward a house. The dog chased after him.

"He saw me," I said. "He's running."

"Don't go after him, Joe," said Delgado. "That's an order. It's two against one. That's too dangerous."

"Understood," I said, already opening my door. "Send me backup."

I tossed my phone onto the passenger seat and pulled my firearm from its holster.

"Stop!" I shouted.

Shane turned and fired three times. Each hit my car with a pop. I ducked behind my engine block as Shane resumed running. Going after Shane and Andy by myself was reckless. Both had extensive firearms training, and both were willing to kill without hesitation. We had already lost them twice, though. We couldn't lose them a third time. This needed to end.

As Shane reached the front porch of a two-story brick-and-siding home, I looked around to make sure Andy Weaver wasn't trying to sneak up on me. Sheriff Delgado had told me to wait for backup, but that wasn't my job. When I became a police officer, I swore an oath to protect people who couldn't protect themselves, and Scarlett Nolan needed help.

I wouldn't let her down again.

# Chapter 42

I jumped back in my car, turned on the ignition, and floored the accelerator. The air whistled through bullet holes in the passenger side door. Glass lay on the seat beside me from a shattered window. When I reached the driveway, I skidded to a stop behind the Weaver's pickup truck. Almost immediately, gunshots slammed into my vehicle.

I opened my door, slipped out of the car, and scurried to its rear for cover. The shooter fired half a dozen times or more before stopping.

"We can still talk about this!" I shouted. "You don't have to die today."

On the plus side, nobody shot at me. I waited and listened.

"Can you hear me?"

A baby cried inside the house. I adjusted my grip on the weapon and crept around the front of my Volvo. The house had a four-car garage, but the doors were shut. A walkway curved around a large flower bed to the front entrance. I held my firearm in front of me and ran through the still open front door.

The house had an open floorplan, allowing me to see into the dining room to my left and into a sitting room to my right. A curving staircase led to the second floor, while hardwood floors led into what looked like a family room straight ahead of me. I almost tripped on a sleeping bag and pillow in front of the door, but I stayed on my feet and followed the sound of crying straight ahead to a living room.

Glass stretched from the floor to the vaulted ceiling, giving the homeowners a beautiful view of the valley below the house. The crying was louder, but the room was empty. I followed the noise to a door, behind which I found carpeted stairs that led to a basement.

"Andy and Shane Weaver, if you can hear me, put your hands up and lie on the ground. No one needs to die today."

Nobody answered, not that I thought they would. I hurried down the steps and found four people—two adults and two teenagers—tied to chairs in a walkout basement. A baby—Scarlett, presumably—wailed from a Pack 'n Play. I swept the room with my firearm, expecting somebody to jump out at me. Nobody did, though, so I ran toward the family. The Weavers had tied them to chairs with nylon cord and then put duct tape over their mouths.

I used my pocketknife to saw away at the restraints of a middle-aged man. The instant his hands were free, he reached up and ripped off the duct tape over his mouth.

"They're armed," he said. "They came early this morning while we were asleep. They brought the baby."

I nodded and cut the cord on his feet, but then a door slammed shut. I looked out the window to see Shane darting across the lawn.

"Get him," said the man. I handed him the knife.

"Help's on the way. Stay inside," I said, already turning. I ran into a laundry room with an exterior door. Outside, the landscape sloped downward to a tree line. Shane and Andy both knew how to maneuver in the woods, and they had demonstrated on multiple occasions that they had escape plans in the works long before they reached an area. If Shane reached those woods before I did, he was as good as gone.

I sprinted after him. Then a pair of shots buzzed past me, and a rifle cracked to my left. My knee buckled, and I fell. My right elbow smacked into the ground, sending a jolt through my body. My left side hit the grass hard, knocking the wind out of me. Another shot rang out from a fallen log in the woods to the west. A round buzzed over my head. I aimed my pistol and returned fire. Shane continued running south down the hill. The shooter must have been Andy. They had set me up.

Shane reached the tree line and then slowed to a jog before turning back and leaning down with his hands on his knees. Andy fired a three-shot burst that went over my head. They had me pinned down. This was a bad position, but I couldn't change it.

Once Shane caught his breath, he straightened and hurried down the hill until I couldn't see him anymore. Maybe he was looping around to a getaway vehicle, or maybe they had an escape route down the hill. It didn't matter. I couldn't go after him until I took care of his brother.

"I've got backup on the way!" I shouted. "Drop your weapon and step out from behind the tree. You don't have to die today, Andy."

He fired twice. Both rounds buzzed over me. Then a different rifle cracked. I looked toward the house to find the homeowner whom I had cut from restraints with a scoped rifle on his deck. He looked at me.

"He's down. Get the other one. Baby's safe."

I hesitated before pushing up. Andy didn't shoot at me, so I presumed the homeowner had killed or incapacitated him. I ran toward the woods. The forest was thick with trees but held little underbrush to slow me down. I couldn't see him at first, but then I caught movement about a quarter of a mile away. Shane was running almost parallel to the hillside as he made his way down.

I didn't have a shot at this distance, but I raised my pistol anyway.

"Shane Weaver. Stop right now! Your brother's dead. You don't need to die, too!"

To my surprise, he stopped. Then he turned straight down the hill. I took two steps after him and then fell to my backside and slid down about thirty feet before I grabbed a root and stopped. Shane didn't have that kind of luck. He hit something and then tumbled head over heels downward. It was almost like watching a tumbleweed blow down the side of a mountain.

Then he stopped with a thud that resounded through the hills. It sounded like a watermelon dropped in the grocery store.

"Shane! Can you hear me?"

He didn't respond. I zigzagged down the hill toward him, but I might as well have stayed at the top and waited for a team with climbing gear. Shane's head had smacked into a piece of limestone, breaking the back of his skull clean open. He had probably died instantly. Somewhere distant, sirens blared as my backup hurried toward us. I leaned against a tree and holstered my weapon as I took a breath.

It would take time to hit me, but Shane and Andy were dead. So was Thomas Becker. Scarlett Nolan wasn't safe, but she was safer than she had been in days. Tara Madison was clinging to life still. I should have felt good. Instead, I couldn't help but feel that three men had wasted their lives and hurt a lot of people for nothing. Nobody won in this case. I was just glad that more people hadn't died.

# Chapter 43

Two days after Shane and Andy Weaver died, I attended the funeral of Lacey Rayner. I tried not to cry, but I did anyway. Aunt Lacey and I had a complicated relationship toward the end of her life, but I loved her all the same. I wished I had gotten to tell her that again before she died.

A day after that, Reuben Terepocki pled guilty to voluntary manslaughter and agreed to serve fifteen years in prison. Reuben still claimed Vic Conroy had ordered his daughter's murder, but I doubted we'd get anywhere with it after he had killed the only witness who could corroborate his story.

From the start, Conroy had misled me. He may not have known exactly what was going on, but he knew I was interested in Reuben, and he saw the opportunity to get rid of a threat. He convinced his dancers to lie to me and told me exactly what I needed to hear when I thought I needed to hear it. My colleagues had warned me about him, but I had still underestimated him. That wouldn't happen again.

After the Weavers died, paramedics had airlifted Scarlett Nolan to a children's hospital in Arkansas, where doctors gave her IV antibiotics for an infection. As soon as her infection cleared up, she would fly to Houston for heart surgery. With modern medicine being what it was, she'd make a full recovery. The Nolans had Tara Madison to thank for that. She kept that baby alive the only way she knew how. I didn't know whether the Nolans realized how lucky they were.

When I got back to St. Augustine, Roy jumped up when he saw me and ran straight at me. I knelt in the yard and pet his back. He danced around me. I couldn't remember the last time someone had been that happy to see me. It felt good to be home.

I spent about a week filling out paperwork and meeting with detectives from the St. Louis County police to close out the case. They helped me fill in some gaps. My notes and some additional research helped me fill in the rest. After a week, I understood most of what happened and why, but I still had one big question unanswered.

On Friday morning, I drove to the home of Wesley and Tara Madison. Wesley knew I was coming, so he was there with his mother, Xavier, and his infant son. I smiled at him when he opened the door.

"Mr. Madison, thanks for having me," I said. "Do you mind if I come in?"

"By all means," he said, taking a step back. "But I still don't know why you're here."

"I just wanted to give you a final update on the case and clear up a few things," I said, stepping into the home. "It won't take long."

Wesley led me down a hallway to an eat-in kitchen. His mother already sat at the table with a cup of coffee in front of her. She nodded.

"Detective," she said. "I understand you saved my daughter-in-law's life. Thank you."

"I don't know whether I saved her, but I tried my best," I said. "How is she?"

Mrs. Madison looked to her son. He sighed and plopped down.

"She's still in the hospital," he said. "She'll be there for a while, and she has a long rehab in front of her, but she'll recover. Her heart's in good shape. She'll watch her kids grow up. That's all that matters."

"That's great," I said, looking around. "Is Xavier around? He should hear this."

Wesley looked over his shoulder.

"X-man!" he called out. "A detective needs to talk to you."

We waited about thirty seconds for Xavier to come out of a doorway. He held a wireless video-game controller in one hand and a can of soda in the other.

"Is this going to take long?"

"Give me fifteen minutes," I said. "Pause your game."

He nodded and put his controller on an end table before joining us around the kitchen table.

"Okay," I said. "Since we're all here, we'll get started. As you guys know, I'm Detective Mary Joe Court with the St. Augustine County Sheriff's Department. I'm here to update you about the homicide of Thomas Becker and the attempted homicide of Tara Madison. I'll keep the graphic details to a minimum, but as you guys know, this case involved some violence. Sound good with you guys?"

They nodded, so I dove into things.

"The case started as an abduction led by a man named Lorenzo Molena. Molena was a former Army officer. He and a team of former soldiers under his command abducted Scarlett Nolan from a hospital in St. Louis. Instead of flying Lorenzo and his team away, though, Thomas Becker double-crossed them. He and the Weavers took Scarlett and left. They hoped to ransom Scarlett back to her family."

I thought Xavier might object to something I said, but he just nodded.

"Thomas flew the helicopter at a low altitude so it wouldn't show up on radar and landed in a field in Illinois, just east of the Mississippi River. He and the Weavers then came back to St. Augustine. They didn't know Jay Pischke was dead, but they soon learned they couldn't use the safe house he had set up. Not only that, Lorenzo Molena proved to be more resourceful than they expected. He came after Thomas and killed him. You with me so far?"

Wesley Madison crossed his arms. The others nodded.

"Shane and Andy Weaver knew they couldn't take care of a baby on their own, so they came to Tara Madison for help. We're not sure how this went down, but we know Shane and Andy held Tara against her will at their compound. She protected Scarlett as if she were her own. Tara's a hero in every sense of the word.

"After an unsuccessful attempt to negotiate, Shane and Andy fled to Taney County in southern Missouri. We tracked them down. Rather than turn themselves in, they fired at me multiple times. A civilian with a hunting rifle shot and killed Andy Weaver. I chased Shane into the woods, where he fell down a hill and smacked his head on a limestone rock formation. His autopsy showed that he died instantly."

I looked to Xavier. "You've lost a lot in the past two weeks, and for that, I'm very sorry. We've done our best to ensure that everyone still alive will be held accountable for their actions."

Wesley drew in a breath through his nose.

"So Shane and Andy shot my wife."

I nodded. "Yeah. This was an ugly case. If there's any good news, it's that Tara and Scarlett survived. I wish it hadn't happened the way it did, but at least you don't have to worry about the Weavers anymore."

The family went quiet, but then Mrs. Madison stood.

"If that's it, thank you for coming by, Detective," she said. "Wesley and I will tell Tara what happened when we visit her. I'm sure she'll be glad to hear the little girl survived."

She moved to escort me out of the room, but I shook my head.

"There's one more thing," I said. "I need to see everyone's cell phones."

Mrs. Madison brought a hand to her throat, while Wesley barked out a laugh.

"Why do you need to see our phones?" asked Wesley.

"Call it a hunch," I said, reaching into my purse. I pulled out my phone and dialed a number from the directory. Down the hall to my left, I heard a beeping noise. No one moved. "Is that Xavier's room down there?"

Wesley's mouth popped open, and he furrowed his brow.

"That's the guest room. Mom's staying there."

My back straightened, and I drew in a sharp breath. I hadn't expected that. Then I cleared my throat to cover my surprise, stood, and stepped between Mrs. Madison and the hallway. The phone rang again.

"We should answer that," I said, putting a hand on her elbow.

"What's going on, Mom?" asked Wesley.

Mrs. Madison gave him a pained expression but said nothing. I escorted her to a neat but impersonal bedroom. She opened a brown leather purse on an end table but didn't reach inside. Her shoulders slumped.

"Why are you doing this?" she asked.

"Can you hand me the phone, please?" I asked. It rang again, but she didn't move. I lowered my chin and let my anger creep into my voice. "Now."

That got her moving. She handed me the phone, but I shook my head.

"Answer it first," I said.

She ran her finger across the smart phone's screen before handing it to me. I hung up but then checked her call history and her most recent text messages. The phone was a burner, and she had only contacted one number. With Mrs. Madison's help, I disabled the phone's password protection and then glanced up.

"Should I tell your family what you've done?"

Mrs. Madison said nothing.

"Tell us what?" asked Wesley. He stood in the doorway with his arm around Xavier's shoulder. Both of them wore worried expressions. Still, Mrs. Madison said nothing.

"A little over a week ago, I was shot twice while trying to negotiate with Andy and Shane Weaver. My vest stopped the rounds from hurting me. Tara Madison was shot multiple times, too, but she wasn't wearing a vest."

"We know that," said Wesley.

"During that attempt at a negotiation, soldiers employed by Nolan Systems used an MH-60 Black Hawk helicopter to infiltrate the Weavers' compound and begin a rescue attempt of their own. If they hadn't come, I might have been able to persuade Shane and Andy to give up. I never got the chance, though. Shane and Andy opened fire as soon as they saw the helicopter. Because of them, Tara and I almost died."

None of the Madisons said anything, so I looked at Mrs. Madison.

"How did you get Gerald Nolan's phone number to tell him where his granddaughter was?"

She swallowed and looked away. I thumbed through text messages on her phone and read a particularly egregious one.

"I know it's dangerous, but get your granddaughter. If Tara dies, Wesley can remarry. He's still young."

Mrs. Madison closed her eyes and sighed.

"Jesus, Mom," said Wesley. "What the hell is going on?"

Mrs. Madison said nothing.

"You should answer. I've only got speculation," I said. Mrs. Madison's eyes remained closed, but her lips moved. She might have been praying. I looked to Wesley and Xavier. "We knew Gerald Nolan had engineered the raid on the Weavers' compound, but we couldn't figure out how he learned of its location. My boss thought he must have searched through old property records. Based on the timing, I suspected he had some help."

Wesley took his arm from his mother's shoulders and cocked his head to the side. His face had grown red.

"Mom?"

She opened her eyes and then covered her mouth with her hand.

"I told him."

A tear slid down Mrs. Madison's cheek. She almost wilted in her son's glare. He stepped forward, but I stepped between them before they could scream at one another.

"Let's everybody take a step back," I said. "Wesley and Xavier, please go back to the living room. I'll talk to you soon. Mrs. Madison, sit on the bed."

Nobody moved, so I let some anger into my voice.

"That wasn't a suggestion," I said, reaching behind me for a pair of handcuffs in a case on my belt. "Do as I ask, or everyone's getting a new pair of shiny metal bracelets."

Wesley glared at me before leading his stepson out of the room. Mrs. Madison sat down. Her back was straight, and she focused straight ahead at a spot on the wall.

"Thank you for letting me talk in private," she said. "My son doesn't need to hear this."

"He'll hear it one way or the other," I said. "And I only asked him to leave because I thought he might have hurt you if he stayed. How do you know Gerald Nolan?"

She made a show of lacing her fingers together on her lap.

"He came to the house after Tara went missing. Xavier was in school, and my son was at work. I was home with Joshua, the baby."

I took a notepad from my purse.

"Tell me about this meeting."

She closed her eyes again and sighed.

"Mr. Nolan was angry, and I couldn't blame him. Tara's ex-husband had taken his granddaughter and murdered his only son. Thomas Becker brought a nightmare to our family."

"So you made a deal," I said.

She looked at me with her brow furrowed.

"Do you have kids, Detective?"

I shook my head.

"No, ma'am," I said.

"Then you have no right to judge me," she said. "Mr. Nolan lost his son and a granddaughter. He deserved my help. And let me tell you something else. You may think my daughter-in-law is some kind of innocent in all this, but she married Thomas Becker. By her own admission, Shane and Andy Weaver were her friends. She even let her son call them Uncle Shane and Uncle Andy. What kind of woman does that?"

I nodded and pretended I didn't want to punch her.

"Tell me about this deal you made."

"Mr. Nolan wanted his granddaughter back, and he was willing to do anything to make that happen. I told him I'd help. If I heard anything, I'd relay the information. That's it. There's no crime there."

"How much did he offer to pay you?"

That seemed to rob her of some of her righteousness. She looked away, so I repeated the question.

"A million cash if my information helped him get his granddaughter back alive."

I almost whistled. "That's a lot of money."

She nodded but said nothing.

"You don't like your daughter-in-law, do you?" I asked.

She considered me and then sighed.

"My daughter-in-law was a tramp who couldn't keep her legs closed in high school. I love Xavier, but my son deserved better than a trollop."

I nodded.

"Did Mr. Nolan give you the cell phone?"

"He did," she said.

"Did he pay you?"

She looked away. "He didn't get his granddaughter back."

"How'd you feel when you heard someone shot your daughter-in-law?"

She hesitated. "What do you mean?"

I shrugged. "Did you feel relieved? Sad? Angry? Disappointed?"

"I was fine."

She was close to shutting down, so I figured I only had one more question. I might as well go for it.

"Was Tara Madison's death part of your deal with Gerald Nolan?"

"I won't dignify that with an answer," she said, shaking her head.

"Answer her, Mom," said Wesley from the doorway. I looked over my shoulder at him. He had crossed his arms and leaned against the doorframe. "Is my wife in the hospital because of you?"

She softened her voice. "Honey, it's not like that."

"From the sound of things, it's exactly like that," he said. He looked at me. "May I see the cell phone you took from her?"

I shook my head.

"I'm sorry, but it's evidence."

Wesley nodded.

"Get out of my house."

"That's a good idea," said Mrs. Madison. "It's past time for you to go, Detective. My son and I need to talk."

"I wasn't talking to her," said Wesley. "Mom, pack your bag, get in your car, and leave. I don't want to hear from you ever again."

Mrs. Madison sighed and softened her voice as if she were explaining the facts of life to a child.

"I was acting in your best interest."

"You engaged in a conspiracy to murder my wife," he said. "Get the fuck out of my house."

She stood. "We'll talk about this later."

"No, we won't," said Wesley. "Are you charging her with a crime, Detective Court?"

"Not yet, but we're still gathering evidence. I need to talk to Mr. Nolan again."

He nodded and looked to his mom.

"Get your bag and get out of my house. Don't call me again."

She held up her hands. "All right. I'm leaving."

I stayed in the room as she packed and then escorted her off the property. Once she drove away, Wesley looked at me.

"Thank you," he said. "I'm sorry you haven't seen my family at our best."

But I had. A week ago, I had seen his wife cradle and hug a baby that wasn't her own while armed men shot at them both, and today I had seen a father protect and comfort his stepson as if he were his own flesh and blood. I had seen a man do what he had to do to protect those he loved, and that meant a lot.

"You guys are doing just fine," I said. "Take care, Mr. Madison."

He thanked me. I left the house with my questions answered but my heart heavy. It was a little after eleven. I didn't want to go back to work right away, so I drove to Able's Diner to grab a sandwich. As I sat in the parking lot, my phone rang, but I didn't recognize the number. I answered with a sigh.

"This is Detective Court," I said. "What can I do for you?"

"Hey, Joe, this is Alexis Koch. You got a minute?"

My back straightened, and I drew in a sharp breath. Though her voice sounded casual, this wasn't a personal call. Alexis Koch was the assistant director of the Criminal Investigative Division of the FBI. I had briefly worked with her after the special agent in charge of the FBI's field office in St. Louis was murdered, but I hadn't spoken to her since.

"Sure, I've got a minute," I said. "What can I do for you?"

"There's an inmate in the United States Penitentiary in Terre Haute, Indiana, who's asked to speak with you. I'm relaying the request."

I allowed myself to sink in my seat. Occasionally, men and women I arrested contacted me from prison, but usually they just wanted to scream at me.

"Who is he?"

"He's a serial murderer. Thirteen years ago, he walked into a police station in Little Rock, Arkansas, with a cooler containing the heads of three women. One was a local college student, a second was a police officer from Memphis, and the third is still unidentified. Before that moment, Mr. Brunelle had no criminal record and had never been suspected of a crime. He walked in because he said he was bored."

I shivered involuntarily at the thought.

"Why does he want to talk to me?"

"He says he liked your work on the Apostate case and had something important to tell you. He thinks you can get his story out."

I shook my head.

"Thank you for your call, but I'm just a detective. If you need a profile on this guy, you've got better people in-house."

"You're right. I have an excellent team," she said. "He doesn't want to see them, though. He wants to see you. It's a mind game. My people have been trying to interview him for years, and he's always refused to cooperate. It's about power. He likes manipulating events and making us do his bidding."

I rolled my eyes a little. "I suppose recreational opportunities are rare in his part of the world."

"We need your help, Joe."

I sighed. "What do you hope to get out of this?"

"He's promised to tell us who the unidentified girl is, but he's got more than that to say. He's admitted to committing three murders, but I suspect there have been a lot more." She paused. "You can become their voice, Joe. Think about it."

I swore under my breath, mostly because I didn't have to think about it. Before becoming a cop, I was a victim without a voice. Captain Julia Green of the St. Louis County Police Department—my adoptive mom—spoke for me, but I was lucky. Most women didn't have an advocate like her. Mom inspired me to become a cop. The women this man killed couldn't hear if I spoke for them, but they mattered all the same. No one could ever put what happened to them right, but at the very least, I could tell their stories. They deserved that.

"He won't see anybody but me?" I asked.

"Correct," she said. "You caught a serial murderer, Joe. You're famous. That draws people to you."

"I was afraid of that," I said. Director Koch began to say something, but I interrupted her. "I'll do it. Email me whatever information you've got on Brunelle. I'll talk to my boss and let him know what's going on."

"Don't worry about your sheriff," she said. "I'll call him. Knowing him, he'll probably send us a bill for your services. This shouldn't be a big deal. You'll drive up, interview Brunelle, and then drive home. I'm thinking two days at most."

I nodded. "Two days doesn't sound so bad."

She and I talked for another minute, but neither of us had anything important to say. I hung up about five minutes after picking up the phone. My belly growled and the diner awaited, but I didn't get out of the car. Instead, I leaned my head back and closed my eyes.

Even in major police departments, very few police officers encountered a serial killer on the job. Brunelle would be my second. Director Koch said this wouldn't be a big deal, but she and I both knew otherwise. Brunelle wouldn't have requested me without reason. He wanted something, and, for some reason, he thought I could give it to him.

I didn't know the first thing about Brunelle, but even locked up, he was a dangerous man. Already he had manipulated an FBI agent who should have known better into calling me. In all likelihood, Director Koch wasn't the only person he had on his mind. There were others out there, doing his bidding wittingly or not.

We needed to find out what he wanted before it bit us all in the ass.

\*\*\*

I hope you liked THE MAN IN THE METH LAB! I thought this was a great mystery, and I hope you did, too. The Joe Court series continues in THE WOMAN WHO WORE ROSES! It's a book with some good twists and a few—hopefully—surprising elements. You can purchase the book directly from Chris Culver's store [store.chrisculver.com] or at Amazon, Barnes & Noble, and other major retailers.

**OR Turn the page for a free Joe Court novella...**

You know what the best part of being an author is? Goofing off while my spouse is at work and my kids are at school. You know what the second part is? Interacting with my readers.

About once a month, I write a newsletter about my books, writing process, research, and funny events from my life. I also include information about sales and discounts. I try to make it fun.

As if hearing from me on a regular basis wasn't enough, if you join, you get a FREE Joe Court novella. The story is a lot of fun, and it's available exclusively to readers on my mailing list. You won't get it anywhere else.

If you're interested, sign up here:

http://www.chrisculver.com/magnet.html

As much as I enjoy writing, I like hearing from readers even more. If you want to keep up with my world, there are a couple of ways you can do that.

First and easiest, I've got a mailing list. If you join, you'll receive an email whenever I have a new novel out or when I run sales. You can join that by going to this address:

http://www.indiecrime.com/mailinglist.html

If my mailing list doesn't appeal to you, you can also connect with me on Facebook here:

https://facebook.com/ChrisCulverBooks

And you can always email me at chris@indiecrime.com. I love receiving email!

C hris Culver is the *New York Times* bestselling author of the Ash Rashid series and other novels. After graduate school, Chris taught courses in ethics and comparative religion at a small liberal arts university in southern Arkansas. While there and when he really should have been grading exams, he wrote *The Abbey*, which spent sixteen weeks on the *New York Times* bestsellers list and introduced the world to Detective Ash Rashid.

Chris has been a storyteller since he was a kid, but he decided to write crime fiction after picking up a dog-eared, coffee-stained paperback copy of Mickey Spillane's *I, the Jury* in a library book sale. Many years later, his wife, despite considerable effort, still can't stop him from bringing more orphan books home. He lives with his family near St. Louis.

Made in the USA
Monee, IL
03 April 2024

55619286R00229